FIND THE LIGHT

FIND THE LIGHT

CELESTE ROWAN

BERKLEY JUNE HUTSON

Book Cover by Miblart

Photography by Christy Stalnaker Photography

First edition Paperback 2025

ISBN 9798993273501 (pbk)
ISBN 9798993273518 (hc)
ISBN 9798993273525 (ebook)

For Mom and Dad,

Who believed even before I did.

PROLOGUE

My name is Celeste Rowan. I live in a small town in southern Tennessee. It is so small that we only have one traffic light. It is not even on a map. It does not really have a name either. I call it Boringsville, USA. Not because I hate it here. There is actually a lot I like about this place. There are lush forests that surround our town and mountains in the distance, plus all the lakes, ponds, and rivers...anyways, you get the idea. I call it Boringsville, USA because nothing exciting ever happens around here. Ever.

My parents chose to move here. Trust me. If I had had a say in where we were moving, I would have voted for Hawaii. However, I was not even born yet, so here we are in the middle of nowhere.

My dad left shortly after I was born. Mom does not like to talk about it. All she will tell me is that he loved me, and he had a good reason for leaving. But I could give him a thousand reasons to come back. Reason one: I really wanted a dad.

Even still, I hated him so much for leaving. If he did ever

come back, I am not sure if I could ever think of him as a dad again. It was a topic I tried to avoid. I did not even like to think about it most of the time, other than on my birthday. My birthday was the only day of the year that I felt brave enough to ask about him. The older I got, the more curious I became. I started asking more questions. On my fourteenth birthday, I decided I wanted answers about my dad. Real answers. Not the usual, "Oh he loved you" or "He really cared." I wanted more. I never realized the price I would have to pay, or the sacrifices I would have to make once I knew.

It all started with a stranger.

ONE

"Celeste! Wake up, you are going to be late for school!" Mom called. I stumbled out of bed in a sleepy daze. I fumbled through my closet, searching for something good to wear today. Finally, I decided on a pair of jeans and a simple blue hoodie. Afterwards, I brushed my teeth in a hurry. I combed my hair hastily, not even bothering to pull it into a ponytail. My long blonde hair was frizzy and slightly wavy from me not blow drying the night before. I did not really care what it looked like. I had bigger things to think about than my hair.

I could not wait to start my day, after all, this was going to be a big day if things went well.

This is it. I am finally going to do it. I am going to ask about dad. I thought to myself.

"Good morning birthday girl!" Mom said in a singsong voice as I sat down at the kitchen table for breakfast.

I looked at the birthday breakfast spread out in front of me. There was bacon, sausage, eggs, and my all-time favorite, blueberry pancakes. Yum! I stuffed a huge bite into my mouth and savored the sweet yet tangy flavor as I smiled at Mom.

"Thanks!" I said.

She laughed because I said it with my mouth full of pancakes. Somehow, she still knew what I meant. That is the thing about moms, they always know exactly what you need. And they tend to understand you like no one else can.

"You're welcome," she said.

Mom always made a huge breakfast for my birthday, and I was always ready to eat a huge breakfast. So, it was always a win-win.

"Soooo, Mom. Remember how you told me when I was ready, you would tell me more about dad? Well, I am ready," I said as Mom drank a sip of coffee.

She almost spit out her coffee, but she managed to gulp it back down. Mom opened her mouth to argue, but I said the rest before she could say anything.

"I know you think I am not ready, but I am fourteen. I cannot go the rest of my life without knowing anything about him. I just need to know. Please."

She looked at me. Her face was unreadable. I was bouncing on the edge of my seat anxiously. However, my hope quickly deflated like a birthday balloon as Mom shook her head.

"I know you think you are ready, but you are not. Look, can we just put this behind us for now and enjoy today. After all, it is not every day you turn fourteen," she said.

Mom's voice was strained and it cracked a little. I could tell she was on the verge of tears. I did not want to make her cry on my birthday. Besides, there would always be another chance to ask about it. Just not today. "Sure, Mom," I mumbled defeatedly.

"I promise, I will tell you one day, but not yet. Now eat up," she said with forced cheerfulness..

She offered me a very forced smile. I, unfortunately, was not in the mood to offer one back. Instead, I stuffed another ginormous bite of pancakes into my mouth. Pancakes made everything better.

She planted a kiss on my cheek and gave me a hug.

I wondered if I would ever get the answers I wanted about my dad. I was going to do everything I could to make sure I did. Not only did I deserve a dad, but mom also deserved to be happy. I knew seeing my dad again would make that happen.

The car ride to school was usually uneventful. I dreaded going to school. Eighth grade kids were jerks. I was not the only person who thought so, yet no one ever spoke up about it. It is like an unwritten rule at my school that you do not speak up about kids doing mean stuff unless you want to be the next target. On occasion I break this rule whenever the school bully, Johnny Welch, picks on other kids. I usually ended up with dirty clothes and a few bruises from being shoved to the ground. Of course, Mom always freaks out when I come home looking like that. I really did not want that to happen on my birthday. Especially not after how that morning had gone. For once, I just wanted to be a normal middle school girl who was virtually invisible to the world.

As I thought about this, a flash of light caught my eye. I looked out the passenger window searching for what it was. Then, I saw someone. They wore a blue hoodie, remarkably similar to mine. The hood covered their face, so I had no idea what the person looked like. Whoever it was, stood there staring at me. Our eyes met and we held each other's gaze, until a bus passed by, obscuring my view. After the bus moved out of the way, the stranger in blue was nowhere to be found. It was like they'd just vanished into thin air.

Anything could have caused that flash of light. I told myself.

Still, I had a strange feeling about the hooded figure.

"Celeste? Celeste? Celeste! Are you even listening to me?" Mom said.

"Oh, yeah. Sorry, Mom. Just…" I paused, uncertain whether or not I had just imagined the stranger.

"Just what?" she asked. I could hear the worry in her tone.

I didn't want to stress her out more. She hadn't been behaving like herself lately. My carefree, easygoing mom was on edge. I had no idea what was causing her to act this way.

"Just lost in thought," I lied.

I decided to chalk it up to hallucinations from eating too many pancakes and turned away from the window. I had the chilling feeling that I was being watched. I decided to ignore it, sighing as Mom picked up where she left off. The rest of the car ride was spent with Mom talking nonstop and me sitting silently. I was trying—and probably failing—to seem interested.

I made it through the first three periods of school without any problems. Well, without any weird, hooded people related problems. Of course, I had other problems to deal with too.

Sidney, a spoiled brat who unfortunately happened to be in both my second and third period classes, seemed to be in the mood to pick on someone today. Apparently, she decided that person was me. I sat through math and English while she and her friends whispered about me, shot me dirty looks, and occasionally hit me in the head with balled up pieces of paper.

Her piercing blue eyes sparkled with excitement, daring me to do something about it. I was not about to make that mistake again. Once, I had gotten so fed up with her and her friends that I had ignored that unspoken rule about jerks and thrown my coincidentally very large textbook at her stupid face. Of course, she had made a big, grand spectacle of it and

I was suspended for a week.

I just rolled my eyes and tried to pay attention to my English teacher's lesson. I fell asleep halfway through, but that was further than I usually made it. So, I was making progress!

My fourth period was of course my favorite. It was Mr. Watomski's science class. Let me be clear, I hate all my school subjects, and I cannot stand all but one of my teachers. Mr. Watomski was the only teacher I liked. Probably because he was the only teacher that liked me. All the other teachers had pinned me as a troublemaker. Which was not entirely a lie but was not entirely true either. I do not try to be a troublemaker; I just do not like sitting there while those teachers ignore all the brats like Sidney.

Mr. Watomski always believed in me, and he constantly pushed me to be better. That's why I loved his class. I actually tried for the first time, and it turns out that I'm not that bad at science. If I studied hard enough, I managed to keep up a B plus average. Which was a lot higher than my grades in other classes.

Today, we were going to talk about volcanoes and rock cycles. Since we were just reviewing stuff we had already learned, I knew most of the answers to the questions he asked. I raised my hand every time, waiting for him to call on me.

Finally, he did. I beamed as he asked me to describe the difference between lava and magma. I knew this answer by heart at this point.

"Magma is below the earth's surface and lava is...." I trailed off.

I saw a flash of light over by the window. I looked outside, and there was the hooded figure again. Then, just like before, I blinked, and the figure was gone.

What the heck is happening? I thought.

Mr. Watomski cleared his throat awkwardly and turned to the rest of the class.

"Can anyone else give the correct and full answer?" Mr. Watomski asked the class. Hands flew up all around the classroom. Practically everyone raised their hands. Everyone but me, because I was too busy dying of embarrassment.

"Guess you're not a teacher's pet anymore," Johnny Welch snickered from the desk behind me. If you can't tell, the guy is an absolute jerk.

My one teacher that I liked had just called me out for my mistake in front of the entire class. I wished I could crawl into a hole and not come out until I graduated. With my grades that would probably be never. I hung my head and pulled my hair around my face to hide my blushing cheeks. I tried very hard to sit at the back of my remaining classes and rarely raised my hand to answer questions.

I sighed with relief as the afternoon bell rang signaling for the school day to end. For a kid like me, there's nothing better than hearing that bell. It's like a big sign with flashing lights that's saying: "Get out of here as fast as your scrawny middle schooler legs can carry you!"

As I walked down the empty hallway, my footsteps echoed around me. School had been out for at least thirty minutes and there wasn't a pickup line since everyone lived close enough to walk. Although some still took the buses, those were long gone by now. I always stayed a little longer to help this girl, Claire, with her homework. She was literally the only person in the school that didn't intentionally stay away from me. She is the sweetest person ever, but math isn't her strong suit. Come to think of it, I guess it wasn't mine either. However, I was still better at it than Claire. Besides, she was literally the closest thing I had to a friend in this town.I had just finished our afternoon study session.

As I put my textbooks away in my locker, I heard loud

shouting in the hallway on my left.

"Huh, I thought everyone already left," I mumbled to myself.

I couldn't think of anyone other than me, Claire, and some of the teachers that stayed later after school. Usually, everybody was ready to high tail it out of school. Even most of the teachers left as soon as the bell rang.

I couldn't resist my curiosity and made my way towards the noise, even though I knew it wasn't wise to run towards people who were yelling. I had no idea what was happening, but I couldn't shake the feeling that something was off.

Okay, I know what you're probably thinking. Celeste, how dumb could you possibly be? Hear me out. When you hear your parents or siblings getting into a fight in the other room do you stay put and mind your own business? Or do you peek around the corner to see what they're doing? Me being the idiot I am, I decided to ignore my solemn oath of no troublemaking for the day and went looking for more trouble. I couldn't help it if I was curious.

I rounded the corner and my jaw dropped. The whole school plus the high school seemed to have stayed to watch Johnny Welch and his entourage beat up Michael Fink, Danny Huggins, and Phillip Mitchell. It was the nerds against the jocks. Newsflash: the nerds were losing, as always. Johnny had Micheal pinned against a locker. Another goof had Danny hanging by his boxers from a second locker. And somebody else was currently trying to stuff Phillip into a third locker.

On top of all that, everyone else was either laughing or videoing it. That made me so angry. How could so many people just stand by and watch while these poor kids got pummeled? As someone who has never really fit in and gets picked on a lot myself, I can't stand to see other people being picked on. Especially people who aren't big enough to fight back. They needed somebody to fight for them. For some reason, I decided that I was going to be that person.

I pushed my way through the throngs of students, which earned me lots of angry shouts of *Ouch! Hey!* and, *Watch it!* Finally, I broke through the crowd and found myself at the front, gazing out at the unfolding scene. My heart raced in my chest as a small voice of doubt whispered in the back of my mind. Who was I to go up against a group of jocks? They were stupid, yes, but they made up for it with brute strength and size. I hardly knew Danny, Michael, or Phillip anyway. Why risk my own butt to save theirs? I ignored the voice of reason in my head, as usual, and faced the bullies.

With my shoulders squared and my resolve steeled, I approached Johnny.

"Leave them alone!" I shouted.

Johnny dropped Michael, his fists balled up so tight that they turned white. Micheal took the opportunity to run and quickly made his escape. Suddenly, all of Johnny's cronies turned their attention to me. Before they could get pummeled again, Danny and Phillip scurried away. I had underestimated the sheer size and brute force of the tenth graders, and a sense of unease crept over me. But I refused to back down.

All around us, the crowd of students chanted, "Fight! Fight! Fight!"

Fear made my stomach tighten. My palms were sweaty, and my heart was racing. This had been a huge mistake, and I was about to pay the price for it.

"We were just having a little fun! Weren't we, guys?" Johnny sneered, and his entourage chuckled in agreement.

"That doesn't seem like much fun to me," I retorted, dismissively waving my hand.

I turned to leave, wanting to get away before things got even more out of hand, but one of the goons blocked my path.

I tried to shove him out of the way, but he was too massive and unwieldy. All of that dumb must have been weighing him down.

The rest of Johnny's gang closed in on me, their faces twisted into malicious grins. Some pounded their fists menacingly, while others mockingly mimed punches or tears. I felt trapped like I was a cornered animal surrounded by a pack of wolves. Big, incredibly dumb, wolves. And for a moment, I wondered if I had made a terrible mistake. I refused to show them my fear, wanting to bluff my way out of this mess. Bracing myself for whatever was to come, I waited for Johnny's next move.

"What are you going to do you little freak. Why don't you go cry to your daddy," he said.

The cruel remark hit me like a punch in the gut. Of course, he knew I didn't have a dad around; everyone did. However, it did not hurt as much as the actual punch in the gut.

I tried to dodge his fist, but I was no match for his speed and strength. I doubled over in pain as spots danced in my vision. There was a chorus of cheers. Some cheered for Michael, and most of the girls cheered for me to get back up. I didn't know any of them, but they were still cheering for me. There are lots of unwritten rules in this world. One of them is 'Guys can't hit a girl.'

I balled my fists, fighting to get back up. Tears welled in my eyes as anger and embarrassment flooded through me. My mom was not going to like this. She would probably be calling the school and Johnny's parents to yell at them.

I struggled to my feet, fueled by anger and adrenaline. Johnny looked at me with dark brown eyes that were full of humorous hostility.

My fists shook with anger. I pulled my arm back and aimed for his big stupid face. I had never been very strong, but

I still hit him hard enough that he staggered backwards. His friends rushed over to help him, leaving room for me to escape.

I shoved my way through the crowd, not bothering to grab my backpack as I fled. I ran as fast as I could through the deserted hallways. The shouts of all the students echoed behind me. I ran as far away from that school as possible. I didn't stop until I reached the safety of the forest.

Every day I take a shortcut home through the woods. I like it more than taking the bus—the serenity of the forest, the rustling leaves, the earthy smell of it all. It made me feel so safe. That's why this was the first place I came after the fight. Today, there was a cool autumn breeze that made for the perfect temperature. It was a cool September day. Autumn was my favorite time of year.

I came to a stop and sat down leaning against a tree to catch my breath. I clutched my stomach. I was sure it would be bruised the next day. I felt like someone was poking it repeatedly with a hot rod.

I sighed as Micheal's cruel words echoed in my head; each one hit me like another punch to the gut. The comment about my dad hit me the hardest.

As a sigh escaped my lips, I found myself instinctively reaching up to touch my necklace. The crystal star pendant was cool and smooth at the touch. At first glance, it was just some old piece of jewelry. To me, it was my only connection to my dad, the only tangible thing I had left of him. It hurt to wonder if he would ever come back. Almost as much as my gut hurt after that punch.

Man, I thought, *I need to learn to fight. Or maybe just learn to stop getting into fights.*

The latter probably wasn't going to happen. I took a deep breath of crisp late September air. A squirrel scurried by me, probably scavenging for nuts to get ready for the coming winter. The leaves that made up the cascading canopy of orange, red, and yellow above me rustled in the wind. The pecking of a woodpecker echoed throughout the forest. A sharp, high-pitched cry rang out from above the trees. Although the trees obscured them from my view, I knew it was the sound of birds flying south.

Despite all of the many noises in the forest, it still felt calm and quiet. Unlike the noisy halls of my school, bustling with people that I have never truly fit in with.

They all knew my dad had left when I was a baby. Somehow, the word spread throughout this small town. When you live in a small town like mine, rumors and stories spread like wildfire. Kids at school laughed at me and made fun of me. It was mostly the jerks like Johnny, but sometimes even the nerds got in on the action. I resented my dad so much. Not only did he leave me and my mom, but he left us with all of the rumors. All my life, I have dealt with the whispers and the stares as I pass by everyone in this town.

No matter how awful my peers are to me, I can't stand to watch them get hurt or picked on by the other kids. I know how it feels to be an outsider and to be scrutinized for it, so I do whatever I can to make sure it doesn't happen to them.

I stayed there, sitting with my back against the tree for longer than I should have. After a while, I decided that I had probably been there for way too long. I knew I would need to be home soon, so I pulled my phone out of my back pocket and checked for texts. It was already around five o'clock in the afternoon.

That's strange, I thought to myself. *Mom always texts me before four o'clock.*

She worked late most days, but she would text me to make sure I was safe and, on my way, home. It had become like our little routine. We never broke our routine, not even if it was an

FIND THE LIGHT   11

emergency. Once, she had gotten into a wreck, nothing fatal just being rear ended. She still texted me as if nothing had happened. I tried not to let it bother me, but I had a bad feeling about it.

I was about to set my phone down, when I saw a flash of light reflected on the screen. My hand shook as I quietly turned my head around to see if someone was there, but there was no one in sight. Then a twig snapped on the other side of the tree.

It could just be another squirrel or something. I thought to myself.

And it could have been. However, a long string of swear words followed closely after. As far as I knew, neither squirrels nor trees could talk.

I quickly jumped to my feet, startled. I quietly stepped around to the other side of the tree. Since the tree was quite large, I didn't see the person until I was face-to-face with him. He was a tall and handsome boy dressed in the same blue hoodie I had seen him in before. Only this time, his hood was down where I could actually see him. Despite the wind, his brown hair was swept back perfectly. The way his sapphire blue eyes twinkled and the way he offered me an awkward, yet somehow charming smile reminded me of a movie star.

I jumped back, dropping my phone.

"Who are you?" I demanded.

He smiled more brightly. He had a beautiful smile that made me melt. I shook my head. What was wrong with me? No boy has ever made me feel the way this boy did, but at the same time, I felt he wasn't like other boys.

Other boys don't stalk you. I thought.

I gathered as much snark as I could before reminding him that he still hadn't answered my question.

"My name is William Hudson, but you can call me Will," he said with a wink.

I felt my cheeks grow warm.

"Why were you following me?" I asked. I tried to ignore his wink, not willing to trust him yet.

"I have no idea what you're talking about," he said.

That made me angry. Of course, he knew what I was talking about.

He had the audacity to grin at me.

"Don't play dumb with me, Will! I know it was you!" I said angrily.

He huffed in frustration and ran a hand through his perfectly styled brown hair. I would have slapped myself if he wasn't standing there. Seriously! What was wrong with me? I didn't even know this guy, and he was a stalker. What about him could be attractive other than his eyes and his hair and his smile....

STOP IT! I chided myself. *He is not cute, not your type, and he is a creepy stalker.*

"Alright, fine. I need to get this over with so here it goes: You're not human, Celeste. Well, you're half-human. Your mom is human; your dad is an Arbitrator. Arbitrators have magical powers and live in a different dimension. I'm here to take you to Enceaf, your father's dimension by order of the Convocation," he explained. He made a bunch of hand gestures and said it all really fast.

I considered his words for a moment. Honestly, part of me wanted to believe him. I wanted that to be the reason I never fit in and why my dad never came back. I just couldn't believe that it would be possible. I mean, could any of that even make sense? My dad left me when I was a baby. In my opinion, the real reason he left was that he didn't care about my mom and me, not because he was in a different dimension. Either way, this guy was a lunatic, and I didn't believe a word he said.

"You're crazy!" I yelled. I backed up slowly, trying to get away from him, but he grabbed me by my wrists.

"I promise you, I'm not," he said.

He looked down at where his hands firmly grasped my wrists. He seemed to realize that grabbing me was not helping his case. After a couple of seconds, he gently released my hands.

"Yeah, sure. I'll believe it when I see it," I huffed as I rubbed my wrists where he had grabbed them.

He had such a strong grip. It had been like trying to get my hand out of a Chinese finger trap. The more I pulled, the tighter his grip got.

"Fine, I'll prove it to you. Just watch, okay?"

He waved his arms out in front of him, almost like he was saying hello to something that wasn't there. That definitely seems like something a crazy person like him would do. I almost ran for it while his back was turned, but before I could, a swirling circle of golden light appeared before us. It shimmered with a kaleidoscope of gold.

"Wow," I breathed. "What is that?"

My brain was having a hard time comprehending what I was seeing. The way the portal swirled and shimmered gave me a chill. A faint memory tugged at the back of my mind, but I couldn't manage to recall anything. Could what he has said been true? Perhaps I was starting to believe him. Either that or I was hallucinating.

Maybe this is all a dream. I thought. I considered smacking him to check. That image put a smile on my face.

"It's a portal to a different dimension," he said.

"Wait…What?!"

I knew he had said stuff about other dimensions, but part of me still refused to believe him.

Before I could protest, he pulled me through the swirling doorway of light. On the other side, we emerged into a void of endless gray nothingness.

TWO

"What is this place?"

"The Grai. It's the void between dimensions. I've never been here before. I don't understand why the portal brought us here. It was supposed to bring us to Enceaf," he said. Panic and frustration clung to every word he spoke.

Something felt wrong. I had a strange feeling that something was off. Other than the fact that I was in another dimension, and I was currently holding hands with a stranger who had followed me all day. Plus, I had a feeling that something was off with my mom. Otherwise, she would have called by now.

A sense of dread settled over me as I realized I didn't even have my phone with me. I had dropped it in the woods. I wanted to groan. I couldn't believe how stupid I had been.

I decided I would worry about that later. I needed to focus on getting answers to all of the crazy questions that were scrambling around inside my head. Some of them were so crazy that I was afraid to say them out loud.

I had always wanted answers. I was finally going to get them. So why did this feel so wrong?

"We can still get out of here though, right?" I asked nervously.

"Of course! Don't worry, I just have to open another portal out of here," he waved his hands, and another swirling golden portal opened.

"This one should take us to Enceaf," he said.

"Should?"

"Well sometimes if I can't concentrate the portals get a little bit iffy," he said.

I did not like the idea of that. Still, I didn't refuse as he pulled me towards the portal. As we approached, I noticed that the Grai was no longer gray. It was enveloped in black fog which had curly wisps of smoke. Suddenly, a shadowy figure emerged from the smoke.

"I am Kilmar," it said in a raspy whisper. "The Arbitrators can keep me contained no longer! My minions are coming. My shadows have begun to corrupt the other dimensions. None of you foolish defenders can stop me now. And you, Celeste Rowan. I will not allow your so-called 'destiny' to be fulfilled. You foolish child! You can try, but you will never defeat me!" The figure broke into a fit of maniacal laughter. Then it just dissipated, but the wisps of curling smoke remained.

"Who was that? What did that guy mean by 'my destiny?' Will—"

He cut me off abruptly. "We need to go. Now!"

He pulled me through the portal. This time it deposited us about five hundred feet in the air. In front of us, gleaming towers of colorful crystals stood tall and elegant, surrounded by a vast landscape of rolling hills. Large, majestic buildings stood encased by a tall golden wall. It would have been quite the sight, had I not been falling to my death.

"Will! Get us out of here!" I called over the wind that was howling around us.

He set his jaw and closed his eyes. After we fell about fifty more feet, he finally opened his eyes. He gasped for breath.

"I'm sorry I can't focus enough to open a portal," He wouldn't meet my eyes.

"What are we going to do?" I screamed. My chest tightened as panic flooded through me.

"You'll have to open the portal!" He cried.

I almost couldn't hear him through the wind that was screaming in my ears. At first, I was terrified. What if I couldn't open the portal? I didn't even think it was possible until five minutes ago. How was I supposed to do it? Then again, I would never know if I didn't try.

I took a deep breath.

I am not going to die today, I thought.

"Okay, how do I do it?" I asked.

His eyes gleamed with grim determination.

"Close your eyes and visualize where you want to go. You see that grass down there? Picture it being closer to us," he said.

He squeezed my hand. I felt my cheeks burn. At least if I died, I would die holding hands with a boy. Sure, he was a stranger, a stalker, and he was from another dimension, but none of that really mattered to me. He was the only boy I knew who had never made fun of me or beat me up. That meant more to me than I had realized.

I looked down at the grass. The ground was getting closer. It was only about one hundred feet away. I closed my eyes and pictured us standing on it. It was really hard to focus on it because it kept shifting to scenes of us splattering all over it.

Seventy feet.

Sixty feet

Fifty feet.

Forty feet.

Thirty feet.

"You can do it, Celeste. Just believe in yourself. I believe in you," Will shouted. It was very sweet, but it made it very hard to concentrate.

Twenty feet.

Ten feet.

Right before we crashed into the ground, I felt a tugging sensation in my gut. It left me sore, like I was stretching a muscle that I didn't use very often. Suddenly, the swirling gold light appeared. Time seemed to slow down as we plummeted through it. My heart was beating so hard that I figured even Helen Keller could have heard it.

Fortunately, it opened onto solid ground. Unfortunately, it opened sideways, so we went tumbling over each other. An agonizing crack came from my ribs. Finally, we stopped rolling, and I landed on top of Will. I rolled off him and winced from the searing pain that tore through my chest.

I gritted my teeth and tried to stand up. Immediately I regretted it. I wheezed and sputtered. My legs collapsed as a wave of nausea hit me. I would have fallen flat on my face if Will hadn't caught me before I hit the ground. "Woah, take it easy," he said, easing me onto my back. "Where are you hurt?"

"My ribs," I said through gritted teeth.

"Hold still," he said.

He placed his hand gently on my chest. I tensed. The only other times a boy had touched me, it had been to punch me or shove me into a locker. To say the least I was uncomfortable. Will must have noticed, because he removed his hand.

"Relax. I'm not going to hurt you," he said.

His tone was sincere enough. Worry lines were etched all over his forehead and his lips were pursed. I decided to trust him. After all, I was stuck there unless he took me home, and he was the only one who could give me the answers I was looking for.

"Okay," I whispered.

He put his hand on my chest. Suddenly, his hand glowed with warmth. A buzz of energy filled my bones. For a moment, it felt like there was fire running through my veins. Then, I felt my ribs mending. He removed his hand. The pain disappeared.

"Is that better?" he asked.

"Yeah. How did you do that?"

"I'm a healer. My magic allows me to heal the sick and injured," he added, "As long as they aren't too close to death."

I suddenly realized how close our faces were. And how close our lips were. Will must have too, because he quickly moved his hand off my chest, and his cheeks turned the cutest shade of pink.

I sat up slowly. That was crazy. One minute I was in excruciating pain and the next I was completely fine.

"So that's what you were talking about when you told me I had magical powers. Why haven't I realized it if I have some kind of magical power? I'm pretty sure that's something I would have noticed," I pointed out.

"Well, most of us don't gain our abilities until we're fourteen or fifteen. I just developed mine a few weeks ago, since I'm only fifteen. I'm still training at Enceaf Academy," he said absently.

I tried to picture an academy filled with other kids like Will, all dressed in immaculate clothes and honing their unique powers. I wondered if I would ever be able to go there someday. I had never fit in at my old school, but maybe I would fit in there. After all, I wasn't completely human. Will had said I wasn't completely Arbitrator either. I was only half human and half Arbitrator. I wondered if that meant I would never truly fit in anywhere.

Once my brain was finished spiraling in turmoil, it focused on the more important part of what he had said.

He was fifteen. That meant he was only a year older than me. My heart did some stupid fluttery thing, and I tried to hide the blush that spread across my face.

I don't even know him. I scolded. *Sure, he's dreamy, and handsome, and has magical powers, but I don't know much about him other than the fact that he's an Arbitrator and a healer. And I still don't really know what those things are either.*

"So, if you're still training, then why were you sent to get me?" I inquired.

"Coming to get you was one of my tests. Guess I didn't do too well, considering I dropped you out of the sky," he didn't look at me as he said it, but I could hear the guilt that crept into the edges of his voice. "Lady Finkle is going to make my life miserable!"

I tried to hold back my laugh, but it was kind of hard too. I never thought I'd hear a name as funny as Finkle in the same sentence as miserable.

"Surely Lady Finkle isn't that bad," I said, trying to suppress a laugh.

"Oh, trust me, her name is very misleading. She's the worst teacher ever, and she hates me," he said.

A hysterical laugh bubbled up in my throat. Evil teachers named Finkle. Smokey figures that talk about my supposed destiny. Magical portals and powers. Different dimensions. All of this shouldn't exist, yet here I was, standing in the middle of it.

"Today has made absolutely no sense. I have so many questions that my brain feels like it's short-circuited. I need answers," I said with a sigh. I buried my face in my hands; my shoulders slumped under the weight of the day's events.

Will put his hand on my shoulder. I lifted my head to meet his eyes. His gaze was so intense. I saw many emotions in them. Worry. Admiration. Fear. Confidence. Every single one made my heart skip a beat.

"I know this seems crazy—it kind of is—but you have been amazing so far. You saved us when I couldn't. You're meant to do extraordinary things, you just don't know it yet," he said comfortingly. His words made my heart swell.

"That thing in the Grai. He called himself Kilmar. Who was he? What did he mean when he said he wouldn't let my destiny be fulfilled?"

"There's this old prophecy. It never made sense, until we found out about you. Now a few of the lines make sense. The prophecy goes like this,

Shining bright,

Will be the savior of light.

Hidden away, out of reach.

They are safe within forbidden keep.

Where shadows reap, a skirmish between darkness and day,

For both sides, there will be a price to pay.

Betrayal of the light, they'll be stuck in a plight.

Powers great and strong,

Will battle for right and wrong.

The greater force will win, with great sacrifice to end.

"How does any of that make you think of me?" I asked.

He ran his hand down his face. He looked at me like I'd just asked the stupidest question ever. Honestly, I couldn't blame him. This whole situation felt pretty stupid. And crazy. And so many other things I am too afraid to unpack. For now, I am just locking those things away until I get more answers.

"Hidden away, out of reach. Safe within forbidden keep—We call the human dimension Fortest. It means forbidden. Nobody is supposed to go there. It's against the Arbitrator code. Your father was safeguarding you in the human dimension with your mom. That line has to mean you," he got so adorably excited when he talked about it.

"Why is Fortest forbidden?"

"A really long time ago, humans and Arbitrators lived in the same dimension. They intermarried and had kids. Those kids were called halflings. Everything was great. But then their children became too powerful. Something about their powers was different from ours. They didn't burn out as quickly from overuse, and they lived way longer than we did. The Elder Arbitrators grew scared of their power and decided to separate us. The humans went to a different dimension. We built walls around our city. Since then, it has been forbidden for anyone to go to the human dimension. Only convocation members can go there on assignment," he explained. I let that information set in.

That was so much information at one time that I only understood half of it. What on earth was a Convocation? Why were halflings so powerful compared to Arbitrators? I couldn't wrap my head around it.

"You said I'm half-human, half-arbitrator, right? So, I'm a halfling and that means I'm super powerful?" I asked him.

"Well, I don't really know. It depends on your family lineage," he explained.

If I was super powerful, it would make sense that my father would hide me. However, I didn't feel powerful. I felt helpless, scared, and confused. None of that made me feel like I was something worth hiding. I mean, if he was embarrassed of me and that's why he decided to hide me, I would totally understand. I was a freak.

"Come on. You see that wall?" Will asked.

He pointed to the speck of gold on the horizon. It was so small, you had to squint and look sideways to see it. But I nodded.

"That's Enceaf. We're almost there. We can teleport closer if you'd like-" I cut him off.

"No! I-I'd rather not. After everything that's happened today, I just want to keep both feet on the ground," I said nervously.

The thought of falling again made me feel like I was going to throw up. He sighed and looked out at the rolling fields.

"It's going to be a long walk," he pointed out.

"Then we better get going!" I said enthusiastically.

Will groaned. Obviously, my enthusiasm was not rubbing off on him.

THREE

We walked in silence for a while. I lost myself in thought. My mind was swamped with a sea of questions. I was so consumed by those questions that I had failed to notice we were being followed.

A large shadow loomed over me. The air had a sudden chill to it. Clouds gathered overhead. I turned around and screamed. A seven-foot-tall beast towered over us. His face was an abomination of mangled red skin. His black eyes twinkled with a murderous rage. His body was covered in shaggy tufts of inky black hair, and its hands and face were the only places that weren't covered in fur.

I should have run or done literally anything. Instead, I just stood there, paralyzed with fear. I couldn't move. I couldn't think. I couldn't speak. Will snapped out of it before I could.

"Celeste, run!" Will yelled

It was too late. The beast had already snatched me up. I squirmed and kicked my legs, but it was no use. His hands were like massive unmovable boulders.

"Come on, don't you want to join your parents?" He grumbled.

Parents. Plural. So, it had Mom and my dad?

That's why my mom hadn't bothered to text me. She probably didn't have her phone. Even if she did, we didn't have a national phone plan, let alone a multi-dimensional phone plan. What if she was hurt or worse? I couldn't bear the thought of losing Mom. She was pretty much all the family I had left.

I guess it would suck if my dad died too. As much as I resented him for leaving us, I didn't want him dead. If anything, I wanted him to come back to me. It occurred to me that the beast might not even have my parents. However, I dismissed the thought. He was too dumb to think of a clever lie. I decided that if this thing really did have my parents, I was going to have to find a way to save them, both of them.

"What did you do to them?" I fumed. I clenched my fists as anger clouded my mind.

"Boss says I can't tell you that!" he said.

I clenched my fists even tighter. I wasn't very strong. As dumb as he was, he was definitely much stronger than me. I couldn't even beat a few boys. My bruised stomach was proof of that. He would easily pummel me. However, he was incredibly stupid. I wasn't the smartest person, but I was smarter than him. I could try to get some information out of him and stall for as long as possible. Once that plan stopped working, well...I would cross that bridge when I got there.

"Who is your boss? I would love to meet him," I said gently. I decided to treat him the way I would a two-year-old. Anger and yelling would never work, so I decided to try being super nice.

A concept very foreign to me after all my years of taking relentless teasing and belittling remarks from my peers. I said it in the politest voice I could muster and offered my friendliest smile.

He blinked at me and scratched his head, clearly perplexed by my sudden change in demeanor.

"You have," he said warily, "In the Grai."

That stopped me in my tracks. A name echoed through my mind leaving a chilling terror in its wake. Kilmar. He had said that he wouldn't let my destiny be fulfilled. Apparently, that included sending this thing after me. What even was he? Some kind of shadow henchman or something? I had the sinking feeling that there would be others like him coming for me as well.

This horrifying realization momentarily made me lose my composure. I shook my head, trying to put the thoughts out of my mind. I struggled to plaster another fake smile on my face.

"Yes, he was...." my voice caught as I struggled to find the right word, ".... lovely. I believe his name was Kilmar. Is that right?"

"Yes," he paused as if he had forgotten something.

I took his moment of confusion to ask him to let me go.

"Would you like to set me down, so we can talk like civilized people?" I suggested.

I wanted to scrape the posh accent off of my tongue and spit it out. I sounded a little bit like someone from England. I had never been there of course since we couldn't afford a vacation. I had still seen a lot of movies about it. Not trying to hate on the English. I just didn't like the way I sounded.

That's probably because I didn't sound like me. Even through all of the teasing and rumors, I had never changed who I was. My instincts screamed that this was wrong, that I shouldn't pretend to be someone I'm not, which was stupid since this plan was currently saving my life.

He shook his head.

"Just put her down," Will said behind me.

I whipped my head around. I had forgotten he was there. He had his arms stretched out in peace. I knew he was just trying to help, but he was ruining my whole plan.

Apparently, the beast wasn't a fan of him.

"You're one of them!" He accused Will.

"Yes, I'm an Arbitrator," Will said calmly. The amount of pride in his voice was a little annoying. Even though I didn't know much about them yet, I still wasn't a very big fan.

"Stay away from me!" The beast screamed. He clenched his fists. Apparently, he had forgotten about the fact that he was still holding me. His grip tightened around my chest. I tried to suck in a breath, but it got caught in my lungs thanks to his crushing grip. His nails dug into my ribcage, not hard enough to break the skin, but enough that it hurt. After everything that had happened, that was the awful little cherry on top.

I felt so much anger bubbling inside of me, like I'd lit a fuse. My blood boiled and I felt as if there was fire running through my veins. Not an agonizing fire, but a warm, empowering one that wanted to destroy everything in its path. I hated that sensation. I wanted to be free of it, but I couldn't control it. I needed to get rid of it. Instinctively, I forced it out.

"Celeste, you're glowing," Will said in awe.

At first, I thought, *well, maybe he's just complimenting me.*

Yes, that would have been nice. However, that is almost never the case when it comes to me and boys. I looked down at myself and sure enough, my body was wrapped in a halo of red light. I looked like a human nightlight.

"Ow! Ow! Ow! Ow!" Cried the beast. The beast dropped me and clutched his singed hand to his chest.

He promptly said, "You're mean!"

I watched, dumbfounded, as he struggled to his feet and ran off crying.

I turned around to face Will, who was lost in thought.

"Now it all makes sense," Will mumbled. He muttered something else under his breath.

"What makes sense?" I asked. "What the heck are you talking about?"

"You were glowing, Celeste. I don't know how you did it, but I do know one thing. You're the Savior of Light from the prophecy. It has to be you," His gaze was so intense I looked away.

"I would love to agree with you. Really, I would, but I'm not special. Never have been. Never will be," I told him. A twang of bitterness crept into my voice.

Being special meant getting a lot of attention. I didn't like attention; it was never a good thing for me. If I got attention in class, it was because I was being sent to the principal's office. If I got attention from boys, they were just teasing me or beating me up, or I had done something super embarrassing like slipping in front of the entire cafeteria.

That had actually happened a few months ago. My pants got all wet and my lunch spilled all over me. Unfortunately, I brought chili from home. Don't get me wrong, I love Mom's chili. However, my pants were soggy and brown. Not a good combination. Everybody pointed and laughed. Everywhere I went people called me 'potty pants.' It took three showers to get all of the chili out of my hair. I wished the water could wash away the embarrassment. Unfortunately, it couldn't. Thinking of that still makes me cringe. Long story short, attention is nothing but trouble for me.

"How do you explain what just happened then?" he asked.

He did have a good point, but that didn't mean I had to like it. The truth was, I couldn't explain what was happening. How could I? I hardly understood anything that had happened that day, let alone what was happening to me.

"I don't know what happened!" I yelled. "I just remember being so mad and frustrated. It's as if there were fireworks going off inside of me. It was so overwhelming, and I couldn't control it. I just needed to get rid of it, so I forced it out. Then I just started glowing."

I spoke as fast as I could, the words pouring out of me like a river. I hadn't realized how much fear and doubt was lying under the surface of the brave facade I was trying to keep up. I had a feeling the strong mask I tried to keep on, the one that was all brave smiles and positive thoughts, was slowly cracking and becoming see-through.

"So, your powers are connected to your emotions?" Will clarified.

"I already told you, I-Don't-Know," I put more emphasis on my words since he clearly wasn't understanding.

"Could you try to channel your powers into other emotions? You said you were mad, so try doing the opposite. Try being happy," he prompted.

"I don't think that will work," I told him.

"Just humor me. Okay?" he said.

I thought about it for a minute. At least I would be getting answers about whatever was happening to me with these new powers. I still needed answers about my dad. What if I got into trouble along the way? I might need to know more about my powers if something happened.

On the other hand, if I ignored my powers completely, maybe they would go away on their own. They could go back to whatever part of me they had been hiding in and leave me alone forever.

Deep down, I knew it was wishful thinking. These powers were a part of me. A scary, overwhelming part that I knew I would have to learn to live with. As much as I hated it, I would have to stop trying to keep them at arm's length and embrace it.

"Okay," I said with a sigh, "I guess it couldn't hurt to try."

I closed my eyes and thought about the things that make me happy: hiking with my mom; being curled up on the couch with a good book; drinking a glass of sweet tea in the summer; my mom's hugs; sitting by a cozy fire when it's cold outside.

Suddenly, my entire body filled with warmth. Not the suffocating warmth I'd felt earlier, the one that felt like a raging inferno. No, this warmth was cozy. More similar to a small steady flame that sent warmth through me with every thump of my heart.

Slowly, I opened my eyes. A yellow halo surrounded me.

"I-I think it worked," I said in disbelief.

I turned my arms over, astonished by my newfound glow. I felt a buzz of energy coursing through me, like I was on a sugar high.

"This is so weird," I mumbled.

"Are you kidding me? This is awesome! You have light powers! And you're a Halfing. If Kilmar is back, you might be the only person alive who could rival him!" Will exclaimed.

I stared at him, stunned into silence. He didn't seriously expect me to just go and battle an evil shadow figure, did he? I just found out I had powers. I didn't know how to use them, let alone use them to fight.

"Why would I be able to beat him?" I asked.

I didn't feel like being confrontational, so I just decided to ask another question that had popped up among the sea of unanswered questions that my mind was swimming through.

"Kilmar is the king of the shadow dimension. He is slowly rising again, but he has one weakness we could exploit: light. If you have light powers, maybe you could beat him," Will explained.

"That's a pretty big maybe, Will," I replied bitterly.

He wanted me to bet my life on a 'maybe.'

Are. You. Kidding. Me?

Will coughed as awkwardness settled between us. He could obviously see how much I resented his words. He did the wise thing and changed the subject before I could get mad enough to throw my second punch of the day.

"You burned the demon when you were red; what do you do when you're yellow?" he asked.

"How am I supposed to know? The only living thing for miles is us so I have nothing to test it on," I pointed out.

I really wanted to find out, but I didn't see how I could, unless Will wanted to take that risk. I didn't think I could use my powers on myself, otherwise I would have burned myself to a crisp earlier.

"Yes, you do," Will said brashly.

He paused as if waiting for me to ask the obvious question. I could have said nothing, stopping him from having the satisfaction of getting to be a smart aleck. However, I was far too anxious to wait.

"What?" I said impetuously.

"The grass!" he said.

A proud smile spread across his face, as if he had just made the most intelligent remark in the history of smart aleck remarks.

"The grass," I repeated.

"Yes!" He said, "The grass is alive too so it shouldn't change how your power affects it."

I sighed, knowing he was probably right. I crouched to the ground and touched a blade of grass. The grass was dry and yellow, as if it hadn't rained here in quite some time. As my fingertips brushed it, the blade of grass changed to bright summer green. I had revived the dry blade of grass.

"So red is for heat and yellow is for healing?" I asked Will.

"That's what it looks like. Maybe we can try to find out more after you meet the Convocation," Will replied.

He sighed and looked out over the landscape, probably picturing how very old we'd be by the time we got to the city. He looked so pitiful and cute that I forgot about my fears of the portal.

"I guess we can portal closer, but only if you promise me we won't drop out of the sky again," I said sternly.

"Don't worry, this time I can focus enough to do it right," he assured me.

He closed his eyes and thrust out his hands. Another swirling circle of gold glimmered into existence in front of us.

"After you," I said nervously.

I was a little anxious about going through another portal. Will rolled his eyes and stepped into the portal. I took a deep breath to steady my nerves. Then I stepped through after him.

FOUR

I landed in the shadow of a massive structure. I looked up and I couldn't help but gasp in awe at the magnificent sight before me. The giant golden gate towering above us was a true work of art. Intricate designs of gold were laced throughout the gates, and pearls dotted the sophisticated pattern, giving it a regal appearance. The gate was so tall that it would have made the towering Redwoods in California look like mere saplings by comparison. It was a breathtaking sight, and I couldn't help but feel a sense of wonder and amazement.

"Why is it so big?" I asked.

"Huh," Will said, "That's not what I thought you'd ask."

I felt my cheeks burn. I could have asked any question, yet I asked that. I felt so stupid.

Quick! Say something smarter! I thought to myself.

I was racking my brain, trying to decide what to say that might be a bit more impressive. Then I realized something: I never cared what boys thought of me before.

Why did I care so much about what Will thought? I had that strange feeling again where I felt like my stomach was swarming with butterflies. I didn't understand what that feeling was. I did understand one thing, though.

I. Hated. It.

"Well, remember how I told you the humans were moved to a different dimension? After they were moved, we built walls around ourselves so that it could never happen again. No one can teleport in or out of the city because of the walls. They create a force field that hinders everyone's ability to portal in and out of the city," he said.

He seemed to be trying very hard to ignore my blushing cheeks and the way I kept looking at him, trying to understand what I was feeling.

Suddenly, there was a loud bang. I jumped and Will chuckled at me.

"Relax. The guards are just opening the gates," he said.

"I guess I'm just a little on edge after everything that's happened today," I said.

The ground beneath us trembled as the gates swung inward. My legs locked and I found it hard to move. I wasn't scared before, but now, standing here in the shadow of a massive glittering city that I hadn't known existed, I was trembling. This was the city of the Arbitrators. I was part Arbitrator, but I had a terrible feeling that didn't mean I would be accepted. This feeling weighed me down. I felt like someone had cemented my feet in place.

"Come on, I'm taking you to see the Convocation," he said confidently.

"Convocation? You mentioned them earlier. Who are they, and what do they want with me?" I asked frantically. I spoke so quickly that Will looked momentarily shocked.

He put his hands on my shoulders. Little bits of warmth seemed to resonate where he was touching me. That warmth seemed to spark another stampede of butterflies in my stomach.

"First of all, chill out. You have no reason to be afraid," he told me.

Actually, I have a lot of reasons to be afraid. I thought. I bit back the scathing remark.

"Second, the Convocation is a group of our most important leaders. Most of them are elders, but some of them are powerful people from our world. Your father used to be one of them. I don't know why they want you though," he said.

I had no idea what elders were. That wasn't what bothered me about Will's explanation.

"My dad used to be one of them? Why isn't he anymore?" I asked.

"I don't really know. I think it had something to do with hiding you, but I could be wrong," he added when I frowned.

My dad used to be one of the most important leaders in this world. He risked his power and importance in this world to protect me? What was he protecting me from? I wondered if it was the Convocation he was trying to protect me from. That did not make me feel any better about walking through those gates.

It would be like jumping into still water. You have no idea what's under the surface or how deep a dive it really is. On one hand, I could just not take that chance at all. I would stay safe and dry. However, I would live the rest of my life with unanswered questions, and I would never stop wondering "what if."

My other option would be to dive blindly into danger. I would gain answers. Maybe, I could even find someone who could help me save my parents from Kilmar. Plus, the only way for Will to pass his test was for me to go in. This seemed really important to him, and for some reason, I didn't want to let him down.

In spite of all of these benefits, my mind kept filling with endless possibilities of danger. Each one was like a knife to my bravery. Soon, all my bravery unraveled, leaving my heart in a cowardly heap.

Will began walking into the city, but I couldn't bring myself to follow. I watched as he stopped and turned to look at me. His expression softened and he looked me in the eyes. He must have seen the fear and the doubt in my gaze.

"What's wrong?" he asked.

"I don't think I can do this, Will," I told him. My voice quivered with fear. I wrung my hands nervously.

"I don't understand," he said. His face was scrunched in confusion.

"I don't belong here. What if the Convocation sees that? What if they decide to hurt me or-or something?" I said despairingly.

I was probably just jumping to conclusions, but in my mind, that or something was killing me. I didn't know these people, and I had no idea what they were capable of.

"I'm not going to let them hurt you. My test was just to bring you to them. They didn't say anything about hurting you or whatever else you think they'll do to you. Besides, they are the fairest leaders in the world. They wouldn't do anything to anyone unless they had done something really wrong," he assured me.

His impatient tone was not very reassuring. In fact, it made me more anxious about going in.

"You don't trust me. I get that. We've known each other

for a few hours, and I've already almost got you killed twice, but I'm trying to pass this test. This is a big deal for me. Do you know how often the Convocation oversees a test? Hardly ever. Like, once in a few decades. The Convocation also chooses their successors. If this goes well, one of them could choose me someday. Please just trust me," he pleaded.

He offered me his hand. I stared at it and my hand hesitated by my side. This was it. If I went in, there would be no going back. I let him take my hand and lead me in through the gates. As we went through, I noticed two guard towers on either side of the gate. A single guard occupied each. They eyed me warily. I kept my head down as we walked through.

The massive glimmering buildings were even bigger than they had seemed while I was plummeting to my death. I didn't think it was physically possible for something to be that tall. While I was walking through the city, I had the strange feeling that if there was even the slightest breeze, the whole city would come toppling down on top of me.

That wasn't the only thing that I noticed about the city. Everything seemed to sparkle as the sun bounced off the buildings. Even the streets sparkled as if they had been dusted in glitter.

The city kind of reminded me of a sparkly, rainbow-colored New York. People were bustling around the sidewalks. Some of them were holding the hands of young children as they waited to cross the crosswalks. Others were coming in and out of shops or chatting while they ate at what I assumed was a restaurant. All of them wore elaborate ruffled gowns or sleek tunics. I noticed that all the kids that I would have pegged as around my age wore plaid skirts or pants with a blazer over a white shirt. It reminded me of what boarding school or private school kids would wear.

I suddenly felt under dressed in my simple blue hoodie and jeans. People whispered as we walked by, probably thinking the same. One young girl, wearing a blue dress with ruffles on the sleeves, pointed at me. Her mother quickly ushered her away. No doubt, she was thinking that she didn't want her daughter anywhere near the strangers in odd clothes.

Carriages rode around, dropping people off and picking up more, like a taxi. If taxis were glittery, plated with gold, and were being pulled by majestic colorful horses with sparkly horns on their heads.

"Are those unicorns?" I gasped.

"Yep," Will replied as if this was just an everyday occurrence.

Of course, for him, it was. For me, however, it seemed like something straight out of a children's book.

Will whistled shrilly and an empty carriage stopped beside us. A beautiful unicorn pulled it.

"Can I pet it?" I asked.

I was perfectly aware that I sounded like a little kid; I didn't care. This was way too cool for me to care.

"Sure," Will said.

I reached out and gently stroked the unicorn's head. Its pink hair was so soft it felt like touching a cloud—which I could tell since I had recently fallen through quite a few of them to get here.

"Climb in," he said as he offered me his hand, a very gentlemanly gesture. This time, I took it without hesitation. After we had both settled into our seats, he told the horse to take us to the "Hall of Convocations."

The carriage lurched forward as the unicorn began to trot. Somehow, the unicorn seemed to know exactly where it was going. I was utterly lost in this glittering city. I was officially more oblivious than a unicorn.

I sat across from Will. He fiddled with the edge of his hoodie sleeves. I felt underdressed and out of place amongst all these people in ruffles, silks, dresses, and heels. Will, despite his human outfit, still looked like he belonged. Something about him just radiated regalness and confidence, despite the fact that he was obviously nervous. He looked less like a scared teenage boy, and more like a model, toying with the sleeves of his shirt to make something that already looked amazing look perfect.

I knew that if we sat in silence, I would start worrying and troubleshooting. Then my mind would spiral, and I would start regretting coming. It would be better if we talked.

"I saw a lot of kids wearing uniforms. Do they go to your school?" I asked.

I thought it was a good conversation starter and a valid question. Besides, deep down, part of me wondered if there was a chance I could go there someday.

"Yeah, Enceaf Academy. They're probably all on their way to take finals. This counts as my finals test, so I don't have to be there today," he explained.

I wondered if he was like me, at the bottom of the social ladder. Probably not, he didn't seem like that kind of guy. As we passed by the two students, the girl looked at Will and blushed. The guy glared at Will. Obviously, the girl agreed with me that Will was quite handsome. By the way the guy grabbed the girl's hand and ushered her away, I got the sense that he had a thing for her. Perhaps they were dating. Will was oblivious to this entire situation and seemed intently focused on me instead.

"Maybe you could go to Enceaf Academy one day," Will suggested.

Hope flared in my chest, but I snuffed it out. I didn't want to get my hopes up.

"Maybe," I said, "As long as this goes well."

"It will," he assured me.

I looked down at my hands. An awkward silence settled over us as I lost myself in my fears and doubts of what was to come. We spent the rest of the ride in silence; however, our ride didn't last long.

Will broke the silence as the carriage came to an abrupt stop.

"We're here," he said grimly.

A large foreboding building loomed over us. Statues of important-looking people stood tall in front of it. This seemed to be the only building in the city that didn't sparkle. It was white as chalk, with large stone columns in the entrance. It had no windows, so I couldn't tell how many floors it had. I guessed it was easily a thousand feet tall.

"Why do I need to come here?" I asked. My voice was small and weak, mirroring the way I felt inside.

"I already told you, I don't know," he said absently.

"Will? What's going to happen to me?" I asked him.

I kept my eyes focused on my feet.

"Celeste, look at me," he said.

Slowly, I lifted my head, so our eyes met.

"I won't let anything bad happen to you. I promise," he assured me.

He sounded so sincere and sure of himself. No matter how many reassuring things he told me, the hollow pit of dread in my stomach grew larger.

"You ready?" Will asked me.

He stood and stepped down from the carriage. I took a breath to steady myself and stood.

"Ready as I'll ever be," I replied.

As I stepped out of the carriage on shaky legs, I braced myself for whatever was to come.

FIVE

The building was even bigger on the inside. The roof was so high that I couldn't see where it ended. Perhaps there simply wasn't one. Extravagant murals and tapestries adorned the walls. The floor was made of white marble. Statues lined the corridor we were walking down. There were hundreds of them. Each one of a different person. All of them wore elaborate gowns or tunics and stood in regal poses as if they were royalty.

"Why are there so many statues?" I asked.

"They're the past Convocation members and the current ones. Every time there's a new member they add a new statue. This hallway is magical, it gets longer and longer every time there's a new statue added," he explained.

The statues looked less regal to me after that. They were more like gargoyles, staring down at me expectantly, waiting for me to prove myself to them.

Will told me that my dad was a member of the Convocation. That made me wonder....

"Does my dad have a statue?" I asked him.

Will didn't answer; he continued walking down the seemingly endless corridor. He motioned for me to follow, and I hurried along after him. We passed so many statues I thought I was walking through China's Terracotta Army, but bigger.

Finally, we stopped in front of a statue of a tall, regal man. His warm smile radiated confidence, and his warm expression seemed out of place among the other statues' scowls. I recognized that smile; I saw it every time I looked in the mirror.

"This is my dad," I guessed.

"Yes. Your father was a favorite of our people," Will replied. "Everyone loved him because of how kind and caring he was."

"Was. As in, he was their favorite, but he isn't anymore because he broke the rules by having me?" I surmised.

Will nodded and stared at the statue. I found myself doing the same.

I couldn't help but feel relieved that I looked a little bit like my dad. He seemed so calm and poised. I, however, tended to act rashly and do impertinent things. I could have stayed there staring at that statue for hours. My mind swimming with questions about who he was and what he was like.

"I don't even know his name," I said aloud.

I wasn't sure why I had said it, it just kind of slipped out. I had learned all this new stuff about him; I had spent years hating him and pining for him at the same time; however, I still didn't know his name. It seemed kind of odd to me.

"His name is Devon. Devon Rowan," Will told me.

"Devon," I whispered to myself. The name felt so raw and new that I was afraid to say it any louder. It felt like something fragile that I would break if I used it too much.

"Celeste, we really need to go," Will said anxiously.

He turned and walked farther down the corridor. I stayed where I was. I couldn't take my eyes off the statue. My dad looked so happy and carefree.

It didn't seem like the face of someone who had defied the Convocation. I was even more determined to find him and my mom. We might not be a normal family, but we could be a family, nonetheless. Mom wouldn't have to worry about all the rumors in our town, and I wouldn't have to worry about all the jerks at school. I could have a dad for the first time in my life.

First, though, I would have to get through whatever the Convocation had in store for me. I took a deep breath, squaring my shoulders and setting my jaw. I ran through the corridors, the statues' faces turning into blurs as I sped past them. Finally, I caught up with Will. Sweaty and out of breath, I put my hands on my knees for support.

He was standing at the end of the hallway when I got to him. Huge golden doors stood tall and threatening before us. They had a similar pattern to the gates, except there was a symbol in the middle. A throne with a single crown sitting in it.

"Why…is this hallway….so long?" I wheezed as I tried to catch my breath.

"Enceaf has existed for far longer than human civilization. We have had thousands of leaders throughout the history of our city," Will supplied.

Will waited until I had caught my breath before he pulled open the doors. I was surprised to find a room that looked like a fancy elevator. The inside was just as white and foreboding as the outside. Everything was white except for two gold buttons labeled up and down, and a gold-encrusted rail.

Will stepped inside. I hesitated for a moment before stepping inside beside him.

"You might want to hold on to something," Will said as he grabbed onto the rail.

I did the same. With one hand still gripping the rail, he pressed the up button. As soon as his fingers pressed it, we shot upward at lightning speed. We continued to gain speed as we climbed higher until I felt like I was going to pass out from the g-force. Finally, we came to a stop. I slumped against the railing. I wondered if I'd left my stomach on the ground floor. I took a few seconds to steady myself and then stood up straight.

"Ready?" Will asked as the doors opened with a ding.

"Honestly? Not really," I said with a heavy sigh.

"Everything is going to be okay. I won't let anyone hurt you," he reassured me.

Inside was a large hall that looked surprisingly like a human courtroom, only it had five judges sitting at the front of it instead of one. I realized those must be the Convocation members. Each one wore frilly gowns and tunics fit for royalty. Their thrones were large enough to hold a full-grown horse. Each member was adorned with golden crowns garnished with colorful jewels. All their faces were grim.

I gulped as my legs started to shake.

Will stepped out of the elevator and bowed to the rulers. I knew I should do the same, but I didn't. These weren't my leaders. They had never done anything for me. They didn't even know I existed until a few days ago. I stood up straighter and squared my shoulders. Some of them raised their eyebrows in question. A few of them glared at me. Still, I didn't budge. Then, one of them laughed. The man in the middle of them. His deep blue eyes were mysterious and wise. His long white beard reminded me of Dumbledore from the Harry Potter books I read in third grade. Will stood back up.

"You're spirited, just like your father," The man said

heartily. His voice was deep, yet soothing.

Will stood. He gave me a look that told me I should have kneeled. I had a feeling I had just made this a lot harder for me.

"William, come over here," said the man.

"Yes, Grandfather," Will replied.

Grandfather? They did resemble one another. They both had the same brilliant blue eyes. I had a feeling he had only gotten assigned to this test because of who his grandfather was. His grandfather seemed quite old, and I wondered if he could possibly be an elder. That would be such big shoes to fill for Will.

Will turned to me before he left. His eyes darted from me to the rulers.

Don't go, I mouthed.

I have to, he mouthed back to me.

This was a big deal for him. I knew that. He couldn't deliberately disobey his grandfather in front of the most important people in his world, especially not for someone he had just met.

"You're going to be okay," he whispered softly in my ear.

He walked over to his grandfather's side. He seemed tense and his face was lined with worry. That definitely didn't make me feel like I was going to be okay.

Beside him, a man with dark olive skin and emerald, green eyes stood. His clothes and the jewel on his crown were the same color as his eyes.

He pointed to me and said, "Seize her."

Two large men seemed to melt out of the shadows. Each grabbed one of my arms and held me still. I tried to get free, but their iron grips held me in place. I looked at Will.

"I trusted you! You said you wouldn't let them hurt me!" I cried out to Will.

"I didn't know. Celeste, I promise you I had no idea!" he replied.

He turned to his grandfather, his fists clenched.

"Can't you see?" Will yelled. "She's the savior of light from the prophecy. It has to be her!"

"She is a danger," the emerald-eyed man replied. "And you are no longer needed here."

Another man melted out of the shadows and grabbed Will. Will was dragged back towards the elevator. He turned back to me as the doors began to slowly close.

"Celeste, I—"

"Save it! Trusting you was a mistake," I yelled.

I turned my face away from him as tears filled my eyes, but I squinted them back. He didn't deserve them. I heard the thud of doors closing. I turned my attention back to the Convocation.

"Orson, what if the boy is right?" another person asked.

Her blonde hair cascaded around her shoulders and her eyes were light pink. Her gown appeared to be made of roses the same color pink as her eyes. She was undeniably beautiful.

"She cannot be, Ophelia. She is nothing but a mistake and a danger," the man, Orson, replied. The way he said Ophelia's name made me wonder if there was something between them, some kind of romantic connection. I already hated this Orson guy, so I decided it was probably nothing.

Orson's words sparked a flurry of murmured arguments amongst the five rulers. The guards grip loosened on my arms as they strained to hear the hushed conversations. I saw this as my chance to get free and struggled against the guards' grasps.

"Stop that!" one cried.

I didn't stop, anger filled me, and I felt that familiar heat buzz through my veins.

"I told you to stop!" he cried again.

He punched me in the gut in the exact spot Johnny had punched me earlier that day. I cried out in pain as I collapsed to the floor. I clutched my stomach as a bile taste filled my mouth. The guards' grips tightened more.

The room fell silent. Everyone's eyes turned to me. Ophelia and Will's grandfather looked at me with pity. The other rulers, Orson, another woman, and another man, kept their faces neutral.

"See, Orson," Ophelia said, "She is just a defenseless child."

"You know what she is, and yet you still defend her," Orson scoffed.

I couldn't just stand there listening to them debate my fate in front of me. I grew tired and impatient. That fiery anger was still sitting at the back of my mind, waiting to be unleashed.

"What do you want with me? I've done nothing wrong!" I screamed.

"You are a danger to everything we have built. You possess powers too vigorous for you to handle. Our job is to stop you from destroying the fragile balance of the dimensions," said Orson.

"And how are you going to do that?" I asked indifferently.

"We'll simply take your powers. You might survive and if you don't, no one will care. Your father is no longer here to protect you. He has escaped us for now, but we will find him.

When we do, he will be severely punished," said the other woman.

She wore a teal dress that matched her eyes. Her auburn hair was swept back in an elaborate bun. She pursed her lips and her eyes narrowed as she looked down at me from her golden throne.

"You won't find my dad! Kilmar has him! Please, you have to let me go. I have to help him!"

"Doing that will definitely kill her, Blanche. If she is the savior of light, and we do this, we will be dooming ourselves," Ophelia pointed out.

With every word the anger bubbled inside me, rising like fireworks. How dare they punish me for existing. I had come here, to this new world that I hadn't known existed until a few hours ago. I had almost fallen to my death, been threatened by a shadowy figure, been attacked by a demon, and taken prisoner by these people-this Convocation. I was tired, confused, and a whole lot of angry.

I had this gut feeling that if I didn't try to control it, the anger would bubble over until it exploded.

"How about we take a vote," offered the other man who had stayed quiet. The other members mumbled their consent.

"All in favor of draining the girl's powers, raise your hand," said Orson.

Ophelia and Will's grandfather were the only ones that didn't raise their hands. A tear slipped down my cheek as bits of fear mixed in with the anger. My two supporters looked away as Orson called out to the guards.

"Sedate her!" he cried.

Quicker than I could react, a cold cloth was pressed over my mouth. A strong scent prickled my nose. I could feel myself drifting off into darkness. I tried to get away. I had to get out of there. I needed to save my parents. I needed to…my thoughts grew hazy, and they trailed off as the sedative started to kick in.

I pulled at the hand that held the cloth to my face. It wouldn't budge; the guard was too strong.

"Don't fight. You will only harm yourself," someone said.

I felt my body get weak as I slid to the ground. Those words echoed in my mind as I slipped into the drug induced, hollow darkness.

SIX

I was surprised to find that the darkness wasn't that bad. There was nothing for me to worry about. Nothing for me to be scared of. The darkness made me feel so numb, but I would rather be numb than have to deal with whatever would be waiting for me when I woke up. I didn't want to wake up and deal with reality. My reality felt more like a nightmare. Missing parents, mysterious powers, people who thought I was dangerous, friends who betrayed me. I didn't want to return to that. Not yet.

I floated in the darkness for what felt like eternity. Then slowly I started to wake up. My eyes fluttered open and I stared up at the sky. But I didn't remember the sky being so close to me. I sat, dazed and sore, and looked around. A cold sense of dread and fear settled over me as I realized that it wasn't the sky at all. It was some kind of force field. I was surrounded by a dome of transparent light. I stood up groggily on shaky legs. However, my legs decided they weren't done sleeping and I fell back down.

"Okay," I said, horrified by how hoarse and weak my voice was. "Let's try this again."

I gritted my teeth and stood back up. I took another shaky step. Thankfully, I didn't fall. I took another step forward and reached out for the force field. I touched the force field with a shaky hand, and it sucked me into it. It electrocuted me and my body jerked in seizure. I was unable to get away. It had an iron grip, and it held me there. When I was sure it would kill me, its grip lessened, and I fell backwards. I grunted as I hit the ground. I lay there breathing heavily, my body searing with pain. Between the sedative and getting electrocuted that was all I had the energy to do. My mind was still foggy.

I licked my dry lips. I had a terrible taste in my mouth, most likely from the sedative.

As I lay there, I thought about what happened. I had been a fool to trust Will. I had fallen for his deceitfully charming charisma and his dashing looks. He was also my only friend, my only ally. Without him I was all alone in this cruel world. How was I supposed to save my parents when I wasn't even sure how to save myself?

I didn't even know where they were or how to get there. I didn't really know how to work my powers either. The only times I had managed to tap into them had been by survival instinct. I needed to know how to use them for self-defense. I sort of knew how to open portals, but I'd only done that when my life depended on it. When every part of my brain was screaming for a solution, my instincts had kicked in. I wasn't even sure I could do it without Will's guidance. Besides, I was in no immediate danger, so those instincts wouldn't be very helpful.

Maybe it was the sedative still fogging up my brain, but I wanted so badly to just give up. There was no one left to help me. No one left to confide in. No one left to care about me. I was utterly alone in a world that hated me for simply existing.

A small voice in the back of my mind reminded me that my parents were still alive. They were with a terrifying, evil shadow guy, but they were alive, nonetheless. They still loved me. Even if they weren't here. I knew in my heart that they loved me. I would have to try and save them myself. Otherwise, my powers would be taken. Then there would be no one to save my parents.

I decided I was done laying there. I didn't know how long I had before my powers would be taken, but I suspected it wouldn't be long. Will had said that no one could teleport in or out of the city, but what if he had been lying? He had been playing me the whole time, lying and scheming to get me to fall right into the Convocation's hands. There was a very good chance that this had been another one of his big fat lies.

Somehow, deep in my heart, I still wanted to believe he hadn't meant for the Convocation to take me. He had seemed so genuinely shocked when I had been restrained. He had stood up for me. The look on his face as they dragged him away still lingered when I closed my eyes. The way his eyes gleamed with fear, pleading with me to listen to his explanations. I had turned him away, refusing to listen.

I wondered if that was a mistake. If I had ruined any alliance I may have found with him.

I sighed and pulled myself back to my shaky feet. It wouldn't do me any good to let myself go any further down that rabbit hole. Instead, I needed to focus on escaping. I needed to see if I could even make a portal inside the walls of Enceaf.

I thought back to what Will had said. Close your eyes and visualize where you want to go. Okay, so I knew what I needed to do, and I sort of knew how to do it. I looked around. I needed to start out small. The force field was in a fenced in, grassy area. There was a small pine tree to my right. Since it was the only thing I could see except for grass and my forcefield.

"Okay Celeste. Visualize where you want to go," I said to myself.

I'll admit. I was probably going a little crazy. Nothing in my world, this world, or whatever other worlds there were, made sense anymore. I was completely alone, and I had little to no idea how to use my powers. I had theories, but those wouldn't be a lot of help. My plan to save my parents was no plan at all, since I had absolutely no clue where they were. My chances were hopelessly slim. Since I had nothing left to lose, all I could do was try.

I closed my eyes. Then I imagined the tree being right in front of me, close enough to touch. I imagined a portal being there, in front of me, swirling in all its golden glory. I felt a small tugging sensation in my gut. It was similar to the one I'd felt before, but not as strong.

I held my breath, a spark of hope coming to life in the hopelessness. That hope died very quickly.

When I opened my eyes, there was a small golden portal in front of me. It was about the size of my head. There was no way I would be able to fit through it. The tugging sensation lessened. My spirits fell as the portal shrunk until it disappeared completely.

There was good news, bad news, and worse news. The good news was that I could make a portal in Enceaf. So, my situation had just gotten a whole lot better. The bad news, although not very important, made my heart sink. If I could portal out of there, that meant Will had been lying to me.

The worse news was that making a tiny little portal that I couldn't even fit through had made me exhausted. My head spun and my knees buckled. I fell to my knees. I stayed there breathing heavily and waiting for my head to stop spinning.

As I sat on my knees still feeling depleted, I heard a small clang. I turned my head slowly in the direction of the noise.

Part of the fence swung open. The last person I wanted to see strode towards me, studying me intently with his blue eyes.

"Will," I growled. "What do you want?"

"I just want to talk," he said gently.

I did not want to talk to him. I wanted him to go away. However, he was impossibly stubborn. Also, I was unfortunately stuck behind a forcefield, so it's not like I could just get up and shut myself in another room. My situation was far from ideal.

The gate swung closed behind Will. He took careful steps towards me, like I was a wild animal he was trying to tame. I wanted to stand up and face him indignantly, but my head was still spinning, and I was too weak from my portal attempt.

"Well, I don't want to talk to you, so you can go ahead and leave!" I snapped.

It was supposed to sound indignant, but it came out as more of a wheezy squeak due to my exhaustion from the portal.

"Lower the force field!" he commanded.

"Are you sure?" Someone on the other side of the fence asked. "The Convocation said she's too dangerous to—"

"Just open it!" Will demanded.

I couldn't see anyone, but there must have been guards stationed on the other side of the gate of the fence. Perhaps there were people on the other side of the gate waiting to make force fields and get rid of them as needed. That would be a pretty cool power. Although, it was not working out to my advantage so far.

Even though the force field was gone, lingering wisps of it remained. They were tiny reminders of how helpless I was at the moment.

Will made his way over to me. I stared down at the ground, not able to meet his gaze.

"Celeste, would you please look at me," he pleaded. I shook my head as my eyes filled with tears.

"Why should I? So, you can lie to me all over again?" I snapped. My voice was so bitter that I almost didn't recognize it as my own.

He winced at my remark. My words were cold and sharp. They seemed to cut him like knives.

Good, I thought. *Let him see how it feels to have someone hurt you.*

I resented him so much, and I was so angry with him. I was angry with the Convocation. Heck, I was angry at the world. I didn't want to be. I wanted to believe that Will was still my friend and that there was still reason to hope. I just couldn't.

"Look, I am sorry. I didn't know they would do that. They just told me to bring you to them. That's it," he said.

That small bit of me that still believed Will was my friend died then and there.

"So what? You just brought me to the Convocation? You didn't stop to think, hey, there's a chance this could ruin her life. Maybe I should just leave her alone?" I shouted.

"Well, no, but—"

"I wish I'd never met you! I hate you!" I screamed at him.

I regretted the words as soon as they left my mouth, but I couldn't take them back. Will's eyes grew wide with shock. His expression fell as he seemed to process what I had said.

"I'm sorry you feel that way," he replied coolly, "but you only have three days, counting today, before they send someone to drain your powers. If you survive that, then they'll have you rot in a cell the rest of your life. Or they might decide to just kill you anyway."

I gasped. Three days till they would take my powers. That wasn't much time. I would have to find a way out. I knew I could make a portal out of there. It took a lot of energy, and I didn't know how to make one out of Enceaf. Still, I was making progress. My mind raced as I began to formulate plans in my head.

Will sighed. "I just wanted to tell you I'm sorry."

Will squared his shoulders and looked at me one last time. He turned and walked away. I watched as the gate opened, and he disappeared through it. Leaving me alone and feeling worse than ever. He had sounded so sincere, and honestly, he sounded sad. How could I stay mad at him when he was truly sorry? Still, I couldn't shake the fact that it was his fault I was in this mess. My heart felt like it was breaking into a thousand little pieces with every second I thought about it.

I buried my face in my hands and wept. I cried until there were no tears left in my eyes and my nose ran out of snot. When the crying finally stopped, I dried my eyes and lay down on the soft grass. I knew what I had to do to get out of there, and it wasn't going to be easy. I also knew that I was going to do whatever it took to save my parents.

My life had officially changed forever. I could never go back to Boringsville, USA and live my normal life there knowing that all of this was out here. I would never be normal again and neither would my family. I guess all the jerks from school were right, I was the freak they thought I was.

As the sky grew dark, I closed my eyes. I was exhausted from the day's events, and I knew I would need my strength if I was going to try and make another portal. Sleep found me instantly. I dreamed I was with my parents, and we were happy together.

SEVEN

I didn't plan on sleeping as late as I did. I went to bed assuming that I wouldn't be able to sleep long; however, my body had other ideas. The sun was high in the sky when I finally awoke. It was probably around midday. That meant I had the rest of the day and the next day before they would take my powers. I'd wasted half a day sleeping.

"Great. Just great," I muttered bitterly.

I stood up feeling much better than I had when I'd fallen asleep. My body felt more rested, except for my back. It ached from sleeping on the hard ground. The grass may have been soft but the ground beneath it was not.

It was a hot and humid day. As far as I could tell, there wasn't a cloud in the sky. I wondered briefly if it ever rained here or if the sun just always shined. The tree's shadow stretched to the edge of the forcefield, so there was no shade to protect me from the blazing sun.

I was already beginning to sweat, and I hadn't realized till then how thirsty I was. My throat still felt dry and scratchy from the sedative. Plus, I hadn't drank any water since I was at school. I was very dehydrated. My stomach growled and cramped from hunger. I hadn't eaten in a while either. I clutched my stomach as the nausea hit me. It's funny how you don't remember things like water and food when you're almost dying every day. Now that I had nothing to do, I remembered those things.

Right on cue, as if he could hear my thoughts, the gates clanged open, and someone walked in. Someone I didn't want to see again: Will. He had impeccable timing, and he came bearing gifts. In one hand, he held a plate full of colorful food. In the other hand he held a silver cup, the scent wafted through the air, and I could smell it through the dome. It smelled sweet and savory. My stomach growled and my mouth watered. He ordered them to let down the dome. It faded away and Will walked towards me.

I glared at him. Then my gaze shifted to the food. I was so hungry, and the food looked so good. Then, my brain started to remember that I was still mad at him and absolutely didn't trust him. I mentally smacked myself to make me snap out of it. I couldn't trust him. For all I knew, the food could be poisoned or something. I wouldn't put it past the Convocation to try a trick like that.

He frowned at me then put the plate and cup down in front of me. I turned my back on him.

"You haven't eaten in days Celeste. You need food," he said.

He was right of course. I was weak, hungry, and dehydrated. Still, I couldn't eat this food without trusting him and trusting him was something I just couldn't do. Not yet. Maybe not ever.

"Why should I trust you?" I asked.

I was thankful my back was still turned to him because it kept him from seeing the tears that were pooling in my eyes. The tears were probably from bitterness towards him, but I was pretty sure a few were over the sight of food and water.

"Because I'm trying to make it up to you. I may never earn your forgiveness, but I won't stop trying to," he said.

I turned around to face him. I looked into his beautiful blue eyes and saw so much emotion in them. I didn't know what to feel or what feelings to trust.

"You'll need your strength to survive what the Convocation has planned for you," he said.

"I'm not going to let them beat me," I said angrily.

"You won't have the strength to do that unless you eat. Please, Celeste," he said.

His tone made me feel like there was a chance he still cared. It was a naive thing to hope for, yet it was one hope that I couldn't snuff out. With this hope, my will crumbled and I gave in to my growling stomach and scratchy throat.

"Okay. I'll eat the food," I said reluctantly.

"Thank you," he said.

He gave me a sad smile and turned to leave. A sense of loneliness crept into my heart. I realized that maybe he wasn't my best friend, but he was still a friend. Correction, my only friend. I was so afraid of being alone with everything that had happened that I couldn't help myself. I wanted him to stay.

"Wait!" I cried. "Would you stay with me a little longer?"

I held my breath as he stopped midstride and turned back towards me. He smiled brightly. Suddenly, I knew I had done the right thing.

He picked the plate up and handed it to me. We both sat

down cross-legged, and I started eating. There was a purple strip of something sweet that tasted a little bit like strawberries, and some gloppy blue stuff that reminded me of Jell-o. The cup was full of clear liquid. I expected it to be water, but it tasted like honey. It was a little bit thinner and slightly less sweet than honey. Whatever it was, my throat felt better as soon as the cool liquid slid down it.

After I finished eating—I may or may not have cleaned my plate; the food was delicious—I turned to Will. He'd sat there silently the entire time I ate. Which was a little embarrassing because I eat like a pig when I'm hungry. I was too exhausted to care.

"You really didn't know the Convocation was going to do this?" I asked as I wiped my mouth with my sleeves.

I was so close to trusting him again; he had given me so many reasons to. I felt like I needed one more reason. Just to be absolutely sure. Guilt washed over his face and settled into his handsome features. He looked me in the eyes. His eyes gleamed with unshed tears. I'd never seen a boy cry. It made me feel a little squirmy inside.

"No. If I did, I wouldn't have taken you there. I can't believe my grandfather would do this to you. He's usually one of the wisest people I know," he said.

"I believe you," I said so quietly that it was barely audible.

Will must have had fantastic hearing. He smiled and said, "Thank you."

An uncomfortable silence settled over us. Neither of us really knew what to say. I was afraid that if I said the wrong things we would be right back to where we had started. I thought about what Will had said. There was so much pain, doubt, and fear behind his words. It mirrored my own internal turmoil.

"Sometimes fear can cloud even the wisest of minds," I

said.

I was shocked by how much older I sounded when I said it. I sounded nothing like me. I sounded like my mom. She was the smartest person I knew, so that was definitely a good thing. I had been through so much the past two days that I guess I had done a little bit of growing up.

Despite my wisdom, Will remained unswayed. He kept his head down, his fingers toying with a blade of grass. I found myself staring at the way his jawline stood out and the way his muscles bulged slightly under his sleeves.

To keep myself from feeling whatever had turned my stomach with butterflies, I decided to change the subject.

"Remember how you said it was impossible to make a portal in Enceaf?" I whispered.

"Yes. Why, what happened?" he asked.

"I made one. It didn't last long, and it took a lot out of me, but it's possible," I said. My voice was full of excitement as I spoke.

I'm not sure why I thought it was a good idea to divulge this information to him. It just felt so good to tell someone. It made me feel like all the other giddy girls at school.

Will's eyes grew wide with shock. His jaw dropped and he shook his head in disbelief.

"That shouldn't be possible," he said.

"Well, it is. I'm going to portal out of here as soon as I figure out how to make a portal big enough for me," I told him.

He nodded. Then he stood up and offered me his hand. I reached out halfway but then hesitated. A small voice of doubt whispered in the back of my mind.

This could still be a trick. He could still be lying, The voice said.

I looked up at his handsome smile and all of those doubts vanished. I took his hand, and he pulled me to my feet. He looked me in the eyes. Our faces were so close, I could feel his breath on my cheek. Then, we both seemed to hold our breath.

Will pulled away, his hand falling limply to his side. He turned toward the gate and started walking slowly toward it.

"Where are you going?" I said abruptly.

Honestly, I was a little miffed that we had a moment and he was leaving so soon. It made me wonder if I'd done something wrong—which was crazy considering he was the one trying to earn my forgiveness—and I questioned every little thing I said or did. Then, I remembered that we shouldn't even have been having a moment in the first place since we were hardly even real friends yet.

"You have work to do. Practice, Celeste. I believe in you," he said passionately. His eyes shined with an intensity that made my heart flutter.

I watched in silence as he flashed a confident smile and left through the gate. I stood there staring at the gate wondering what to feel—and wasting my time—for a moment. Once I remembered that the Convocation was probably going to kill me the next day, I snapped out of it.

I thought back to how I'd made the portal the last time. I thought about where I wanted to go, thought happy thoughts, and imagined a portal forming. There was the same tugging sensation in my gut. When I opened my eyes, there was the portal in all its swirling golden glory. However, it was too small and closed almost instantly. The only difference was that I didn't feel as drained. I was a little bit tired, but it wasn't unbearable like the last time.

I huffed in outrage. How was I supposed to get out of there if I couldn't get my portal to last more than two seconds?

I paced back and forth trying to figure out what I could change to get the portal to work.

As I paced, I noticed that my stomach still hurt a little from the strange tugging sensation. I remembered how vague the tug was. How I could barely feel it.

Maybe I'm not tugging hard enough. I thought to myself.

I figured it couldn't hurt to try tugging harder. After all, there wasn't much left for me to lose.

I mimicked what I'd done every other time to make my portal. Except this time, when I started to feel the tug, I pulled harder. It was as if I was grabbing onto an invisible string and pulling at it with all my strength. It didn't feel uncomfortable like the other tugs. This one felt right. I felt like I was stretching a muscle I'd never known I'd had.

I continued pulling from my gut and when I couldn't pull any harder the portal began to form. It started small like the others, but this one didn't stop growing. The portal continued to expand until it was as tall as me. When the portal opened, I had to fight to keep control of it. Every step I took towards the portal was heavy and hard. The portal shrank and expanded continuously.

I was so close to going through the portal. It was only a foot or two away from me. Then someone shouted behind me.

"She's trying to escape! Get her!" they called. Before I could turn my head to see who it was, something slammed into me. It pushed me to the ground with such force that it knocked the breath out of me.

"Let me go," I said in between gasps.

"Not a chance," one man growled. I gasped as they pulled me to my feet. He pulled my arms behind my back. I cried out as sharp pain shot through my arm and up my shoulder. I made the mistake of looking back at my captor. He was one of the creepy large men from the Convocation Hall. The same one who had drugged me the first time.

In front of me, the other one appeared out of thin air. I wanted to ask how he'd done it. He had just appeared out of nowhere. That shouldn't have been possible. Before I could open my mouth, the man kicked me behind my knees, and my legs gave out. I grunted as I hit the ground.

"What do we do with her?" the one who had kicked me said.

"Drug her. She can't escape if she's not conscious," said the other.

"No!" I screamed as I struggled to get free.

My efforts were in vain. The man yanked hard on my arms. I screamed in pain.

"Hurry up, Harry! I want to get this over with," he said. The boredom in his voice made me so angry.

I screamed as cold cloth was clamped over my mouth for the second time. Fear and sadness tore at my heart. Tears streamed down my cheeks.

My vision turned fuzzy. A cloud of darkness swam into my mind, and it became harder and harder for me to think clearly.

No. Not again. I thought desperately as the darkness tried to take me again.

There was no fighting it this time. I slipped back into the hollow darkness. The darkness wasn't that bad. Actually, it felt good for a little while. There was no pain, no sadness, nothing.

Then I started to feel my energy slowly slipping away. My powers were being taken away. I knew that. I could feel it slowly killing me bit by bit, with every passing second. I was ready to wake up. The darkness seemed suffocating.

I needed to escape the darkness, but the grip it had on me was as tight and strong as the guards'. If I couldn't escape, I could at least fight with the only weapon I had against it: light. I channeled all the emotions I was feeling into a wave of light. It was so strong that it was hard to control. I let it roll over my mind and wash away the darkness.

My eyes fluttered open. I was still inside the forcefield. I had hoped that when I woke up the pain would stop, but it didn't. I gritted my teeth and stood up.

The woman in the teal dress stood outside the dome. I recognized her as a Convocation member. Blanche, they had called her. I could see her hands drawing a beam of light directly from me. She was draining me, my powers, and my energy. She was taking away my life force, and I could feel it. This is what they had meant by taking my powers.

I knew I only had one shot at getting out of there. Just one shot.

You can do this Celeste; you can do this! I thought to myself.

I gathered all my anger and searched for the familiar feeling I had when the demon had grabbed me. Instead of just forcing it out, I used all my mental energy to form it into a sphere. I didn't have the strength to wonder how I did it. I assumed it was by instincts since that was how it had happened with everything else. I held the red sphere in my hand feeling its powerful, fiery warmth coursing through my veins. I threw it with as much strength as I could, like a pitcher in a tied game of baseball.

It was as if time slowed as the red sphere flew towards the edge of the force field.

The light exploded when it touched the force field and sent a blast wave that knocked me off my feet. I groaned as I sat up.

When the dust from the blast had cleared the dome was

gone, and Blanche was out cold. I tried to open a portal. I felt like that invisible string I was pulling on snapped. It took all of the strength I had left, but the portal opened.

I thought that once the woman had been knocked out my strength and energy would return. Unfortunately, opening that portal made me feel like a dinosaur had trampled over me. My entire body ached, my head throbbed, and my vision was starting to get blurry.

I realized that this portal was blue, not gold. It vaguely occurred to me that this portal might not lead anywhere in Enceaf since all the previous portals had been gold, but I didn't care. I was so desperate, and the agony was too much. All I knew was that it would take me away from where I was. Without looking back, I staggered through the portal.

On the other side, I found myself on the beach of a small tropical island. The salty ocean air hit my nose, and the wind blew through my hair. The ocean stretched out as far as I could see. I had just enough time to take in its beauty. Then, I collapsed. I felt my consciousness drift away.

EIGHT

Suddenly, a wave of light trickled through my mind. My entire body was filled with familiar warmth. A gasped escaped my mouth as my eyes fluttered open. I groaned as the sunlight seared my corneas. A shiver ran down my spine despite the tropical heat. I felt two strong arms cradling me. Two blurry figures were leaning over me. When the one holding me came into focus, I had no idea what to feel.

"Will?" I said weakly.

"Are you okay?" he asked.

The answer? I quite obviously was not. I had no idea where I was, my entire body ached, and I still felt overwhelmingly exhausted.

"Define okay," I said. I offered him a small smile; he didn't return it.

"How did you find me?" I asked, needing to change the subject.

He bit his lip, as if trying to figure out how to answer. I could see the wheels turning in his mind as he tried to figure out how to say the right thing.

I tried to sit up, but I couldn't. I felt like I had a bunch of bricks on top of me, and my choice was either to fight against it and try to get up, or let it crush me. I was too tired to fight, so I melted into Will's strong embrace.

"Long story short, I came to see you. I got there right as Blanche was draining you. When you created that blast, I ducked behind the tree. Then you were gone. The portal was still open, so I followed you," he explained.

I looked up into his eyes, his mesmerizing blue eyes. They sparkled with something that made me feel those familiar butterflies. The ones I had absolutely hated at first, but that I was beginning to tolerate. Will's face was beaded with sweat, the same way it had been when he'd healed me on the way to Enceaf. His hands shook as he held me, and he breathed heavily. I realized that he and his healing powers were the only reason I was alive. Otherwise, whatever Blanche had done would have killed me.

It suddenly occurred to me that there was another person there. He had dark amber eyes, and his blond hair was expertly styled. He wore the same style clothes as Will, except his was all black. He seemed to be about Will's age, so he was probably around fifteen or sixteen.

"Who are you?" I asked.

"I'm Edward Jenkins. I'm Will's best friend. He told me what happened in the Convocation Hall. I agree with him. It wasn't right," he said with empathy in his voice.

He was obviously an a Arbitrator, but I didn't know what his powers were. He reminded me of those kids at school that always wore black, lurked at the back of the class, and rarely had anything to say to anyone. He had this quiet strength to him, he didn't radiate confidence like Will, but there was something else there that I couldn't quite put my finger on. It made me kind of nervous.

"Nice to meet you, Edward. I'm Celeste Rowan," I told him.

"Oh, I know. Will hasn't quit talking about you since he met you," Edward replied. He gave me a lopsided grin.

Will shot him a pointed look that made Edward drop his gaze. For them to be best friends, they sure didn't act like it.

"Can you stand up?" Will asked.

He seemed very eager to change the subject, which left me wondering what he was so worried about that topic leading to.

"I'll manage," I said through gritted teeth.

With Will's help, I stood up. A spell of dizziness hit me as soon as I got to my feet. I would have collapsed if Will hadn't put his arm around my waist.

"Celeste, can you try to portal us out of here? This is pirate territory, and I don't want to be here when they get back," he said.

"You can't?" I asked.

The look I gave him must have been more severe than I thought, because his cheeks turned bright red.

"Arbitrators can only teleport in and out of Enceaf and Fortest. Our dimension and the human dimension," he explained, "Speaking of which, how on earth did you teleport us to Aquaria? You're not even supposed to be able to teleport out of the city! How did you teleport to another dimension?"

It took me a second to pick up on the fact that Aquaria was the name of this dimension, and I had somehow teleported to. Then it took me another few seconds to figure out how the heck I had managed to get to Aquaria. I needed another moment or two to celebrate the fact that I had teleported to another dimension, because this was pretty freaking cool. Except for the whole, almost dying thing. That was not cool at all.

"I don't know how I did it. I felt so many emotions when I teleported. They must have mixed together and made whatever light I needed to make that portal. Mainly I felt so sad and hopeless," I paused, wincing at the memory. Then I added, "You said we're in Aquaria. What dimension is this?"

"The sea dimension," Edward said quietly.

I should have guessed that. All I could see was ocean, ocean, and would you look at that, more ocean. There were a few tiny specks on the horizon that I guessed were other islands. Other than that, the only thing on the horizon were the pearly whitecaps of the turquoise waves that shined like diamonds as the sun bounced off them.

"I can try to open a portal, but I don't know where it will go," I warned them.

"That's okay. Most of the other dimensions are safer than this one," Will replied.

I stared at him. My exhausted brain was struggling to keep up with all this big, new information.

"There are other dimensions?" I asked.

"Yeah, but this is one of the more dangerous ones because of the pirates and the sea monsters," Will replied casually.

I was baffled by the way he was able to talk so casually about it. I blinked at him as my mind started to spiral through endless thoughts and possibilities of the other dimensions. I knew that if I let myself do that, then I would keep going down, and down until I hit rock bottom. I decided that the best thing to do was to put it out of my mind for a while. Instead, I had a portal to make.

I pulled all my energy into making it. I could only picture one place I wanted to go: home. I forced the portal into existence. A silver portal opened in front of me. I hadn't realized how much energy it would take to open another portal. I couldn't keep it open, I just didn't have the strength. As soon as it opened, it closed again. I blacked out from the exhaustion.

When I came to, Will and Edward were leaning over me again.

"S—sorry. I don't know what happened," I said weakly.

"Don't be. It's not your fault. When Blanche drained you, she didn't just take part of your powers. She took part of your spark," Will said.

"But that doesn't make any sense. How can her powers be connected to her spark?" Edward said.

"What's a spark?" I asked.

"Her powers are connected to her emotions, so maybe it is also attached to her spark. That would explain why she is so powerful," Will countered.

"Guys! What is a spark?" I yelled over them, both puzzled and annoyed that they had yet to answer my question.

Both of them looked at me.

"It's like your core. It's the center of your being and the most powerful people have powers that are connected to their sparks. If you lost part of your spark, then it's going to take a while to recover from that," Will explained.

His face was lined with guilt. I knew he was sorry for taking me to the Convocation, and being mad at him would do nothing for me.

I sat up. Intense pain flooded my body, and all of the

blood rushed from my head. I felt wobbly and dizzy, but I ignored the pain. Shakily I stood up. I breathed a sigh of relief when my legs didn't buckle.

"It's going to be a little bit before I can portal us out of here. I need to let my spark heal," I added, "Also, I believe you mentioned something about pirates."

"Yeah, this is the sea dimension, Aquaria. Pirates, mermaids, sea monsters, you name it, they all live here. We really don't want to be here when the pirates come," Will said.

"We should set up camp for the night. Pirates don't come ashore during the night, and Celeste needs to rest," Edward said.

I wanted to argue and say that I was fine. However, I was still a teenager, and my body demanded rest. I'd tried portaling and that hadn't worked. We were on a small island in the middle of a gigantic ocean with no way to leave. I supposed I had time to rest. Maybe just for a little while.

"Yeah, you're right. Do you want some help setting up camp?" I asked.

"I can handle it," Will said.

Edward opened his mouth to argue, but Will cut him off.

"Someone needs to stay with Celeste. She's too weak to protect herself right now," Will said.

This time, I opened my mouth to argue, but Will was on an interrupting roll.

"I know you are perfectly capable of protecting yourself, but you are in no state to do that right now," Will said.

He gave me a pleading look. I sighed and agreed to stay put. I watched as Will disappeared into the forest, leaving me alone with Edward. I turned back toward Edward, who was sitting on the beach. I came to sit beside him. Edward wrung his hands, not meeting my gaze.

I decided that I wanted to get to know Edward. If he was going to be on this journey, or whatever we decided to call this mess we had found ourselves in, we needed to learn to trust each other. Trust was one thing we both seemed to be running low on.

"Why did you come with Will?" I asked Edward suspiciously.

He looked very confused. His eyebrows furrowed and he lifted his gaze to meet mine.

"I already told you," he replied impatiently.

"You said you didn't think it was right. I think a lot of things are wrong or unfair, but that doesn't make me want to leave behind my entire life. Besides, you don't even know me. I just want to know why you would do this for me," I said. I spoke rapidly, and it all just came tumbling out like a waterfall.

Edward was quiet for a moment.

"I may not know you, but I understand what it is like to not fit in. I'm tired of not living up to the Convocation's standards of a perfect Arbitrator. Maybe I just wanted a fresh start and that's why I came through that portal. Perhaps, I also wanted to do something good for a change and stick up for someone the way I wish people would stick up for me," he said.

The pain and heartbreak in his voice made me feel for him. I knew exactly how he felt. All those times of sticking up for nerds and other kids that I didn't even know, I had really been doing what I had always wanted others to do for me. When you're a normal teenager, fitting in is everything. When you don't have that, it feels like you've got nothing. I knew I would never fit in again, and I had made my peace with it.

"I guess we are a lot alike, you and I," I told him solemnly.

"Neither of us knows what it is like to truly fit in, and we are both tired of it."

"I guess so," he said.

After that, we fell into silence. We were both lost in our own thoughts.

Night had already fallen, and I looked out over the black sea. The lapping of waves against the sandy shore rang through my ears and the salty sea breeze blew through my hair, sending a slight chill down my spine.

Eventually, Will returned with logs, twigs, leaves, and two rocks in hand. He struck two rocks against each other. After a few tries, sparks flew from them and towards the sticks creating a small flame. Will blew on it and continued adding sticks until we had a mighty campfire.

"Huh. I thought that only worked in the movies," I told him.

"What's a movie?" he asked.

I stared at him, dumbfounded. Had he been deprived of the sacred pastime of television? I made myself a solemn vow that if we ever made it back to my house, I would turn on all my favorite movies and we would binge-watch them together.

"It's kind of like a story told with a bunch of moving pictures," I explained.

"It sounds confusing," he said.

I decided that it was no use explaining it to him. There was no way he could understand the beauty of television if he wasn't human.

Neither am I, I thought bitterly.

I was only part human. However, in my opinion, that was the best part of me. It was the part that didn't do potentially life-threatening things; the part that didn't care what other people thought of me; the part that knew I would always be different. It didn't matter as long as I had my mom.

I watched as sparks burst out from the fire and drifted like glitter up to the stars. I was shocked to realize that I could see the Earth's constellations. My mom had taught me how to spot them. Not only could I see the ones that would have been out on Earth during this time, but I could see the other ones as well. I was able to see all of them. I named them off in my head. Every time I named one off, it was a bittersweet reminder of my mom and my old life. After everything that happened, it felt good to have a piece of my old life here with me. Even if it was a small one.

I yawned. My eyelids had begun to fill heavy, and my entire body ached.

"You should rest. We can take the first watch," Will said.

"Are you sure?" I asked hesitantly.

"Yeah, don't worry about it," Will replied casually. Then he added, "Besides, you look like you could use some sleep."

Did I really look that bad? I certainly felt that bad, but I would never admit it to him. I definitely wanted some sleep, but I felt terrible about leaving them to stay up all night. Edward must have seen how hesitant I was about it.

"It's fine, Celeste," Edward reassured me. He gave me one of his lopsided grins.

"I guess a little sleep couldn't hurt," I said with a sigh.

I laid down, and my eyes began to close as soon as my head hit the ground. Gratitude swelled in my heart. I wasn't alone. I was terrified and tired, but I had Will. I knew he would be there for me if I got into any trouble. (Which was probably inevitable.) Even though this whole mess had started with him bringing me to Enceaf, I was confident that it would end with us by each other's side. It may sound stupid, but Will was the one person I trusted with all my heart—other than my mom of course—and I wanted to let him know how grateful I was for him.

"You know Will, I'm actually glad you took me to Enceaf," I told him sleepily. I didn't know where any of this was coming from. Drowsiness and exhaustion fueled every word.

"Oh yeah, and why is that?" he asked.

Although my eyes were closed and I was half asleep, I knew he was smiling. I could tell by the teasing tone in his voice and the way he spoke softly back to me.

"Because I met you," I whispered softly.

Sleep cut off Will's response. I would never know what he thought of what I had said. I'm not sure why I said it the way I did. It just sort of slipped out. I didn't have time to think about it; I slipped into a land of dreams.

NINE

At first, I dreamed about my old life and being back with my mom. Then the nightmares came. Shadows ravaged the blissful dreams. Images of my parents' unconscious bodies surrounded by more demons flashed through my mind. Kilmar's words echoed throughout all of them, "I'm coming. I'm coming. I'm coming."

I wanted to scream and cry. I wanted to curl up and hide. Somewhere deep inside my mind, I knew it wasn't really happening. It was just a dream. A terrible, awful dream. The rest of me still screamed that it was real. I felt something break inside of me, every time a new image of my parents' lifeless bodies came into focus. Any hope I had ever had that my parents would be okay crumbled. I wondered if anything would be okay. Fear consumed me until it was all I had left.

I could hear people calling my name.

"Wake up," they said.

But I couldn't. The nightmares weren't over. Kilmar's

terrible, evil laugh rang out in the nightmares. Then he opened his mouth to speak, but it wasn't his voice that spoke.

Celeste, wake up. Wake up. Wake up. The voice demanded.

It got louder and louder, drowning out my nightmares.

The nightmares faded and I woke up with a start. My eyelids fluttered open, and I gasped. My heart hammered in my chest. Flickers of my parents and images of Kilmar still lingered when I opened my eyes. I breathed heavily, icy terror running through my veins.

When I looked up, I soon realized why Will and Edward had been trying to wake me. I jumped to my feet.

We were surrounded by pirates. I knew Will had said that this was pirate territory, but I guess I thought he was kidding.

Some of them had eye patches. A few had hooks for hands or wooden stubs for legs. They all had swords, sharp and deadly. I knew with absolute certainty that they could end my life in a single slash. Their worn leather outfits reeked of alcohol, fish, salt, and body odor. I saw a few of them with black or gold teeth. The pirates appeared to be an assortment of ages and races. However, they were all male. There wasn't a single woman or girl in their motley group.

The youngest of them seemed to be about my age, maybe a few years older. His clothes clung to his biceps, showing off how large his muscles were. He had dirty blonde hair and blue eyes that were a similar shade of my own. The oldest was a scrawny, old man. His grey hair had thinned so much in some places that his head was almost completely bald. His jerkin hung limply over his petite, skinny form.

Our tiny fire had been reduced to a pile of ash and smoke. It was covered in water. I assumed the pirates had put it out. It could have been the waves, but the rest of the beach was dry except for the fire. However, the fire was the least of my worries.

Will and Edward were back-to-back, with swords in their hands as well. Where they had gotten them, I had no earthly idea. Perhaps they had stolen them from the pirates. Maybe Edward had brought them along and I just did not realize it.

They seemed to be in a sort of standoff with the pirates. They all had their swords drawn, however, none of them brandished, swiped, or jabbed at Will and Edward. It occurred to me that they might not actually know how to use the swords and were probably completely defenseless.

Sweat dripped from the boys' faces; their breathing was heavy. They looked tired, as if they had fought already. If so, it was a miracle I didn't wake up. I must have been more tired than I thought if I slept that hard.

One pirate stepped forward. He looked like he was in his mid-thirties. He had long raven black hair, and a goatee. I figured he was the captain, because he wore a large hat with a bright red feather poking out. He reminded me of Captain Hook without the hook, or maybe Blackbeard.

"Ahoy ye landlubbers! I be Captain Grimes! What brings ye here?" he said. His ascent was thick, although I couldn't quite recognize where it was from. It sounded a little Jamaican.

"We don't want any trouble," I said calmly.

"Well, Lasse, I wouldn't mind causing a bit of trouble," the captain replied with a sneer.

"This doesn't have to turn into a big spectacle," I told him.

The captain refused to see reason. He was painfully stubborn. And his accent was painfully annoying.

"Maybe that's exactly what I want Lasse," he retorted.

The way he called me Lasse made my skin crawl. It rolled off his tongue like it was acid. As if the very thought of referring to a girl made him want to hurl. I guess this group of pirates didn't understand that whole "men and women are equal" thing like humans did.

Actually, I was pretty sure that the pirates were human. Just by looking at them I could tell that they weren't Arbitrators. I had only met a few Arbitrators, but it was clear that they valued things these men did not. Things like the way they dressed or the way they held their heads a bit higher than they had to. The way Arbitrators walked as if they were all royalty. There are also other things like soap and water. Some of them looked as if they had no idea what a shower was.

Clearly, the captain wasn't going to let us go. I decided that we needed a plan. I turned to Will and there was a moment of understanding between us. Somehow without words he knew what I was going to do. He nodded. His expression was grim. His features were set with determination. That gave me all the reassurance I needed.

I wasn't even sure if it would work or not. What did I have to lose if it didn't? All I could do was try.

I gathered up all my anger, remembering how I had done it to the demon. It swelled inside me, building and swirling until I couldn't contain it anymore. I forced it out and willed it to turn into a sphere of light. The pirates were mesmerized by it. All except for Grimes, who seemed to realize what I was going to do with it.

"Get down!" I screamed at the boys. They ducked behind me, and I chucked the ball of fiery light right at the pirates.

"No!" Grimes cried.

Unfortunately, my aim was terrible, and it hit the ground at his feet with a disappointing thud. Fate was on my side though, because the pirates had just begun to laugh at me when the orb exploded. Sand shot up all around them. A blast wave of red light sent me flying backwards. The world swam as I hit the ground. My vision was blurred and my ever-present friend, dizziness, paid me another visit.

After a few seconds, the dust settled. I sat up slowly and discovered that everyone lay flat on their backs, except for Will and Edward who had dropped onto their stomachs before I'd thrown the sphere. Whether it was because they had faith in me, or knew something would go horribly wrong, I was thankful they had moved out of harm's way. The two boys were running around grabbing all the pirates' cutlasses. I got to my feet and began to collect cutlasses as well.

I reached down and grabbed the captain's cutlass.

"Check it out," I said as I brandished the sword. "I be Captain Celeste!"

Both of them broke out laughing. A small laugh escaped my lips. Then another, and another and another. Suddenly, I found myself in a fit of hysterical laughter that was completely inappropriate in our current situation. I knew I should have been more focused on the pirates, but it just felt so good to laugh. I realized that this was the first time that someone other than my mom had laughed at my joke. Usually, people just laugh at me. As much as I missed my old life, there wasn't anything worth living for there. Except my mom of course, but she wasn't there anymore.

Suddenly, the boys stopped laughing and their eyes grew wide with terror. I was about to ask them what was wrong when I saw movement out of the corner of my eye. Before I could react, the captain was back on his feet. He grabbed the cutlass from my hand and wrapped his arm around me to keep me from running. Cold sweat ran down my back as he whipped his sword around with a terrifying *shink!* He stopped that shiny sword just as it would have cut my throat. He held it there threateningly. I gulped at the sight of the sharp blade.

"And I be Captain Grimes," he said in a low, cold voice.

Terror coursed through my veins like ice. Will and Edward remained frozen, as if they were afraid to move. I feared for them to move as well, as Grimes could lash out at any sudden movements. I was quite attached to keeping my head connected to my body.

"Wake up ye scallywags!" Grimes called to his band of pirates. His crew slowly groaned back to life at his command.

Despite the icy terror, I was sweating like a dog. The sun was beating down on us harshly, and it was terribly humid. You know what else was terrible? The way Grimes smelled. He smelled like someone had heated rotten fish and mixed it with the body odor of a middle-aged man who's never bathed. Combine that with the salty smell and the nausea the sight of the blade gave me, and it was enough to make me gag.

"Let her go!" Will shouted.

"Stop it! Ye bilge sucking landlubbers! Drop the swords, or the wench gets it!" He held his sword closer to my throat for emphasis.

The edge of it glazed my skin. I saw my own blood trickle across the blade. I felt something warm and sticky ooze down my neck, and I knew with certainty that it was more blood. The scratch wasn't large enough to be fatal, but it was still painful enough that I had to grit my teeth to keep from crying out.

"Don't do it! Will, please, I'm not worth it," I pleaded.

I knew that if he gave up for my sake, my parents would have to wait even longer. They would spend more time at the hands of Kilmar. They were more important to me than my own life.

"Shut up wench!" Grimes ordered.

He dug his sword farther into my neck. I winced as more blood spilled from the gash that had formed.

The pain in Will's eyes was unmistakable. However, there was a quiet determination behind the pain. I knew that look. I made it just before I was about to pick a fight I knew I couldn't win. It was the kind of look that would get us into trouble.

"You're worth it to me," he said.

I wondered if he felt the same way I did. If maybe, just maybe, he got those inexplicable butterflies, or if his cheeks burned the same way mine did whenever he glanced at me. I wondered if he felt that notorious feeling where it seemed like we were the only two people in the world. Did he search my face, memorizing every detail like I did his?

Our eyes met. I silently pleaded with him not to lay down his sword. I wanted him to fight, after all, we hadn't come this far to be beaten by a band of pirates. Despite this, Will dropped his sword. The captain laughed maliciously. He knew he had won. However, Edward grasped his cutlass with an even firmer grip. He seemed to be weighing his options, a look of uncertainty crossing his face. The negatives must have outweighed the positives because after a moment, he reluctantly followed Will's example. I watched as his grip loosened on the handle.

The blade fell to the ground. Although the sand muffled the sound of the impact, in my head the bang was deafening, drowning out any hope of escape. Two pirates swooped in and restrained the boys' arms behind their backs.

I wanted to scream. Part of me wanted to break down, curl up, and cry. But another part, the sensible part, took one look at our current predicament, and I knew I needed to be brave. I looked at my friends. Both were restrained, held at sword point, and were only here because of me. One look at them, and I decided I would do everything in my power to protect them. Even at the risk of my own life. A plan had begun to form inside my mind. My plans had gotten me into a whole lot of trouble in the past few days, but maybe trouble was exactly what I needed.

I closed my eyes and channeled all of my anger. I found that I was angry for reasons I hadn't anticipated. I found that yes, I was angry with myself for being captured when I should have been searching for my parents. But that wasn't what surprised me. I was angry with myself because I knew that if Will hadn't shown up and worked his magic on me, I would be dead. I need to be stronger than that. Allowing Will and Edward to help me will only get more people I care about hurt. A pang of sadness mixed in with the anger. I realized that as soon as I found a way out of this, I would have to say goodbye to Will. It was just too dangerous for him.

Suddenly, a cold voice brought me crashing back to reality.

"Don't go tryin' nothin'," warned Grimes. "Otherwise, your friends are going to get it!"

I couldn't let that happen. All of my anger had turned into a bundle of energy, and it was fighting against my control. I was terrified of what would happen if I couldn't control this power.

Then my instincts kicked in. I imagined stuffing all my anger into a bottle and putting a cork in it. Although I had lost my chance to use it at that moment, I had a feeling that I could use it later.

A sound somewhere between a sigh and a growl escaped my throat when my eyes came back into focus and I saw the disappointment in my friends' eyes.

"Take em' back to the Calypso's Cutlass!" ordered Grimes.

I took that to be the name of their ship. The name sounded familiar, maybe the name of a goddess from Greek mythology. She had something to do with the oceans, but I couldn't quite put my finger on it. I had taken a course on Greek mythology for my elective in school one year, but I couldn't recall much from the course since I had slept through most of it.

Knowing that fighting would only bring my friends harm, I did not resist. Our hands were tied behind our backs, and we were loaded into a large rowboat. I lifted my head to the sky.

The sun had just begun to rise, and the beautiful array of orange, yellow and pink was breathtaking. I wondered if I would ever get a chance to enjoy it again. Will sat to my right and Edward sat across from us between two pirates that were quite overweight.

"What are we going to do? I know you're planning something," Will whispered in my ear.

I could hear the hopefulness in his voice. He thought I had a plan, but my plan hadn't worked. I had planned to blast the pirates again, but that hadn't gone well. That made it so much harder to say my next words because I knew they would snuff out his hope.

"Nothing," I told him.

For now. I thought to myself.

The stone-cold glare Grimes shot at us may have been enough to silence our conversation, but it wasn't enough to stop the plans that had begun to form in my mind. If anything, it only motivated me more.

TEN

When we arrived at the ship, shackles were put on the boys' ankles. I figured it was to prevent them from jumping ship. If they did, they'd sink like rocks. That was going to be a problem. I would have to work my plan around it.

My wrists were bound instead of my feet. I guess they thought that my hands were how I used my powers. My hands seemed to be an important part of my powers, but I was hoping my powers still worked without them. Maybe, I could just melt off the chains if I needed to. If my powers even worked that way. I barely even understood them, let alone how they worked.

As I was thinking about my powers, I realized I had no idea what Edward's powers were, or if he had any at all. Was he even an Arbitrator? Probably. I wondered what he could do. Did everyone have a different power? Are there people with the same powers?

I would have to ask Will these questions the next time I got a chance.

A young boy was checking my chains to make sure they were secure. I remembered him from the beach. He hadn't talked much and had been on the opposite side of the boat from us. He seemed too young to be hanging out with a crew of pirates. The way he kept his head down, never making eye contact with anyone, made me wonder if he knew that too. If so, perhaps I could get him to see reason.

"Please just let me go. You can pretend I used my powers and blasted you. They'll never know," I pleaded.

"Sorry. I just can't. If they found out they'd make me walk the plank," he said as he tightened my chains. He didn't look at me while he spoke. He kept his eyes glued on my wrists, as if they held infinite secrets of the universe.

I winced as the metal dug farther into my wrists. The boy stared at me. For a moment we were locked together, neither of us wanting to look away. He gazed at me with big blue eyes that seemed to look right through me. He broke away first. He looked around to make sure no one was looking and discretely loosened the cuffs of my chains.

"Thank you," I whispered.

"Don't mention it. Seriously, don't," he said. He scurried away from me without another word.

I was to report to the captain's quarters since I was going to be his chambermaid. When I got there, I found the door closed. I knocked quietly. After someone called for me to come in, I gently opened the door. I found the captain in a chair behind an oak desk. The entire back of the room was made of windows overlooking the sea. The desk caught my eye because of the beautiful designs carved on the front of it. A woman stood on a chariot of pearls being pulled by dolphins. I guess the woman was Calypso, the Greek mythology goddess the ship was named after.

"Tis' a fine carving. Isn't it?" the captain asked.

I had lost myself in a daydream admiring it. However, I snapped out of my daze at the sound of Grimes's voice. His voice gave me the same feeling Johnny's did, when he'd teased me at school. They were just so similar. Both were obnoxiously cocky and absolute jerks.

"I guess. Maybe I'd be able to enjoy it more if I weren't chained up," I snapped back.

He tilted his head back and laughed hysterically. I glared at him. Hatred flaring in my heart.

"I like you. Perhaps ye'll make a fine maid after all," he said.

"I'm nobody's maid. The only reason I haven't blown this ship to shreds is the fact that my friends are on it," I growled.

I clenched my fists as my blood boiled with anger. Grimes's expression shifted from his usual cocky smile. He arched one eyebrow. His brown, almond shaped eyes, which usually gleamed with humor, turned dark and stormy like the sea.

"You couldn't really do that. You aren't strong enough," he snorted. While his voice suggested he was confident and certain about his words, his body language suggested otherwise.

"Aren't I? You saw what I did on the beach, and that wasn't even half of my full power," I countered.

I was bluffing slightly; although, not for the reason you might think. I was confident in the fact that I could blow a good size hole in the ship, one big enough to sink it. However, I did not know the full extent of my powers. While I could always learn more about them with trial and error, there were a lot of ways it could go wrong. Therefore, I considered it a "no man's land."

I could tell my words had gotten to him, and I could see

the wheels beginning to turn in his head. A few drops of sweat rolled down his forehead, leaving lines in the dirt that had caked on his face. I supposed he hadn't had a bath in a long time. He seemed to shrink more and more by the second. I imagined my words echoing in his mind, creating cracks in his confidence.

I smirked, knowing he hadn't won. I had lost the first battle, but I was going to win the war.

After moments of us sitting in silence, he cleared his throat loudly.

"Enough talking! Time for you to get to work. You can start by organizing my cupboard," he blustered.

He pointed to a cabinet to my right that was overflowing with plates, bottles of what appeared to be liquor, and glowing vials of different colored substances. The substances reminded me of moonlight, the way it cast a faint glow over the storage space.

In stark contrast to the mesmerizing liquid, everything was covered in layers of dirt and grime. I wondered if that was where he had gotten the name Grimes. Was it from having a messy cabin or smelling and looking so disgusting? Either way I felt like I was going to vomit. The only thing that stopped me was knowing that I would probably be the one that had to clean it up. Instead, I sighed and started the tedious task of cleaning the captain's gross, smelly cabinets that looked like they hadn't been cleaned since the day the ship was built.

I started by taking everything out of the cupboards and sorting them into piles. The captain eyed me closely at first. I could feel him watching me, and his gaze was a cruel reminder of my predicament. After a few boring minutes of sorting, he grew impatient, lost interest, propped his feet up on the desk, and went to sleep. I rolled my eyes at the sound of his obnoxiously loud snoring.

This guy snores like a foghorn, I thought to myself.

Once I had taken everything out, I started to put things back in. I grabbed a bottle of the glowing liquid. It splashed around inside the bottle as I moved it, glittery puffs appearing with the movement. I was placing it near the back corner when something shimmered along the back wall. Curiously, I put the bottle down beside me and ran my fingers down the wood. My fingers brushed a smooth cool surface that stood out among the splintery wood. I pressed against it and then I heard a soft click. A small section of the wood slid back revealing a hidden compartment.

I felt around inside of it. When my fingers touched it, I pulled out the strange object. I marveled at the strange sight: a bottle, almost identical to the others, except this one was filled with a black substance. Touching it made a chill run through my arms and spread throughout the rest of my body. Despite the fact that I wasn't afraid of the captain, a terrifying fear clawed its way into my heart. I shivered from the feeling. I almost dropped the bottle and cried out as I reached out and caught it just before it shattered.

Fearing I had woken him, I glanced over at the captain. The drool dripping from the corners of his mouth indicated that he was still sleeping. With shaky hands, I placed the mysterious bottle back into its hiding place in the cupboard. After that, I put everything neatly back inside the cupboard, carefully rearranging everything so that it was nice and neat.

When I finished, I stalked over to the captain's desk. He was asleep so there wasn't a way for him to know I had finished.

What do I do now? I wondered.

Could I just leave and go down to my sleeping quarters? Would I get in trouble if I woke him? Was I to report to somewhere else? I had no idea what I was supposed to do.

In an attempt to wake him subtly, I cleared my throat. I did so a few more times but he continued to snore. I debated shaking him awake. I changed my mind, deciding it would probably anger him if I woke him. I quietly tiptoed towards the door, wincing every time the floorboards creaked beneath my feet. I gently opened the door. After I closed it, I sighed at what my life had become. I had been reduced to a scullery maid.

"Is the captain asleep?" someone behind me said.

I jumped at the sound of the stranger's voice. I tried to compose myself as I turned around. I came to find the same boy from earlier, the young, blonde one.

"Oh, uhh, yeah," I muttered in reply.

"Sorry, didn't mean to scare you," he apologized.

"Man, he snores like a foghorn," I whispered. A light laugh slipped from my lips. It was my sorry attempt at a joke. The boy didn't share my humor. Instead, his icy blue eyes turned cold.

"You don't want to wake him. Trust me. The last guy to do that didn't survive the flogging," he shuddered.

He looked over at a post. I suspected it was no ordinary post. Red was splattered all over it. I had a bad feeling it wasn't just red paint. I shuddered as well. I would have to be careful not to wake the captain.

I remembered how kind this stranger had been to me—for a pirate. The way he had known he would get into trouble if he was caught loosening my chains; yet he did it anyway. I felt a need to know who he was.

"What's your name?" I asked him.

"I'm Oliver," he replied.

"Celeste, Celeste Rowan," I replied. He offered me his hand, and I shook it awkwardly. As that feeling of awkwardness that I had come to be so familiar with settled over us, I felt the need to change the subject.

"Anyways…how old are you? You seem a bit young to be hanging out with a band of pirates," I pointed out.

I immediately regretted my words. His pained expression made him look like a different boy. His bright blue eyes seemed to get darker. Clearly, I had struck a nerve.

He sighed and said, "I don't even know how old I am. I'm an orphan. Nobody knows when my birthday is. The pirates found me when I was little. I was too young to remember where I came from. The pirates took me in. I guess even this cruel band of pirates wasn't heartless enough to kill a defenseless little boy."

Yet they are cruel enough to take people prisoner.

I thought about this for a moment. He had no reason to treat me so well. Surely, he had no reason to be kind to a prisoner of the pirates who had saved him. It just didn't make sense to me. Nothing really did at the moment. My life has been a series of mishaps, screw ups, and unfortunate events.

"Why have you been so kind to me?" I inquired.

He didn't answer immediately. Instead, he paused for a moment. I could tell he was choosing his words carefully.

"I have two reasons. One, I saw how brave you were when the captain held you at sword point. You were willing to sacrifice your own life so that your friends could live. I admire that. And the second—" he faltered.

"And the second?" I prompted.

"The second reason is…is…I can't tell you. Not here. There are too many eyes and ears," he fretted.

I looked around. We were completely alone on the deck. The captain was still snoring away in his cabin.

"There's no one here," I conceded.

"It doesn't matter; someone is always watching. I'll tell you tonight, when everyone else is asleep," he whispered in my ear.

Then he was off, going below deck. I assumed he was doing his daily chores. I figured I was probably supposed to go do mine. I had been ordered to serve in the galley.

I stood there stunned, my heart hammering in my chest. I felt like I had just committed a crime. I was blindly trusting Oliver. The fact that I knew his name didn't mean I knew him. He was still just as much a stranger to me.

At the same time, I was ready to take that leap of faith, so long as it didn't end with Will and Edward getting hurt or worse. Oliver had been right about one thing, I was willing to sacrifice everything for the sake of my friends.

ELEVEN

The rest of that day I spent down below deck serving all of the men. A large table big enough to seat the entire crew stood in the center of the room. The men came and went. Some stayed longer than others—since they became too drunk to do anything else.

I served them beer, terrible tasting bread that passed for biscuits on this retched ship, and water that was more dirt than actual water. That was the entirety of the terrible menu. I was not looking forward to staying here. However, I wasn't going to be here very long. I was simply biding my time until I could find a way to escape.

After a long while, I realized that this motley crew of pirates was not only smelly, but they were boisterous and constantly drunk. All except for Oliver, who didn't show up at all throughout the course of the day. I figured he was too young to drink anyway. I wondered what he was doing and hoped it was better than what I was enduring.

There was one upside to my serving the pirates though. I listened for information as to when we would be stopping. I gathered that in three days' time we'd be stopping at a large island with a vast jungle. They were searching for a treasure that resided on the island. They called it the "Eye of Azure."

"I heard it can grant you the ability to see the future," said one guy.

"I heard that there's a maze of thorns around it," said another.

"Those are just children's tales compared to what the captain told me," boasted one guy. He looked to be middle aged. He wore a bandana around his head and a sword strapped around his waist. "The captain told me that the terrors that lurk on that island are like nothing you've ever seen before."

"Oh, yeah! Like what?" said a rueful man in his mid-twenties.

"You mock me now, but you won't be laughing when you see the beasts. Big as a boat, they are. With big black eyes and fangs that'll tear you in two," he said.

Some of the other men laughed along with the rueful man from earlier. They did not believe the stories. Neither did I. He was drunk after all.

I listened to the pirates and maneuvered my way around them to bring them food. It wasn't that bad until one, severely drunk guy decided it was his mission to make me miserable.

"Wench, bring me more beer," he cried.

He downed the rest of the one he was currently drinking. He burped and smashed the glass bottle on the floor. I sighed, knowing I would have to clean it up and bring him another beer.

I was shocked that none of the men had passed out yet.

After all, they had to be ruined already. Some of them were starting their tenth round of drinks.

I marched over to the corner and grabbed the broom. It was covered in cobwebs and the wooden handle had termite holes all over it. It seemed like it hadn't been used in a while.

I grabbed a bucket to put the glass in.

I trudged back to the mess. After sweeping all of it into a pile, I stooped down and began putting the glass into the bucket. I picked up each piece carefully, trying not to cut myself on the sharp glass shards. My fingers were sticky from the beer, and they smelled wretched.

I stood up and the man's cruel laughter echoed behind me. I knew he was enjoying this and that made me angry.

I kept my steps even and my back straightened as I walked back to the kitchen and placed the bucket of shards there. The only chef was a stout, gray-haired old lady named Jessie. She didn't acknowledge me. She simply took the bucket from my hand and replaced it with a pitcher of beer. Then, I returned the broom to its spot in the corner.

The man watched me like a hawk as I strutted towards him, beer in hand.

I had dealt with a lot of bullies over the years. I found that if you really wanted to make them mad without getting in trouble, you had to kill them with kindness, though it didn't have to be real kindness. I just always faked a smile and spoke as politely as I possibly could. Not only did it confuse them, but it upset them to know that they weren't getting any kind of reaction out of you.

"Here you go sir," I said as I passed him the bottle of beer. I plastered the biggest smile I could muster to my face. "Will that be all?"

He seemed hopelessly confused by my kindness. He

stumbled over his words as he tried to figure out how to respond.

"I-yes that....will be all," he faltered.

Just then, a bell rang, signaling that it was time for curfew. I was literally saved by the bell.

Since we were prisoners, we had to sleep in a cell in the lowest, deepest corners of the ship, where you could easily feel the nauseating rocking of the ship. When I got there, I carefully tucked the bottle of black stuff in a pile of rope in the corner.

I didn't even attempt to sleep. There was no way for me to tell time down there. The only light came from a rusty old lantern that sat atop one of the numerous barrels surrounding us. We were on the level where they stored all of the liquids. Stale water made the ship smell like damp wood. The stench of alcohol burned my nose. I shivered as I watched a rat shimmy down the wall of the ship and run across the floorboards.

Word had reached me that the cells above us were much nicer than ours. They had better lighting, mats to sleep on, no alcohol, and they even had sacks of food right outside of the bars. The slaves that slept there weren't herded into their cells like cattle. They just walk about willingly. Those cells had to be earned, and we were far from earning them. I had decided not to tell Will and Edward about my conversation with Oliver. They were both exhausted and sore. The two boys had been working, rowing the giant oars that moved the boat.

All day, they had been forced to do that. All day, while I was serving people. Not working hard, excruciatingly painful labor for hours like they had. I felt guilty knowing that I had gotten off easy. To me, it was just another reason that I had to save them. They were in this mess because of me, and I needed to fix it.

I sat there thinking for what felt like hours. There was so

much to think about. Mostly I thought about my dad. I had never known him. I couldn't remember anything about him. Mom used to sing me to sleep with the same songs he had sang to me as a baby. At least, that's what Mom had told me.

It was the only thing I allowed myself to cherish about him before now. Before they had only stood as bittersweet memories of a father who didn't love me. Now they meant so much more than that. They're a reminder that he has always loved me, and that someway, somehow, a part of me has always loved him.

Other than a few, hazy memories, I only have one thing from my time with him: a small necklace with a crystal star charm on it.

I guess, to me, it had always been too painful to think about what could have been. It hurt too much to think about how happy we could have been if he hadn't left us. It hurt to wonder if he would ever come back. That's why I only asked on my birthday. Somehow, being a year older gave me the courage to wonder about him.

Now I know why he left us. Not only had he been protecting us from the harshness of this world, but he had also been protecting us from people who thought I was dangerous. People like the Convocation.

I realized this when I woke up on the beach after my encounter with the Convocation. They treated me like a monster. I'd seen a monster. I'd seen a demon. I was neither of those things.

But Kilmar is. I thought. *And he has my parents.*

I couldn't hold back my tears anymore, and I let myself cry. I clutched my necklace like a lifeline. I could feel the tears slipping down my cheek. These were hot tears that burned. I could feel them slide through the layers of dirt and grime that had caked my face after not bathing in so long. It had been five days since Will first took me to Enceaf. Or was it Six? How long had I been out before I woke up in the forcefield? Minutes? Hours? Days? I continued to cry, trying to keep quiet to not wake the boys.

In an effort to calm down, I found myself softly humming one of my dad's old songs. My mom had sung it to me as she tucked me into bed when I was younger.

Songbird sing.

Songbird fly.

Songbird soaring through the night.

Songbird sing.

Songbird soar.

See the dawn rise once more.

Songbird sing.

Fly away.

Songbird bring a brand new day.

I hummed these lines over and over again until the tears stopped. I had done this many times when no one was watching. Except this time someone was watching.

"You have a great voice," someone said from the direction of the stairwell.

I whipped my head around and saw that the speaker was Oliver. I felt my cheeks getting warm. I hoped I didn't seem embarrassed. I was embarrassed, but I didn't want Oliver, the only pirate on this ship that seemed to actually treat me like a human being, to see me embarrassed. I guess I was afraid that I would lose what little respect I had gained from him.

"Thanks," I said as I turned away to wipe my tear-stained cheeks. "What song is that? It seems so familiar," he said.

"It's a song my dad made up. He used to sing to me when I was little," I said as I touched my necklace. I wondered how he could have heard it if my dad made it up.

"Oh," he said, "I must have just heard something like it."

"I guess so," I replied dryly. I felt a little bit offended because that song was mine and my dad's thing. After losing him it felt so fragile. Like, if I let someone else hold it, it might shatter. I didn't want to lose my favorite thing about him.

Of course this was all just an overreaction. He had just heard something similar to it. That's all it was. That's what I told myself; I tried my hardest to believe it.

"Man, your friends are out cold!" he said as he walked towards the cell.

I glanced at my friends who were both snoring away constantly. Their snores could rival the captain's.

"They had to row all day. The man overseeing them refused to let them take a break. I wish I could take their places. It's my fault they're in this mess in the first place," I fretted.

"That sounds like a heavy burden. I'm sorry you are bearing it. Guilt is both a good and a bad thing. It's fine in small doses because it keeps us in check. But the amount you are putting on yourself will weigh you down," he told me.

"That doesn't change the fact that it's my fault," I groaned, "The only way for me to fix it is to get out of here."

"There's no chance that the captain will let you go now. He seems to think that there is something special about you. Your only chance of getting out of here is by escaping when no one is watching. I'll help you," he said.

I stared at him blankly; my brain seemed to come to an abrupt stop. I had not been expecting that. He didn't even know me, and he was offering to help me escape these pirates. The same pirates that had raised him. They were the only family he'd known, yet he was betraying them for me. I was utterly confused.

"Thank you…. but……why?" I asked him.

"That's what I came to talk to you about," he answered.

I realized he still hadn't told me his reason two. The reason he had been so kind to me when all the other pirates were such jerks. I was anxious to understand.

"Reason two?" I prompted.

He gave me a slight nod. My heart hammered in my chest as he opened his mouth to speak.

"Okay, this is going to sound crazy. Are you absolutely sure you want to know?" he checked.

I gave him an exasperated yes. I was dying to know, and it was killing me that he was dragging out the answer. His blue eyes seemed to see right through me. His gaze remained so intense, so questioning that I feared he might see right through me, right to the scared little girl who is buried inside.

He took a deep breath.

"Reason two is that…I have the same powers as you," he said.

I couldn't think enough to say anything. There were too many questions to ask and too many emotions to feel. All I could do was stare and blink and try to sort through everything that was clambering around in my mind. I slammed my eyes shut as the walls started closing in around me from the force of my newfound revelation: he was like me, he was a halfling.

"I know this is a lot to take in, but you need to calm down," I heard Oliver say.

Okay. I thought. *He's right. You need to calm down. Take deep breaths and calm down.*

"Sorry," I said once I had calmed down. "I've just been through so much. My emotions are a little on the fritz."

I felt my cheeks blush as a fresh wave of shame ran over me.

"It's okay," he assured me.

Although, I could tell by the way his cheeks had turned red that he was uncomfortable with my outburst.

"It's just that before now I thought I was the only halfling," I said.

His face contorted in confusion.

"Halfling?" he inquired.

"Half-human, half-Arbitrator. That's what we are, I think," I explained.

I wasn't completely sure that he was telling the truth. He had yet to give me any reason to believe he had the same powers as me. Yet, he also said he would help me escape so I didn't really have a reason to question him.

"Show me what you can do," I prompted.

"Alright, but we need to be quiet, so we don't wake the others," he said.

We both glanced at the two snoring boys. He seemed to have realized the same as me: we had been talking quite loudly. It was a miracle we hadn't caused any suspicions. We hadn't made any effort to be quiet before that moment.

I stared at him, motioning for him to go on.

He closed his eyes and sure enough he began to glow. He glowed the darkest shade of blue I had ever seen. The light was so bright and intense, it made me wonder what he was thinking about. Whatever it was, it couldn't be good. I almost asked him, but then I remembered what had made me glow blue. I had thought about my parents and the fact that I might never save them. I never wanted to feel that hopeless sadness again. It was awful.

Powerful fear followed that sadness. It was so powerful that it cut deep into the darkest corners of my heart and left nothing but terrible feelings in its wake. His pain and sorrow must have been even worse to make him glow that intensely.

"Can you do this?" I asked.

I imagined opening the bottle I had stored my power in when the pirates captured us and letting all of the bottled-up anger flow out. Then I shaped it back into an orb. Soon I had a glowing red ball of pure anger in my hand.

"No," he said with a sigh. Then his eyes lit up. "Could you teach me?"

"You want me to teach you?" I repeated skeptically.

"Yes! And anything else that you know would be great too. I haven't been able to practice. I was scared that I would be found out if I did," he replied.

"I haven't had much time to practice either, so the orb is about all that I know how to do. I guess I could try to teach you but I'm still learning myself," I explained.

"I don't care; I just want to learn. These powers, they are getting harder to control," he whispered, "Whenever my emotions spike, it feels like there are fireworks going off inside of me and it's all I can do to keep them in."

I understood what it was like to fear my own powers. It was terrifying to know something that powerful was lurking inside you. If I didn't control it, then I feared it would control me. That kind of fear gnaws at you until it overtakes you completely.

"Okay," I concurred.

"So, what do I do?" he inquired.

I had to think about that for a moment. What did I do? What did I feel? What did I think?

"So first, I find a really powerful emotion. It's like the same thing you do when you glow," I explained.

He closed his eyes, scrunching his features from the effort. He stayed normal for quite some time, and I started to fear that it wasn't working. Suddenly, he glowed bright yellow.

"Great job!" I crooned. "Hold onto that feeling; imagine having complete control over it. Got it?"

He tensed and I could tell the effort was draining him. I didn't want to stop though. I didn't plan to unless he told me he needed to.

"Got it!" he exclaimed.

I shushed him. He mumbled an apology, realizing he had been too loud. We both instinctively looked toward the stairwell. There wasn't any evidence of footsteps. I sighed, exasperated.

"Now you need to imagine it forming into a ball. That's it," I told him.

I waited patiently. I didn't have to wait very long though. Soon, he had a glowing yellow orb in his hand. I quietly applauded and praised him for getting it on his first try.

He practiced some more. He did it over and over again, turning a different color each time. I was happy for him, but we still had important things to discuss.

"Um, Oliver? This has been really great, but we've gotten off track," I reminded him. "You said you could help me and my friends escape?"

"You're right. We've gotten completely off track," he

conceded. "I think that I can help you escape. I know where the keys are. If we can get them, then we can escape when the ship arrives at the island."

It was a risky plan, but it made sense, except for one part that I didn't understand.

"Why wait until then? We could always just portal away from here when no one is looking," I felt the need to point out.

"I know you think that, but your chains are made of Embrasium. It's an indestructible metal. It also keeps Arbitrators from portaling. It messes with their sparks so that if they try to portal…." he cut off.

He shivered. I did not want to find out what would happen if we attempted to teleport. I wanted to play it as safe as we could. There wasn't a lot of breathing room for that seeing how we were surrounded by ruthless pirates that were all armed. Still, it is better to be safe than sorry.

He continued, "Let's just say it won't be good. The only way that you are going to get them off is by using the keys. When you are in the captain's cabin, grab the keys. They're in the bottom drawer on the right side of the captain's desk. Then we can escape."

I sighed. My life has gotten so complicated. At least I wasn't alone; I had Will and Edward. Plus, I had someone just like me, someone who understood how scary it was to be a halfling: Oliver. It was going to be so hard rescuing my parents, but at least I had friends to help me.

"I should go before I get caught," he said. He turned and walked towards the stairs.

Say something! I thought to myself.

"Hey, Oliver," I called out in a whisper voice, "Thanks."

"For what?" he asked.

"For everything."

TWELVE

In the morning, I woke to the sound of one of the pirates banging their sword against the metal bars of the cell. The bars rattled, and the bangs echoed around the room. We all groaned at our rude awakening.

As the pirate did this, he called out, "Wake up maggots! Time to work!"

Will groaned and stretched. Edward muttered something under his breath, probably a complaint. He was wise to keep it quiet enough that the pirate never heard it. This pirate reminded me of one of my teachers. They were the type that if you even breathed wrong, you were in big trouble.

"Hurry up wench! You're to report to the captain's quarters again," the pirate ordered.

I sluggishly got to my feet and tried to mentally prepare myself for the captain. This was my shot at saving my friends. I just had to grab those keys.

If it goes anything like yesterday, I can grab them when he's asleep,

I thought.

I made my way up the staircase. My legs were still stiff from sleeping on the hard wooden floors, so I tripped a few times as I climbed the stairs.

Soon I stumbled onto the deck. I was shocked by the scene I walked into.

Thunder clapped loudly in the sky above me. Lightning flashed. Wind howled all around me. Huge waves battered the boat and made it rock dangerously. Sheets of rain fell, making the deck more of a pond. I could barely see through the storm.

Absolute dread filled me as I stared out at the raging storm. My only thought: I needed those keys. There was only one way for me to get them, I had to go through the storm.

I blindly moved in the direction I thought the captain's quarters were in. I took careful, small steps. The ship was rocking so violently, I was struggling to keep my balance. I stumbled and slipped my way across the deck.

I had just spotted the faint outline of the captain's door when out of nowhere, a huge wave smashed into the boat. The ship tipped to one side, and I slid across the deck. I clawed against the deck, desperately trying to find something to grip onto. I slid all the way down to the railing. I reached for the railing. I barely managed to grab the rails in time to stop myself from plunging into the sea.

"Help!" I called out, even though I knew it was probably hopeless. No one would hear me over the raging storm.

"Someone, anyone! Please help me!" I cried out again.

One by one, my fingers began to slip from the slick railing. I tried to grab on with the other hand, but I lost my grip. I started to fall. I closed my eyes, resigned to my fate. Suddenly, I felt a sharp jolt to my wrist, and I stopped falling. I opened my eyes warily. Two hands grasped my own. I looked up to find Oliver leaning over the deck.

"Need a little help?" he chuckled warily.

"Yes, please!"

I grinned up at him. He didn't return my smile, as he was struggling to pull me back aboard. His face was red from the effort. I did my best to help him, but the side of the ship was slick with algae and rain. I sighed as he hauled me back up to the deck and we both collapsed.

"Thanks for the save!" I rasped.

"No problem! Better get going, you're late!" he wheezed. I could barely hear him over the storm.

I pulled myself to my feet. I made a mad dash to the captain's quarters. It was a miracle I made it at all. Between the storm, gale force winds, and battering waves I felt like the world wanted me dead.

I breathed a sigh of relief as my fingers finally grasped the cool metal handle. I pushed the door open. It opened with ease; however, I had to fight against the wind to close the door. It took a moment, but I got it closed. I slumped against the door, feeling both physically and mentally depleted.

"You're late!" The captain fumed.

He glared at me from behind his desk, his whole face turning red from rage.

Suddenly, I was eight years old again, surrounded by a group of older boys who had been beating up a younger boy that I went to school with. When I tried to get them to stop, they shoved me to the ground. I sat there crying on the ground while they shoved and bullied the other boy. When I told my mom what happened, she was furious. She had marched up to the school and demanded that the older boys be punished. However, it didn't happen on school grounds, so there was nothing the school could do about it. I felt terrified and helpless. Here I was, six years later feeling the same way. The only difference? I wasn't fighting alone anymore.

"S-sorry. It won't happen again!" I stammered.

"It better not, or you won't like what happens," he let the threat hang in the air for a moment before continuing, "Time to sweep the floors. And when you're done with that you can mop them. Then you need to dust off the cabinets."

I winced at the threat, remembering the flogging post that Oliver had warned me about. Not wishing to meet that fate, I sighed and set about my work. Sweeping was such a tedious task; even more so with the promise of escape lingering in the back of my mind. I just needed the captain to fall asleep. I took my time sweeping, knowing it would bore him. Occasionally, I glanced over at the captain. I needed him to fall asleep so I could grab the keys.

I had finished sweeping and was halfway finished mopping before I heard the tell-tale snoring. I coughed loudly to test if he was sleeping hard enough.

"Five more minutes mummy," he mumbled sluggishly.

Yeah, he is out cold, I thought to myself.

I quietly sat my mop down and tiptoed over to the desk. I tried to open the drawer as quietly as possible. I winced as the wood squeaked a little, but it was not enough to wake him. I looked inside the drawer, thankful when I spotted the ring of keys. There were probably forty keys on the ring. It would take me forever to figure out which key would unlock our chains.

"Dang it!" I whispered.

It certainly wasn't ideal, but at least I had the keys. I slowly shuffled back to my mop and tucked the keys away in my pocket. The keys jingled as I moved, so I decided to move slower. I didn't want the jingles to arouse suspicion.

I rushed to finish mopping and dusting. Then I reported

to the dining hall to serve the men again. I prayed that it would go better than the previous night.

This time, Oliver was there. He stayed in the corner where his face was hidden in the shadows, but his presence was comforting. He was the only other halfling I knew, and I felt as if that connected us somehow.

I glanced at him. He noticed and we locked eyes. I gave him a slight nod. It was barely even a nod at all. However, he seemed to understand because he winked back. His gaze shifted to the pirates seated at the large table. I suppose he was checking to make sure no one had seen him. They didn't, of course, as they were completely drunk again. There wasn't a single sober man in the galley. There never was, except for Oliver, who was far too young to partake.

Once he realized that no one had seen him, he walked swiftly up the stairs and out of view. I turned and went back to serving the men.

They were talking about going to the island. The storm had hastened our journey to the island. We were due to arrive in the morning.

There was also more talk about what we would find on the island. One man claimed that there were giant scorpions, and another said that there were giant mosquitoes. Someone said that there were fish that could walk on land. Somebody else claimed that the butterflies were made of actual butter. This time, even I didn't believe the tall tales. I tried my hardest to listen, hoping I could gain some helpful information, but the tales just got more unbelievable.

I gave up listening after an hour or so. Instead, I focused on moving carefully, as to not make the keys jingle. I was counting down the time until I could make my way back to the cell.

When I heard the bell, I was anxious to get back to the

cell. However, when I got there, my heart broke at the sight of my friends. Their eyes had dark shadows underneath. Their clothes were covered in dirt. They looked exhausted.

Guilt weighed heavily in my heart. I knew it was my fault, but I was doing everything I could to fix it.

Since I had gained my powers, I learned that letting my emotions spiral was not a good idea. I needed to learn to control my emotions and bend them to my will, so that I could use them to fuel my powers.

I could tell that Will and Edward could use some cheering up. I wanted to show them the keys so badly. I could see their hope had all but faded. Telling them mine and Oliver's plan would bring that hope back. However, showing them too soon would put them at risk. I needed to wait until the pirates were asleep.

"So, what did they make you do today," I asked instead.

"They had us swab the entire deck," Edward replied.

I thought back to the storm that had rocked the boat that morning. Not only was it unfair since the deck didn't even need to be mopped, but it was dangerous. I had almost drowned, and I had only been out there in the storm for a few minutes. They were out there all day. It was a miracle they were still alive. I hated that captain and those dreaded pirates. They were cruel and heartless.

I wanted them to know Will and Edward's pain. I wanted them to suffer the same way the boys had. The thought absolutely terrified me because it wasn't me. Even when I had been held prisoner by the Convocation, I hadn't wanted them to suffer the same way I had.

Oliver had been right, if I let the guilt weigh on me, it would tear me down. I knew I should listen to his words. However, I was terrible at doing what I was told. The guilt was slowly eating away at me.

"I'm so sorry. It's my fault you guys are in this mess in the first place," I said. I was the reason they'd been on that beach in the first place. If it weren't for me, they would never have been there or been taken by the pirates.

Will seemed so taken aback by this. He took my hands in his.

"No. Celeste. It's not your fault. We made our choice," Will said.

"Will's right," Edward added.

I was so glad that they didn't hold any of this against me. However, I still held myself solely accountable for our predicament. Their suffering was my fault.

"You should have just left me," I scoffed bitterly. "I told you I wasn't worth it."

It was a selfish thing to say. He and Edward had both risked their lives to save mine. I should have been grateful. However, guilt is so much stronger than gratitude.

I turned my head away from him to keep him from seeing the tears that had started to roll down my cheeks. I closed my eyes, knowing I didn't deserve this. I didn't deserve to feel sorry for myself.

"I believe I already told you: you're worth it to me," he whispered. He somehow managed to fit an endless amount of passion into those quiet words.

He ran his thumb along my cheek, brushing away my tears. If the occasion were different, I might have turned away, repulsed by a boy's touch. However, his touch sparked a feeling deep within me, one that I had been trying very hard to snuff out.

As much as I wanted to put my feelings for him on hold, I just couldn't anymore. After all we'd been through, it didn't feel right. I had been trying so hard to control my emotions, but what if I didn't? What if I just listened to them instead?

That was what I had always done when things got hard. When did I stop listening to my heart? After all, it may have gotten me in trouble, but it had never led me astray.

Before I could change my mind, I wrapped my arms around his neck.

"Thank you," I whispered in his ears.

For a second, Will did nothing. Then he hugged me back. His embrace made me feel so warm, and it made me feel something else that I hadn't felt since he pulled me through the portal: safe.

THIRTEEN

I could have stayed that way forever.

Of course, Oliver chose this moment to come barreling down the stairs. Will and I quickly separated. A moment of awkward silence settled over us, interrupted only by Edward's just as awkward cough. I had honestly forgotten he was there. I felt a little bit guilty about it, but it was worth it for that hug.

"You need to get the chains off right now. They know the keys are missing and they've ordered a mandatory search of the entire ship," he insisted.

"What the—" Will stuttered.

"No time to explain!" I cried as I scrambled to get the keys out of my pocket.

There was a problem though. "I don't know what key it is!"

Oliver stared at the keys. He looked from the keys to where the chains rubbed my wrists, then back to the keys.

"Look for one that is the same color as the chains," he said matter of fact. As soon as one problem was solved, another replaced it.

"There are four that are the same color!"

"Just try all four until one fits," he said.

Of course! Why hadn't I thought of that? At that moment, I was so panicked that I couldn't think straight enough to be of any use. I knew I was hindering us; however, if Oliver felt similarly, he didn't say.

I set to work trying to get the chains off Will. The first key was too large for the hole. The second one was too wide. I stuck the third one in and prayed that it would work. It fit the hole perfectly, and when I turned it, I heard a soft click. My mind screamed with relief as Will's chains fell with a clang to the ground. I got Edward's chains off and was working on getting mine off when the captain came down the stairs. He took in the scene with a gaping mouth, and eyes wide from shock. Will and Edward with their chains off; me with one free wrist; and Oliver in the middle of it all.

"You dare betray us boy?!" he cried to Oliver as two more pirates climbed down. They each flanked one side of him. "You will pay dearly for this crime!"

I wasted no time getting my chains the rest of the way off. Free of their burden, I shaped a sphere in my hands. This one was red hot. My entire body hummed with energy from the sphere. I wanted with all my being to toss it right at the captain's face.

"Take one step closer and I'll blow this entire ship up!" I warned the pirates.

Oliver followed my lead. He shaped a dark blue sphere in his hands. There was a collective gasp. Will and Edward's jaws dropped. The two pirates flanking the captain looked as if they might faint. The captain's reaction was what truly bothered me.

He seemed calm and unsurprised by the sudden revelation. It occurred to me that perhaps he had known Oliver was a halfling. I dismissed the thought. He would have exploited Oliver if he had known.

We all watched as Oliver did something even more unexpected. He shaped a blue sword from the sphere. It was my turn to gape at him.

"How did you do that?" I gasped. I was absolutely mesmerized by his new skill. I envied him for it, and I wanted to know more.

"How about I tell you after we get out of here?" he urged.

"Good point!" I agreed.

We would definitely come back to this topic later.

Oliver turned to the pirates. He pointed his sword at the captain's chest.

"You are going to give us a ship. Then you are going to let us go," he demanded.

"We could just portal out of here like we planned," I whispered my protest.

Oliver was changing the plan, but I liked our plan. It was safe; it was simple; it was good. I didn't want to change the plan.

"Where would you suggest we go? Enceaf? I know how the Convocation feels about halfings, Celeste," Oliver argued.

I winced at the painful reminder. I knew all too well what they thought of me. I was not eager to return to them. Nonetheless, there were other dimensions we could portal to. We could go to back to Fortest, or some other dimension. I knew there were others out there. I just needed a different colored portal.

Oliver gave me a look that begged me not to argue. I sighed and resigned myself to our new plan.

The pirate on the captain's right asked nervously, "What do you want us to do captain?"

He glanced at us nervously. His eyes settled on Oliver's glowing blade. The fellow gulped. I suppressed a smirk. At least the captain's crew feared us. We had that advantage.

The captain sighed heavily.

"Let them go. We have other slaves," he ordered reluctantly.

"B-but captain, he's a traitor. He should have to answer for this," the broodier pirate on the captain's right pointed out.

"I said let them go!" the captain snapped.

Oliver seemed to decide it was time to go.

We walked up the stairs. Oliver was in the front since he knew where the boats were. I brought up the rear since I had my sphere. Will and Edward were unarmed so they stayed in between us. Both of them kept looking around nervously. Their eyes stayed wild, and uncertain. They were confused, and they had a right to be.

As we climbed through the levels, I saw more than one slave glare at us. Maybe they were jealous. I would be, if I had been captured and taken away from everything I've ever known, I would be jealous of someone fighting for their freedom. Part of me ached for these people. I wanted to help them, and perhaps someday I would. Today was not that day.

Once we were on the deck, Oliver led us over to a small rowboat.

"This will do. Hop in," he told us.

We scrambled into the boat, and Oliver came on

afterwards. After we were all in, the boat was lowered into the ocean.

"Good luck!" the captain said with a laugh.

This seemed very odd to me. He had just lost three servants and a crewmember. His laugh was so foreboding, like he knew something we didn't. Even as the ship sailed away from us, his words and his laughter still rang clearly in my ears. So strange. So very strange.

Something else bothered me. Our escape seemed too easy. I had a feeling that the captain wouldn't have just yielded. He didn't even fight back at all. He just let us go.

I looked around in every direction. Searching for something, anything. I had the strangest feeling that there was some trick, some catch that I hadn't seen yet. After all, the captain wasn't a fool. A sick jerk maybe, but not a fool.

That's when I saw it, the storm. The one that had almost thrown me into the sea. The same storm that the Calypso's Cutlass was sailing away from. The same one that was heading straight for us.

"I knew it was too easy," I said aloud. I curled my knees up to my chest.

"What are you talking about?" Will asked.

He was on the other side of the small boat from me. Edward sat beside him at the front and Oliver sat beside me at the back.

I squeezed my eyes shut, as if that could block out my situation. We were adrift in the middle of the ocean. No matter how fast we paddled, we couldn't outrun that storm. As soon as one problem was solved, another bigger, more life-threatening one popped up.

I felt the boat rock slightly. I opened my eyes and grasped the side of the boat in alarm. Will had swapped seats with

Oliver. He was staring at me now, probably still expecting a response that I couldn't yet bring myself to give. I uncurled myself.

Will repeated his question.

I didn't answer for a moment. Instead, I looked out toward the storm. The stormy grey clouds seemed to reflect my mood. I tried to be calm and not let my emotions control me. I knew I didn't need to control them either. I needed to work with them, but I was feeling so many emotions, too many to stay calm. Then, I turned to look at the boys.

"It's a trick. They didn't just let us go. The storm is heading right toward us, and they knew it," I said as I pointed at the wall of big dark clouds behind us. They all turned toward the storm.

I was barely able to keep myself together. I guess I had been hoping that maybe I could finally catch a break. The last few days have been one bad thing after another. I just wanted a little bit of calm. But by some sick twist of fate, we were about to be in even bigger trouble.

I turned away from everyone else. I fought against the tears that were threatening to spill onto my cheeks. I hugged myself and curled my knees back up to my chest. This wasn't supposed to happen. Fourteen-year-old girls aren't supposed to lose their parents. They aren't supposed to be captured by corrupt rulers. They aren't supposed to be enslaved by pirates and then set adrift to drown in a storm. Fourteen-year-old girls shouldn't have to endure this madness. However, as I was constantly reminded, I am not like other fourteen-year-old girls.

I felt myself slipping into despair. My thoughts spiraled more and more the longer I thought about it.

"She's right. Can we outrun it?" Edward asked Oliver.

Oliver shook his head. I knew what he would say. So, I

wasn't really listening when he told us that the ocean was too vast and the storm was too fast. There was no way to outrun it in a rowboat. I snorted bitterly, knowing I had been thinking the same thing.

"Celeste, could you use your powers to propel us away from it?" Will asked.

I perked up at this. He looked at me hopefully as I considered the question. The optimism in his eyes pulled me from my stupor.

"I guess it could work. Maybe we could make a beam of light. I think it should be similar to forming an orb. It needs to be red though. I think it packs the most punch," I told Oliver.

He nodded, his hopefulness suddenly turning to grim determination. He set his jaw. He and Will switched seats.

"Let's give it a shot! On the count of three," he replied.

"Okay, I'm ready," I said. I wasn't sure if I was trying to reassure him or myself.

I closed my eyes, focusing on every bit of rage I had ever felt. I let it swell inside of me until it was all I had left.

"One! Two! Three!" We shouted in unison.

When we got to three, I opened my eyes. A beam of red light was shooting from our hands. We were propelled forward so hard that Will and Edward fell forwards.

"Woohoo!" Will shouted as he struggled to sit back up.

Edward laughed and smiled at me.

The pirates may have tricked us, I thought, *but they haven't beaten us.*

I found that making a beam of light powerful enough to propel us was not easy. I knew that Oliver and I had to keep it going no matter what. We seemed to have a silent understanding of this. The storm was right behind us. If we slowed down even a little, we would be enveloped in it. That was not an option.

It was also very tiring. It didn't just drain my energy. It drained something deep down inside me: my spark. I guessed that happened every time I used my powers, but it was just in smaller doses since the orbs were smaller than the beam. Also, once you made the orb, that was it. You didn't have to do anything else. With the beam though, it just kept draining you.

I looked at Oliver. He looked tired as well. He was gritting his teeth and sweat was beading his face. His chest heaved from breathing so hard.

"Do you feel it too?" I asked him.

Will and Edward, who had been in deep conversation, turned to look at us. Oliver turned to look at me too. Oliver cocked his head.

"Feel what?" he replied. He seemed confused.

"Do you feel like it's draining you, like it's draining something inside of you?" I elaborated.

He breathed what I think was a sigh of relief. "I'm glad I'm not the only one who noticed. Why is it happening?"

I was thankful that he was talking to me. It kept my mind somewhat free from the drowsiness. Don't get me wrong; I was also thankful that I had Edward and Will with me, but it felt good to know that someone truly understood what I was going through. Oliver felt the same things as me. I had a feeling he also understood how important our powers were; how much they had changed our lives.

"I think our powers are connected to our sparks. I think we draw energy from our sparks to make our powers work," I explained.

"What is a spark exactly?" he asked me.

I barely knew the answer myself. So, I turned to Will, seeking his explanation.

"Will, do you want to explain this part? I think you'll do a better job than I will," I asked him.

"Sure," he said with a shrug.

I still had questions of my own, so I decided that Will would be better at explaining it. Plus, it was getting kind of hard to make the beam and talk at the same time. I could see Oliver breathing hard too as Will spoke, and I knew he was as tired as I was.

I was glad I was sitting down. If I weren't, my legs probably would have buckled already. I had passed out my fair share of times in the past few days—Or had it been a week already? I kind of lost track of time. So much happened that the days mixed together in one giant blur—but I was determined to be stronger. I had three friends who had risked their lives for me. I needed to be strong for them. I needed to be strong for my parents as well. After all, they were counting on me too.

After Will finished explaining, silence overtook our boat. Everyone seemed lost in thought. I could see Will staring at the horizon. His hair, which used to be neatly swept back, was now a tangled mess—I didn't even want to know what my hair looked like. I hadn't brushed my hair since the morning before Will pulled me through that swirling gold portal—and his clothes were covered in dirt. Another wave of guilt swept over me. I had grown accustomed to it. I had so much guilt weighing on my shoulders but letting it overtake me would not make anything right. In fact, it would make it worse. I had learned my lesson, and I wasn't going to give into the guilt.

Instead of focusing on my guilt, I tried to imagine what must have been going through everyone's mind. Oliver had to be wondering about what he would find. He had no family and new powers. He had just left behind the only life he'd ever known. There was no clear path in front of him. His moral compass was probably going haywire.

I could never ask him to join me in finding my parents, but I couldn't help but hope he would come. I still had this feeling that we were connected. There was something about him that I just couldn't quite put my finger on. I wanted to get to know him better. Perhaps we would find somewhere for him to stay, somewhere he would be safe and happy.

Then my thoughts shifted to Edward. He hadn't even met me, and he still came with Will because he thought what had happened to me wasn't right. He left his entire life behind so he could do what was right. Even though I had no idea what his life was like before we met, I figured it had to be better than this: always in danger; the future never being certain; pining for answers that never come.

I would have given anything to make things go back to normal, to go back to the way things were, just my mom and me. Back when we were both happy, and we had each other. However, now where there was happiness in the memories of my old life, a pang of sadness and regret came with them. I was so sad that Mom was gone. My heart broke at the thought of what Kilmar could be doing to her.

I also regretted that I had let myself hate my father for so long. I wished I could be with him just once and tell him that I loved him. I wanted to thank him for keeping me safe all these years. I was sure that if my dad had been there, he wouldn't have let the Convocation hurt me.

"I don't know how much longer I can keep my beam going," Oliver said weakly.

"Just hold on. We can do this. We have to," I blustered.

"I-I can't," he said.

His eyelids drooped. I knew what was going to happen next, but I couldn't do anything about it. I could only stare in terror.

His beam flickered. Then it began to fade until it was completely diminished. Oliver collapsed along with his beam.

I looked at Will and Edward as we started to slow down. That was all it took for me to decide what to do. It was up to me to keep us out of the storm. I was determined to do whatever it took to keep them safe.

My entire body seemed to go into overdrive. A burst of energy thrummed through my body. It traveled from my toes all the way to the tips of my fingertips. Suddenly, my beam fired with twice as much power. It propelled us forward even faster than Oliver and I combined.

I tried not to think about what would happen if I used too much of my spark. But I couldn't help it. I remembered how I had felt when it was being drained, how helpless I had been.

What if I used too much? Would it kill me? I wondered.

No. I don't need to think about this. I chided myself.

I tried to expel these thoughts from my mind, but they still lingered no matter how hard I tried.

I had no idea where the sudden burst of energy had come from. Perhaps adrenaline? Whatever it was, it was fading fast. I could feel the beam getting weaker. Our pace continued to slow. The storm was closing in fast. I was ready to give in and let the exhaustion take me.

Then, Will shouted out the most beautiful words I had ever heard.

"Look," he said, "I can see land!"

These were beautiful, beautiful words. They filled me with the strength to keep going. They ignited the ember of hope inside me that had all but gone out. This strength kept me going until I saw the trees. I was so close. I didn't want to give up yet, but my strength was fading. I could only watch helplessly as my beam flickered. Then, it sputtered out completely. When the beam was gone, my legs collapsed. I could feel someone shaking me, begging me to wake up. I was not unconscious yet, but I couldn't move.

The desperation in the voice broke me. My vision was going dark, but I knew it was Will shaking me. I wanted to get up, for Will's sake. I wanted to be strong for him and Edward, but I had no strength left.

"I'm sorry," I said weakly. As my consciousness left me, I was left with one thought in my mind.

I was so close.

FOURTEEN

I have no idea how we survived. I can vaguely recall the storm overtaking us. Then there was a huge wave. After that, everything was foggy. It was a miracle we didn't drown. Our small boat had been reduced to splinters of wood that lay scattered along the beach.

I remember waking up on the beach. My hair and my clothes were wet. Despite the tropical heat and the sun beating down on us, I was chilled to the bone. Sand stuck to my wet skin. I rubbed my arms trying to get warm, but it felt like I was rubbing sandpaper across my skin.

I had awoken with a terrible fear consuming me. This was fear like I had never felt before. It was greater than the fear I had felt when Will and I fell through the sky. It was greater than the fear that I would die. It was the fear that I would be the reason someone died.

It was the kind of fear that buried itself deep down inside you, so that you would always remember it; always be able to feel it; and never forget it. It makes you want to do everything in your power to make sure you never feel it again.

The sun was high in the sky. It was nearly sunset when we were overtaken by the storm. That meant we must have been unconscious for the entire night. If I had to guess, it was probably late morning. So much time had passed. I have no idea exactly how much. I knew one thing for sure, Kilmar had been in possession of my parents for far too long.

I found everyone except Will unconscious. I was still trying to figure out how I felt about him. I couldn't stop thinking about our hug. I felt a little bit awkward about being alone with Will, but I was thankful for the company, nonetheless. I would rather be with him than alone. My thoughts were disturbing and frightening. I did not want to be left alone with those thoughts, for fear that I would spiral in them.

While we waited for the others to wake up, he asked me how I had retrieved the keys. I told him how I had found an ally in Oliver and how we had talked while he and Edward were asleep. I recounted our conversation; how we formed our plan; and how I discovered that Oliver had the same powers as me. I recounted how I had taught him how to make the orb.

"I can't believe he figured out how to make a sword out of light," I scoffed.

"Can you do that too?" Will asked giddily.

"I don't know how to. I didn't even know Oliver could do that. I'll have to get him to teach me when he wakes up," I replied.

I glanced over at Oliver and Edward. They must have hit the sand a lot harder than I did, because they were still out cold. I hoped they didn't have concussions.

Together, Will and I built a fire. Will gathered wood and I used my red light to start a flame. I had plenty of red light. The red light was fueled by my anger, and the imaginary bottle of anger I had hidden away in my heart—or I guess my spark—was overflowing. I still wasn't sure how I managed to tap into that hidden reserve of emotion. My body just naturally sent all of my extra, built-up emotions there.

I was still a little confused about how my powers worked though. They were just so complicated. Emotions make different colors of light. Different colors of light do different things. There were so many emotions and colors and powers. How could I keep track of them all?

While we waited for the others to wake up, we tried to dry off a bit by the fire. Occasionally, Will would toss a stick in the fire to keep it going. Every time, I marveled at the way the sparks burst up from the fire and filled my frozen fingertips with warmth.

I tried to make a mental list of my powers: Anger made red light, and the red light made fire. Happiness made yellow light, and the yellow light healed things.

Plus, different colored lights made different portals. I knew that a gold portal sent me to Enceaf, the Arbitrator dimension. Green portals sent me to Fortest, the human dimension. So, how had I gotten here, Aquaria? My memory of how I got here was hazy. I remembered how I had felt so sad and hopeless. I made a blue portal and landed on the beach. So, a blue portal sent me here, the sea dimension. Sadness created blue light. I wondered what powers blue light would make. Would it be the opposite of anger? I pondered this for a while.

Soon enough, everyone was awake. We were all sore and tired. Will and Oliver talked quietly by the fire. Edward was resting in a soft patch of beach grass he had discovered. They all looked at ease. A faint grin tugged at the edges of Oliver's mouth. Will leaned forward, relaxing by the fire while he and Oliver conversed. I didn't care what they were talking about and the fact that they were whispering didn't bother me. After all we'd been through, I couldn't imagine Edward or Will keeping secrets from me, or Oliver for that matter.

I stood leaning against a tree, surveying the area. Ever since I had gone through that portal with Will, we hadn't been safe. The last few days had been very frightening and perilous. I had a hard time believing that we were finally safe. I just couldn't let my guard down, not after everything that had happened.

Maybe I was just imagining things, but I got the feeling I was being watched. I got a chill down my spine that made the hair stand up on the back of my neck. I looked all around, my eyes frantically searching the beach, the edge of the jungle, the ocean surface. But I didn't see anything. Surely, I wasn't crazy.

Out of the corner of my eye, I saw a blur of movement from near the fire. I whipped my head towards it. Will and Oliver stopped mid-conversation. Both of them looked at me with worried expressions. Will stood and came over to me.

"What's wrong?" he asked.

"Something just doesn't feel right," I told him.

He looked around as well. He must not have seen anything either, because he shrugged.

"We've been through a lot, and I get why you are stressed out, but it's alright to let yourself relax a little," he coaxed.

I wanted to tell him he was wrong. That terrible feeling still lingered in my gut. My entire body was on guard, every nerve on edge. It had been this way for so long. I reveled in the idea of finally relaxing. My willpower crumbled and I gave in.

"Okay," I said.

I followed Will back to the fire and took a seat beside him. I watched the fire, letting its warmth roll over me. I took a deep breath.

Maybe Will is right. I could let my guard down, just for a little while. I thought.

For a moment, I was able to believe this. I leaned back on my elbows and extended my feet towards the fire.

Then the ground began to shake. It shook the trees. Birds erupted from the canopy, frightened by the sudden movement. I bolted to my feet. The boys all followed suit.

A chorus of hisses erupted from somewhere within the jungle. I had never heard a sound like that before. I felt my heart thumping in my chest as the hisses grew louder. I knew with absolute certainty that whatever was making them was getting closer.

"What do you think is in there?" Will asked.

I wheeled on him. After I had that terrible feeling, after I'd explicitly told him something wasn't right, he had the audacity to tell me everything was fine.

"I don't know, but I do know that I told you so!" I snapped back.

"Do you have to be so smug about it?" Will retorted.

"Yes! Yes, I do!" I yelled over the hissing.

Our conversation ended abruptly when something erupted from the jungle. It was a giant scorpion, easily the size of a car. Its black body gleamed in the sunlight. It clicked its pincers menacingly.

I couldn't look away from its eyes. They were black and hollow like a night sky without stars. There was no emotion in them. I knew that this creature wouldn't lose any sleep over killing us.

For a moment nobody moved. The scorpion stood there with its tail arched and pincers ready. I held my breath. None of us said a word. The only sound was the waves crashing on the beach and the thumping of my heart. We were locked in a standstill.

That standstill did not last very long.

The scorpion lunged for me. Instinctively, I rolled out of the way. It hissed in outrage as its stinger missed me. It then turned its attention to the others. Both Will and Edward managed to dodge the scorpion's attacks, but Oliver wasn't as lucky. He didn't get out of the way soon enough and the scorpion's stinger pierced his chest.

Oliver looked down at the stinger protruding from his chest. The scorpion let out a low hiss. I could have sworn it was laughing at him. It stayed there staring Oliver down for what felt like forever before it withdrew its stinger. Oliver collapsed with a groan.

The fear and anger clouded my mind, and my vision dimmed to a dark red haze. All the anger and fear I'd felt in the past few days burned inside that imaginary bottle within me. It begged me to let it out, and I did, not because I wanted to, but because I had to. I couldn't suppress my emotions anymore. They felt like fire burning inside me.

Suddenly, a beam of maroon light shot out of my hands and straight at the scorpion. The beam slammed into the scorpion, sending it tumbling backward. It struggled to get back on its feet. Its body hissed and steamed from the intense heat. It gave one final roar before it exploded with a sickening pop. Well, the shell exploded at least. Underneath, a dark shadowy outline of the scorpion remained.

The shadow scorpion looked at me. Its black eyes locked with mine. A whisper came from it.

I will win. The voice said. I knew it was Kilmar's voice. I had heard it before, in the Grai, and in all of my nightmares.

The shadow scorpion hissed one last time. Then it dissipated into black smoke. I watched in horror and outrage as the shadowy tendrils slithered away. I kept my gaze fixed on those awful shadows until they were gone completely.

I knew for certain that the shadow scorpion had been sent by Kilmar. He wanted me to be afraid; he wanted me to fear him. He had sent that thing as a reminder of how powerless I was in this whole mess. Kilmar was going to hurt everyone I cared about: Will, Edward, Oliver, my parents. The only way for me to keep any of them safe would be to push them all away.

My emotions became too overwhelming again. Red hatred and black fear swarmed around me. My emotions were no longer mine. I sank to my knees as they consumed me. I wanted to lose myself in them. I buried my face in my hands. Then, in the midst of all my chaos, I felt someone shaking my shoulders. At first, I could barely feel it. It was hard to feel anything but the red and black all around me. Then they shook me harder, hard enough to knock me back to reality.

I opened my eyes.

"Will?" I whispered, because that was all I knew to do. Something new mixed in with the anger and fear at the sight of Will.

"Celeste, snap out of it," he urged. His eyes searched mine.

"I can't," I whimpered.

I wanted to, I really did. I just didn't know how. I hugged myself, as a tear slipped down my cheek.

"Yes, you can," he assured me.

Something in his voice finally snapped me out of my daze.

I focused on the red and black that was swirling around me. The red light burned with hatred and the blackness stung me with its icy coldness. My hatred and fear would be the death of me if I didn't stop this madness. I knew I couldn't just get rid of it. That wasn't possible. These emotions were too strong, too raw.

Instead, I closed my eyes and imagined that tiny little bottle inside me. Dubiously, I tried stuffing it all in there, but it wouldn't fit. It was too much. I panicked as I realized this. If it wouldn't fit, I would just have to make the bottle bigger. I imagined stretching and pulling the bottle until it was large enough to hold the emotions. Then I shoved the hatred and fear into that bottle with every ounce of strength I could muster. Once I was sure every last trace of it had been put in the bottle, I imagined putting the cork back on it.

When I opened my eyes Will was still looking at me and his hands still rested on my shoulders.

"Are you okay?" he asked me.

I was anything but okay. I felt like my entire world was on fire and I was stuck in the middle of it as it collapsed around me. I was unable to escape or cry out for help.

"I'm fine," I lied.

He stood and offered me a hand. I took it gladly.

My cheeks burned with embarrassment at what I had done. I couldn't lose control of my emotions again. I was finished listening to my heart. From this point forward, I would be shoving all of my emotions into that imaginary bottle and burying it deep, deep down inside me. Then they couldn't cause any more problems.

I was about to open my mouth to thank Will for snapping me out of it when my focus wandered over to where Edward was bent over Oliver. I felt so stupid. Here I was making a fool of myself while Oliver was dying.

I ran over to him.

His skin was pale, and his lips were turning blue. His face was sweaty, and he was breathing raggedly. There was a big ugly gash from where the scorpion's stinger had punctured his chest. The wound was smoking and turning black. Looking at it made me want to hurl. If it had been any farther over, it would have hit his heart.

"Will, can you heal him?" I asked. My voice cracked and tears threatened to spill onto my cheeks.

Don't cry. I told myself. *Don't cry. Don't cry. Don't cry.*

Oliver was only in this mess because he stuck his neck out for me. How had I repaid him? I'd gotten him impaled by a giant shadow scorpion. I'd found a friend in Oliver. He was one of my first true friends. I couldn't lose him. I couldn't let him die because of me. I couldn't let Kilmar take anyone else away from me.

"I don't know. It's not a normal injury. Look at the way it's turning black. Powerful magic made that wound. It was a powerful poison. We need something powerful to heal it," Will explained. He shook his head in despair.

"What if we do it together?" I asked desperately.

"That might work, but it's a long shot and—"

"I don't care if it's a long shot! This is my fault. Please, Will. I can't let him die because of me," I said.

I looked into his eyes, pleading with him. He sighed.

"Okay, let's do this," he said.

He offered me his hand. I took it, even though I didn't really know how it could help. I was grateful nonetheless because it provided me with an anchor. It gave me a way to steady myself. I focused on happy thoughts until I saw myself glow bright yellow. I relished the warmth that flowed through me.

However, thoughts about Oliver threatened my yellow aura and made it flicker. Whenever I closed my eyes, I could still see Oliver collapsing, I could still hear the sickening thud as he hit the sand. I battled these memories for a while, fighting to keep my glow. Finally, I managed to steady it.

"Ready?" Will asked.

Not trusting my voice, I nodded. Will placed his hand on Oliver's chest, and I followed suit. Warmth flowed through my fingertips and into his chest.

I closed my eyes as our warmth collided with the wound. The poison from the stinger fought back with sharp jagged bits of shadow. It was cold and black. The shadows were too powerful. It latched onto our warmth, shredding away at it.

By the time Will and I pulled away, we were both sweaty and gasping for breath. Our efforts had seemingly no effect on Oliver. He was still sweaty and feverish. His wound was still smoking. The only difference was that he looked a little green, probably from the poison, which made him look even worse.

It didn't work. Those words echoed in my mind. The realization hit me like a knife.

"No!" I cried. "There has to be something we can do!"

I closed my eyes, ready to try again. Edward pulled my hands away, taking them in his.

"There has to be something!" I cried. "There has to!"

"Celeste, I'm sorry. There's nothing we can do," Edward gently told me. He ran his thumbs over the back of my hands before releasing them.

I sank to my knees beside Oliver. I desperately begged him to stay with me, to keep fighting. As I held his hand, I could feel his pulse growing weaker by the minute. His breathing was becoming more ragged.

I couldn't fight the tears anymore. I was tired and angry, and very sad. I sank to my knees beside Oliver. I desperately begged him to stay with me. To keep fighting. I held his hand. I could feel his pulse growing weaker by the minute and his breathing more ragged.

"I'm so sorry," I said. "This is all my fault."

Then with those words a fresh wave of tears came. These tears burned as they rolled down my cheeks. Guilt churned around in my heart, and it weighed me down.

I don't know how long I cried alone, but it felt like forever before I felt someone's hand on my shoulder. I turned to find Will with his arms extended. It took all the strength I had to stand but I stumbled into Will's arms. I sank into his warm embrace. I was so tired, and his arms were so steady. At that moment, it didn't matter whether or not I had feelings for him. All I cared about was that he was a shoulder I could cry on.

"It's not your fault," Will whispered in my ear.

I responded with a sob that came out as more of a hiccup. He had no idea how wrong he was. Oliver was going to die, and it was all my fault. I knew I was being selfish by crying, but I couldn't help it. It was the only way to keep from letting my emotions consume me again.

I thought I had hit rock bottom, and there was no way on earth that things could get any worse. Well, the universe grabbed a shovel and started digging deeper. Little did I know, things were about to get a whole lot worse.

FIFTEEN

"Does anyone else hear laughter?" Will said abruptly.

I pulled away from him. Neither of us were laughing. I was literally standing there crying on his shoulder.

I was about to open my mouth to call him crazy when Edward—who I'd completely forgotten was there—said, "You're right. I can hear it too."

"It's coming from over there," Will remarked.

He pointed to the right where there was a grove of palm trees. I stared at the trees for a minute or two. It was hard to hear anything over my own thumping heart. Then I heard it. Laughter. Loud, obnoxious laughter coming from within the jungle canopy.

Suddenly, they emerged. They were lousy, smelly pirates! Why? Why did it have to be pirates? I would have given anything for it to be a unicorn or a mermaid. Heck, I'd even take a dragon. This world had pirates, sea monsters, shadow monsters, and people with magical powers. Couldn't I just have something cute and fluffy? No, the answer was no.

The universe must have it out for me big time, I thought to myself.

Then I remembered that Oliver was lying on the sand dying behind me. I realized my life could be a lot worse.

The pirates were carrying a large chest. It was gold, with a golden eye on it. It glowed faintly. I figured they must have found the treasure they were searching for. If that was true, then we had washed up on the very island they had been going to. We must have somehow passed them without me realizing it. Great. Just great.

The pirates seemed very preoccupied with their laughing and their treasure. I didn't think they'd notice us. Unfortunately, I thought wrong. Captain Grimes turned his head in our direction. When he saw me, his eyes narrowed.

"Well look what we have here. The lads survived!" he said. He looked at our group and frowned. "But I seem to recall there bein' four of you."

There was a hint of something else in his voice: worry. Mostly though, he seemed to be trying to get to me. He quickly regained his cocky smirk.

That did it. Oliver was dying. We were stuck on an island in the middle of the freaking ocean, and now of all the things that could possibly happen, we ran into these guys, again. Are you kidding me?

"The only thing that kept me from kicking your lousy butts last time was that you had my friends. Now we're free and there's nothing stopping me. So, you can either keep bothering us and get the snot beat out of you, or you can leave us alone!" I snapped at them, my voice dripping with venomous hatred.

I hated these pirates with every fiber of my being. Even

looking at them made my blood boil.

The captain was the only one who wasn't taken aback by my outburst. Even Will, who had moved to my side, now had his mouth hanging open. Not that I cared at the moment. All I cared about was getting these stupid pirates away from Oliver.

"Alright, missy. We'll leave you be. Just answer me one question," he said.

"Fine," I growled.

Whatever gets them far away from here. I thought to myself.

"Where's Oliver?" he asked.

His voice was serious, and his features were scrunched with worry. Was this some kind of a joke, or was he seriously worried about Oliver? I didn't think he deserved to be worried about Oliver after what they did.

I almost decided not to show them. I could have denied that he was there and sent them on their way. However, part of me wanted to believe that they still cared about Oliver. Maybe they could find a way to help him. I decided it was worth it to let them see him. At that moment, I hated those stupid pirates more than I had hated anything or anyone in my entire life. I despised the very ground they walked on. Part of me wanted to make them hurt, because I was hurting and Oliver was hurting, and they were only making it worse. But I cared too much about Oliver to pass up a chance to help him.

Tears pooled in my eyes as I pointed at Oliver. He was wheezing and coughing now, his breathing shallow. Oliver groaned and I felt my heart break into a million pieces.

The captain hurried over to Oliver. The other pirates solemnly removed their hats.

"Poor lad. He was so brave," said one of them.

"He was the kindest pirate I've ever met," said another.

On and on they went, talking about how good he was to them. I didn't really know whether to be touched that the pirates actually cared about him, or to smack each one of them, and remind them that if they really cared this much about him, they wouldn't have sent him adrift.

Will knelt beside Oliver, along with Edward and the captain. I couldn't bring myself to let my guard down with all these pirates around. I was willing to cooperate with them, not trust them.

"How did this happen?" asked the captain.

"Kilmar sent a scorpion to attack me and my friends. When it lunged for Oliver, he couldn't get out of the way in time and—" my voice cut off.

I didn't have it in me to finish that sentence. I hung my head as a fresh wave of guilt washed over me. I wrapped my arms around myself, choking back the sobs that tried to escape my throat. I knew I needed to be brave and have hope. The problem was: my hope was almost gone. How could I be brave without any hope? After all, hope is what gives someone the power to be brave. It gives them the strength to keep moving forward despite wanting to give up.

I needed that strength now, and I was clinging to my own fading hope. I felt as if it were a small, delicate, string that was holding my entire life together, and at any moment, it might snap. Then my world would come crashing down, the walls would cave in, and I would lose what little I had left.

"Kilmar? You mean the king of the shadow realm?" The captain asked, not quite masking the fear in his voice.

"Yes. He has my parents. I don't know why he took them, maybe he wants something from me," I said.

"What would the King of Darkness want with you?" The

captain asked dubiously.

"I'm a halfling. And so is Oliver. That's why he helped us on the ship. He knew I was like him," I replied.

He didn't seem at all shocked by this new information.

"I have something to tell you, but it can wait for a later time. I know a way to save Oliver. There's a giant oak tree in Sproot, the forest dimension, that can heal any person who touches it," he said.

A way to save Oliver. My heart clung to those words. I let them lift me up and away from the dark place that guilt had brought me to.

Part of me was curious as to what he wanted to tell me. The rest of me screamed with joy. I immediately felt determined to save Oliver.

"How do we get to Sproot?" I asked.

He scratched his chin as he thought about it.

"How did you get here?" he asked.

That was a very good question, one I struggled to find the answer to. While I sat there, silently fumbling for the answer, the captain turned to the group of pirates.

"Take the treasure back to the ship. I will accompany them to Sproot," he ordered.

It took two men to lift the bulky chest. Its contents rattled as they heaved it up onto their shoulders. They stumbled back into the jungle canopy.

Grimes turned back to me then. He fixed me with his gaze and asked again, "How did you get here?"

I thought about that a little bit longer. It had taken blue light to make a blue portal, and I had been really sad, so I made the blue light.

"I made a blue portal," I replied.

"You need a green portal to get to Sproot," he said.

What emotion would make green light? I knew happiness and sadness didn't make green light. So, what would?

I was racking my brain trying to figure it out. Then a light bulb went off in my mind. I remembered something my mom said when I was little. I was in preschool and one of the other kids had this really cool new toy that had just hit the market. I knew I could never get that toy. Mom simply couldn't afford it. I wanted it anyway, because it was cool, and it belonged to someone else. I cried to mom when she picked me up that day.

I want one of those! I fumed.

I crossed my arms and huffed stubbornly.

Mom just laughed. She had this laugh that instantly made you feel lighter inside.

She chided, *I spy the green-eyed monster.*

The green-eyed monster. It was a silly thought, but what if jealousy made green? It couldn't hurt to try.

"I have an idea!" I exclaimed.

"Just do what you have to do. I don't know how much longer Oliver has," Will said.

I followed his gaze toward Oliver.

"Will's right. He doesn't have long," Edward added.

I closed my eyes as I thought back to how I'd felt that day at preschool, how I resented that kid for having something I wanted, something that I thought I should have. I focused on that feeling. I fed it like a flame, adding more of that jealous feeling until it was like a massive inferno in my heart. Then I set it free, shaping it into a portal.

When I opened my eyes there was a green portal in front of us.

"Come on. Help me carry him through the portal," Edward barked.

The portal was every shade of green you could possibly imagine. All of the different shades of green swirled together in a dazzling display of light. I didn't have time to enjoy its breathtaking beauty. It was taking all my concentration to hold it open, long enough for them to carry Oliver through. I watched as Edward and Will carried a limp Oliver through the portal. Seeing him like that filled me with so much guilt and sadness that it almost broke my concentration. I had to fight to hold onto my jealousy. It's really hard to stay jealous when you are sad.

Once the captain was through, I began to take careful steps toward the portal. I knew I had to hold my concentration while going through the portal.

No matter how hard I tried to fight the guilt, I knew deep down that everything was my fault. An image of Oliver's limp body being carried through the portal filled my mind, and my concentration broke. The portal started to close.

No! I thought.

I sprinted towards the portal and threw myself into it. Then the portal closed behind me.

I ended up in an endless gray space that seemed oddly familiar. I couldn't quite put my finger on it; I was sure Grimes had said Sproot was the forest dimension. This wasn't a forest. It was simply nothingness. If I wasn't in Sproot, then where was I?

Then it hit me: I was in the Grai again. Like last time the endless gray turned black. Smoky tendrils appeared in the space around me. Cruel, cold laughter echoed all around me. I saw a familiar shadowy figure; the same one I saw in every single nightmare: Kilmar.

SIXTEEN

"You," I snarled.

"Hello Celeste Rowan," he sneered.

This time Kilmar was more solid. His form was no longer smudgy, and it didn't swirl and fade like the last time. His red eyes were cold and calculated. His grin wasn't just cold; it was the kind of grin a murderer would wear on his face. It was pure evil.

I knew I should have been trying to portal out of there, should have been trying my hardest to get back to Oliver and the others. That would have been the logical, responsible thing to do, but since when was I logical or responsible? I had a lot of unanswered questions. Questions that only he had the answers to. I was determined to get those answers.

"What do you want?" I growled.

"There are many things I want. The list is endless, but before you go asking me more questions, keep in mind that I will only answer one. So, choose your question wisely," he said.

He was toying with me. That much was obvious. I clenched my fists as anger washed over me.

I pinched the bridge of my nose and cursed under my breath.

"One question? I mean, are you kidding me?" I fumed.

I had so many questions bouncing around in my head. How was I supposed to choose? I thought long and hard. I knew he had my parents. I knew he needed me for something. I knew that going to save my parents would mean walking into a trap—which I was mostly okay with as long as I saved them. The only reason I had to save them was because Kilmar wanted me, but what did he want me for? What did I, of all people, have that he wanted?

"I am quite serious," he snarked.

I wanted to scream at him and call him all the names under the sun. However, that wouldn't get me anywhere. I sighed, tried to calm myself, and gathered my thoughts.

"What do you want with me?" I asked.

"Ahh, that is a question I can answer. I want your power. My own has grown weak. My form is not solid, as you can see. Your kind are the ones who trapped me in my realm and stole my powers so long ago. Only by taking the power of a halfling can I fully regain mine. My powers have slowly started to return, though they are still weak. I was able to disrupt your portaling and bring you here. As I did the first time we crossed paths. You can give me the one thing I crave more than anything else: power," he explained.

He almost seemed sad. In his red eyes I saw a tiny glint of pain and sorrow, you know, if I looked past his dark, evil, and psychotic nature.

I shivered as I thought about how I had felt to have my spark drained. It had taken me a full day to recover from a few seconds of it. If he'd had his spark completely drained….the thought made a chill run down my spine. How had he even survived it? I didn't know much about sparks, but I knew enough to know that if I lost it all, I most likely wouldn't survive. Had what he did been so bad that he would be made to spend an eternity in that suffering?

If it had just been the Arbitrators that took away his powers, then I might question the justice of it. After all, they had tried to do the same to me. I hadn't even done anything to deserve it; I had simply existed. However, it wasn't the Arbitrators who drained his powers, it was the halflings. And I believed in my heart they would never do anything that painful to someone unless they had a good reason. I had to believe that, because I was one of them.

"You could help me. You could willingly give up your powers to me. I'd let your parents go free and we could go our separate ways. Then no one gets hurt," he coaxed.

If I gave him my powers, it might save my parents for a little while, but then Kilmar could practically do whatever he wanted with them. He could hurt a lot of people.

"You promise you wouldn't hurt anyone?" I asked warily.

"Promises are such fickle things. They don't mean anything really. I trusted those halflings and believed their promises. In the end, they were just empty words without meaning," he said sincerely. "They betrayed me and drained me of my powers."

What was that supposed to mean? The halflings had betrayed him. No, it couldn't be. They were the good guys in this equation. Weren't they?

He's manipulating me. I thought. *He's trying to make me feel sorry for him, so that I'll do what he wants.*

I decided that I needed to go before it actually worked. I'd asked my one question. Anything else he said would either be a trick or an outright lie.

I set to work making my portal. I thought back to the jealous feeling I'd found earlier. This time I imagined it wrapping around my brain and my heart, that way nothing could break my concentration again. I waited until I was completely consumed by jealousy. Then I looked down at my body as it began to glow green.

I imagined the light forming into a green portal. I felt a tug in my gut and the portal swirled into existence in front of me. Just to be safe, I waited until I was sure the portal was solid. Then I kicked my legs trying to move through the portal. It sort of worked. I felt like an astronaut in space. I moved slowly in the direction of the portal. The whole time, Kilmar watched me with an evil grin.

Finally, I drifted completely into the portal.

On the other side, I tumbled onto soft grass. I grunted as gravity made a reappearance. I didn't even have to try to suppress my jealousy or cram it into that imaginary jar. It simply evaporated like water in a hot summer. I was too afraid and confused to feel much of anything else.

SEVENTEEN

I closed my eyes as I lay there on the soft green grass. I was trying to calm my nerves. My mind spun with so many questions, and far too many possibilities for my future. Every aspect of my life felt intangible like a stream of water. I tried grabbing it, but alas, you cannot grasp water.

My heart thumped wildly in my chest. I found peace in the steady rhythm.

Tha-thump, tha-thump, tha-thump.

Tha-thump, tha-thump, tha-thump.

When my nerves finally settled, and felt like I could actually breathe again, I stood up. I needed to figure out what to do and where to go.

I surveyed my surroundings. I landed in a breathtaking forest. The trees were every color imaginable. Some were purple with pink bark. Others were completely blue or green. There was one that was a vibrant combination of red, orange, and yellow, and it looked like the leaves were on fire.

As the wind rustled through them, the leaves shifted, giving the illusion of flames dancing.

Turning in a circle, I took in the scene. I looked for any sign of the giant oak the captain had described, but there was no sign of it—or anyone for that matter. I was completely and utterly alone. I sat down with my legs crossed and rested my chin on my fist. I needed to figure out what to do. On one hand, if I stayed put, I wouldn't get lost. On the other hand, there was a chance no one would ever come looking for me. After all, I left my friends and the captain in a state of crisis.

Maybe they will just forget about me all together, I thought bitterly. *I deserve it for getting Oliver hurt.*

I huffed in frustration. It was my fault Oliver got hurt in the first place. For all I knew he could be dead, and I wasn't even there for him. I could have made another portal as soon as I'd seen Kilmar, but no, I just had to be selfish and stay. I felt terrible, and I blamed myself.

I thought I had learned my lesson about guilt on the ship. Clearly, I hadn't, because here I was feeling guilty all over again. Perhaps if I stopped screwing up so much and being such a burden to everyone around me, I would not have a reason to feel so guilty all the time.

Suddenly, I saw movement out of the corner of my eye. I whipped my head around, fearing more danger. What I saw wasn't dangerous at all. I was amazed to find a tiny girl about the size of my palm. She had glittering pink wings. She fluttered them, effortlessly floating through the air. Her red hair bounced as she flew around me, looking me up and down.

"What are you?" I gasped.

Her tiny mouth moved as if she was speaking, but all I heard were jingles. She reminded me of Tinkerbell. She was so magical, much like everything in the forest. I had the sudden urge to reach out and touch her. I felt as if by proving she was tangible and real, I could prove that I wasn't losing it.

"I can't understand you," I whispered.

I still half-believed that I was imagining her.

She flailed her little arms around, jingling aggressively at me. However, I still failed to understand her. The tiny girl seemed to realize this. She stopped flailing and gave a defeated jingle. She kicked the air with her heel as if she were still on the ground. I figured she was probably just as frustrated as me that I couldn't understand her. In her eyes, I was probably some dumb giant that had stumbled into her land. I certainly felt dumb, standing there playing charades with a tiny, winged girl. She jingled frustratedly a little bit longer. Then her eyes lit up, like she'd gotten an idea. She flew to me, then to our right, then back to me. She did it a couple more times before I finally got the message.

"You want me to follow you?"

She jingled more and circled around me doing small loopty-loops.

"I'll take that as a yes," I chuckled.

She fluttered around me. Then she began to fly toward the woods. I hurried after her. It may seem crazy that I would put my faith and trust into a creature that I couldn't even understand, but I knew, somehow, I just knew that this tiny creature would take me where I needed to go.

She didn't fly too fast. I had plenty of time to take in the forest as I plodded along after her. We wound our way around more vibrant colored trees. When I say these trees were colorful, what I really mean is it looked like a rainbow barfed all over them. It wasn't just the trees that were colorful, the fauna was as well.

Once, I saw a family of purple squirrels that were collecting blue nuts from a dark blue tree. I saw other strange colored animals too. I saw a bear that was green, an owl that was yellow, and a bright red rabbit. However, not everything was bright and colorful.

There were some trees that contrasted greatly from the vibrant ones. Some of them were ominous black. Their leaves were in crumpled heaps on the ground, and their trunks were shriveled and flakey. They seemed so fragile, as if they would crumble to dust at the slightest breeze. It almost looked like they had been burned, yet the air around them didn't smell of smoke. Nor did I see any evidence of a forest fire. Something else had happened to these trees. I had a sinking feeling that this was Kilmar's doing. He was destroying this beautiful forest with his shadows, taking something bright, and colorful and replacing it with something dark and evil. I wanted to stop and explore more.

However, as I turned my attention back to the tiny girl, I found that she was far ahead of me. Too far. If I didn't hurry, I would lose her tiny form in the maze of trees that surrounded me. I immediately raced after her. I leapt over logs and stumbled over roots as I ran at a full sprint. She seemed to be going as fast as her wings could carry her. Somehow, she always stayed far ahead of me. I knew that if I stopped, I would fall so far behind that I wouldn't be able to see her anymore. So, I didn't stop. I just kept running, pumping my legs as hard as I could.

Soon, we came to a golden river that was easily a hundred feet wide. The water sparkled in the rays of sunlight that leaked between the leaves of the trees above me. I didn't have time to admire its beauty though, because the tiny girl was already halfway across. it. She crossed with ease, floating over the water. I didn't have the luxury of wings. Us normal-sized people have to walk—or rather jump—if we want to cross rivers.

My only path to the other side was a series of slippery rocks and unsteady logs. If I hesitated for too long, the tiny girl would leave me in the dust. I didn't hesitate, nor did I think. I just moved.

As I hopped onto a small log it rolled sideways. I struggled to find my balance on the slippery log, and I fell into the water. I struggled against the current's pull, kicking my legs until I was able to climb back on. I sighed with relief, clinging to the log, then continued crossing. The rocks were slippery with moss and algae, and every so often I would lose my footing and slip. I always managed to catch myself before I fell in though. The current was strong, and I was afraid that if I fell in again, I wouldn't be able to get back out.

My legs and arms ached from the effort of staying on top of the logs and rocks. Finally, when I was sure my legs would give out, I made it to the other side of the river, just in time to watch the tiny girl disappear into a grove of green willow trees. These seemed to be the only trees that weren't a crazy color. They were just normal. It almost felt wrong to see them here in the midst of this forest that could have been from a fairytale.

The grove was so thick with branches that I couldn't see through it. There was no way I would be able to find that tiny girl in that dense grove. I knew I had to catch back up with her.

"Wait!" I cried as I began to push my way through the grove.

I shoved the branches out of my way, blindly stumbling along. I kept tripping over what were probably tree roots. I didn't know for sure. I couldn't see anything. All I could see were leaves. Normal green leaves. The only ones I had seen so far.

I found myself wondering if something was hiding deep within the grove. Something someone didn't want to be found. Something like the giant oak I was searching for. It was a profound thought, but one I clung to.

I continued stumbling along for what felt like eternity.

Then suddenly I tripped on something big and fell face first. I tried to get back up, but I couldn't. I had nothing to grab hold of. Where my hands should have been able to find a tree root or trunk, it grasped only air.

I felt wind whipping against my face and realized I was moving. Or rather, sliding. For a moment everything was pitch black. I felt like I was free falling. My stomach twisted into knots. I screamed as I started to panic. Then my descent slowed, and I felt my body go horizontal again.

The pitch black gave way to a large open meadow surrounded by the willow tree grove on all sides, with a single gigantic oak tree in the center. It was the biggest tree I'd ever seen. It was almost as big as a skyscraper. I would have sobbed with relief, had there not been a pressing matter still at hand.

I realized I was on a wooden slide. It wound around the giant oak tree. I looked up ahead and was horrified to see that the slide was about to end. This wasn't the kind of ending where you came to a gentle stop at the end of the slide and hopped down like a little kid. No. This was the kind of slide that lived in my nightmares. I was still extremely high above the ground. Also, I had no way to stop myself. I tried running my hands along the walls to stop, but the sides were too smooth, and I had too much momentum.

As I got closer, I saw the same golden river I had crossed earlier. It flowed from one side of the meadow, under the slide, and out to the other side of the meadow. At least I wouldn't be falling onto solid ground. Still, a fall from this height would be like hitting concrete.

I screamed as the slide dropped off and I fell headfirst towards the water. Time seemed to slow down as I fell—Isn't it funny how the moments you wish would end are the ones that last the longest?—Each second felt like a century. I closed my eyes and braced myself for the brutal impact.

Oh man! I groaned internally. *This is going to hurt!*

However, the impact never came. Just before I hit the water, something wrapped around my waist and caught me. I grunted as my descent stopped abruptly. I craned my neck around, struggling to see who—or rather what—my savior was. I was shocked to find a large tree limb wrapped around me. The giant oak had stretched out one of its limbs and caught me.

"Th-thanks," I stammered as it gently lowered me to the ground.

I stared up at it, half expecting it to reply. It didn't, because it's a tree and trees can't talk. At least, I thought they couldn't. I was kind of new to this dimension. For all I knew the trees could talk, the sky could be pink, and the squirrels could juggle. (These are all hypothetical examples of course. But hey, it could happen.)

I stared in awe at the oak tree. It was one of the tallest things I had ever seen. It was easily as tall as the gates in Enceaf. Its leaves were an oddly normal shade of green, and its bark was deep brown with majestic lines inlaid in it. and so were its trunk and limbs. Yet somehow, it seemed just as magical as the rest of this forest.

It better be magic, I thought to myself. *Oliver's life depends on it.*

I hadn't known Oliver for long, yet I felt as though I had known him my entire life. I felt as if we were old friends. Which was crazy, since I didn't even know his middle name, or his favorite color, or any of those things friends are supposed to know. I didn't know any of that stuff about Will or Edward either. I didn't have to. We shared a bond that connected us more than those things ever could. It's crazy what chaos and crises can do to people. In a lot of cases, it can tear people apart. Instead, this brought all of us strangers together. Will and Edward weren't strangers to each other of course, but they were strangers to me. Strangers that were the best friends I had ever had. Granted I hadn't had any real friends before, so that was setting the standards pretty low.

As I studied the tree, I realized for the first time that there were huts in the top of the tree. It looked like a village of some sort. As the wind rustled through the leaves, the branches swayed ever so slightly. It was absolutely beautiful. And breathtaking. And so…different.

I felt like nothing was familiar anymore. Everywhere I turned there was something new, something unknown. What I wouldn't give to go back to Boringsville, USA. Despite all the years of torment, I missed my old school. I missed Johnny and his familiar ugly face. I missed those old familiar forests that were my shelter all throughout my life.

As much as I ached to have my old life back, a question still lingered in the back of my mind. What if I didn't want to go back to the way things were before?

Did I really want to go back to pining for answers about my dad? All the ridicule of him leaving us? What about my new friends? Edward had been brave enough to come help me, when he didn't even know me. Oliver helped me escape the pirates by betraying the only family he had ever known. And then there is Will. My life hadn't been the same since I met him. He had been the beginning of my new life, of this new journey. No matter how hard I tried, I couldn't picture myself living without him. Even when I pictured myself with my parents, with my new family, Will was always there beside me.

Suddenly, my thoughts were interrupted. I heard familiar mocking jingles and turned to find the tiny, winged girl floating behind me. I glared at her.

"You little twerp! You knew that would happen, didn't you?" I growled, wagging my finger in her tiny, mischievous face.

All I got in reply were more jingles. I could have sworn I heard her snicker. I rolled my eyes, huffing in frustration. This earned me more jingles that were probably her making fun of me.

"What now?" I asked, ready to move on.

She jingled loudly. I gasped as more tiny, winged people joined her, both boys and girls. Their wings were all different colors; although I noticed that the boys' wings were darker than the girls.

The creatures fluttered around until they rearranged themselves into a pattern. I recognized it as a letter.

"P," I read aloud.

This earned me some satisfied jingles from the tiny, winged people.

In case you're sitting there, wondering if I'm completely off my rocker for going along with all this, don't worry, I probably am. I realize it's crazy, but then again so was everything else in my life. I didn't think there was much left in the world that could surprise me. At least that's what I thought.

They fluttered around forming letter after letter until they had made a word.

"I-X-I-E," I finished reading.

"P-I-X-I-E," I said again. "You're Pixies?"

They twirled around me jingling. It sounded like jingle bells being played by a bunch of kindergarteners. The sound was definitely cringe worthy, but I couldn't help smiling at them. They were just so adorably cute, in their own frustrating, mischievous kind of way.

"Okay Pixies! Where to now?"

They flew around and lined up to create a path. So far, they haven't steered me wrong. While that slide had certainly felt wrong, it led me to where I needed to be. I decided that it was useless to stop trusting them now.

I started to follow the trail of pixies. Every time I passed a pixie it would flutter off to who knows where. The trail wound all the way around the tree and into a small gap in the trunk that I would have missed if there wasn't a jingling pixie in front of it.

I hesitated outside of the opening. A voice of reason echoed in the back of my mind, reminding me of the doubts that I was supposed to be having.

What if this is the wrong way? It said. *What if this doesn't lead to the boys?*

However, there was also another voice. A louder one. This one told me I was right, and it urged me to keep going. I decided to trust the second one, the one that gave me hope. When my world felt like it was falling to pieces around me, hope was the only steady thing I could cling to.

The inside of the tree would have been dark, but the pixies' wings illuminated the space, casting a warm, colorful glow over the passage. A winding staircase was carved into the tree that led all the way to the top. I sighed, thinking of the long climb I had ahead of me.

Then I began my ascent. There were so many stairs! I was sweaty and breathing heavily by the time I made it to the top. My legs felt like lead, and I was a bit dizzy. I guess it was from over exertion. I looked down into the darkness. Whoever lived here really needed to consider getting an elevator.

I turned around to look at the village. The huts were constructed of wood with leaves as the roofs. Some of the huts hung from branches while others sat on top of them. All of the huts were connected by a series of rope bridges and wooden platforms.

In the center of the village was the largest branch. It grew straight up and giant leaves sprouted out of it. A cot sat at the foot of it on a raised platform. Beautiful women with golden wings and dressed in emerald gowns were tending to a very pale blonde-haired boy: Oliver.

My breath caught at the sight of him. He still looked the same as before: sweaty, pale, and in a truckload of pain, but as I watched the winged women shuffling around him, I realized everything was going to be okay. I don't know how, I just knew.

Every part of me wanted to go to him, to apologize for this mess, but the pixies weren't leading me that way. The pixie path led to a hut on the far side of the tree that was larger than the rest.

I sighed, knowing I needed to trust the pixies. I walked toward the hut. Other than the winged women tending to Oliver, I saw no one else in the village. It was quiet, but not in a creepy, foreboding way. It felt peaceful.

Since there wasn't a single person in sight, I was alone with my thoughts. As I walked, I had plenty of time to imagine all kinds of terrible things waiting for me inside the hut. The downside of having a vivid imagination is that you can picture all kinds of terrifying things. Then you get stuck worrying about all the things that could happen, and you get too sidetracked with those things to worry about any of the cool, amazing things that are going on around you.

That is precisely what I did. Instead of focusing on the beauty of this magical forest and this enchanting tree hut village, I was stuck troubleshooting about what awaited me inside that hut.

I crossed the last rope bridge and came to a stop at the door. I raised my fist to knock, but I couldn't make myself do it.

"You can do this Celeste. Just knock," I told myself. Then I scowled at myself for being such a baby about this.

"Great, now I'm talking to myself."

I took a deep breath, raised my fist, and rapped hard on the door. The seconds of silence that followed were agonizing. I felt like every single one took another year off my life.

Suddenly the silence ended and someone opened the door. That someone had beautiful blue eyes and perfect brown hair, that was slightly messy. The sight of him replaced my anxiety with something different, but just as terrifying, something that made my stomach twist into knots from the butterflies that had just taken flight inside of me.

EIGHTEEN

"**W**ill?"

He gaped at me, hand still clutching the side of the door. His loss for words made me uncomfortable. I fumbled to find the right words to replace the silence and explain my absence.

"I'm so sorry it took me so long to get here, I lost my concentration and the portal closed. So, I had to open a new one, but then that one took me to the wrong place. Then these pixies took me on this super long path and there was a giant slide, and the tree saved me and now here I am," I said.

I realized I was rambling, but I didn't care. I just wanted to explain myself before he had time to start asking questions and I started having to lie to him about what happened with Kilmar.

I hung my head as I spoke, squeezing my eyes closed to protect myself from whatever look of disdain I knew would be plastered on his face. I couldn't bring myself to look him in the eyes while I straight up lied to his face.

I held my breath, waiting for the inevitable questions and the dubious looks he would give me.

Then he did something completely unexpected.

He wrapped his arms around me and hugged me. He clung to me like I was his lifeline. For a moment I was too stunned to move. I was afraid that this moment was like glass, so fragile that if I moved it might crack and crumble. I tensed up, not daring to move. This was the second time we had hugged. Last time, I initiated it. This time, he hugged me first. It didn't seem real.

I finally came to my senses and hugged him back. My hands came to rest on the small of his back. He rested his chin on top of my head, gently smoothing my tangled hair with one hand. The warmth of him against me sent butterflies through me. I'd never had a boy treat me like that. I didn't quite know how to feel.

I buried my head in the crook of his neck and smiled. He still smelled like Aquaria, the sea dimension. He smelled of salt, and the ocean, and a little bit like a sweaty boy, but I was willing to overlook that for the fact that Will was hugging me!

His arms were strong and steady. They were safe.

"I was so worried something had happened to you," he whispered in my ear. His voice was tight with emotion.

He squeezed me tighter, so tightly I couldn't breathe. It was so worth it to hug him though. Even if I could breathe, I still would have been holding my breath, praying with every fiber of my being that this moment would never end.

Then of course, with my luck, it ended.

"Ahem," someone cleared their throat loudly.

Will backed away from the door and ushered me inside.

I was shocked to see at least fifty winged men—normal

sized ones— huddled together in the hut. Grimes and Edward were also there. They were gathered around a large map that lay spread out across a big round table in the center of the room.

All of them looked at us with their eyebrows raised. I moved away from Will and pulled my hair around my face to hide my blushing cheeks. I felt the familiar weight of awkwardness settle over the room.

My nerves were already on edge, not just from the awkwardness, but from the tense atmosphere of the room.

The way they had all been gathered around the table, speaking in hushed voices, pointing to certain places on the large map that was sprawled across the table in the center of the room reminded me of a war counsel. I wondered if that was what it was. If I had seen the map I would have been able to tell, but I couldn't see it very well. Some of the men had strategically moved so that it was obscured from my view.

They didn't trust me, and honestly, I couldn't blame them. I was a halfling after all. In every world, Aquaria, Enceaf, and even my world, halflings meant trouble. I didn't like it, nor did I understand it. That's just how it was.

"Is this her? The girl from the prophecy?" asked one of the winged men.

I automatically singled him out as the oldest. He had gray hair and a short grey beard. He had dazzling sage green eyes. His tunic seemed to be made of leaves, the design swirled and dipped up and down around his feet. In his hands, he held a staff made of wood with a simple green crystal jutting out from the top. His head was adorned with a matching wooden crown, set with emeralds.

"Yes, Your Majesty," Will replied with a nod. "Celeste, meet Alaric, King of the Fairies."

King of the Fairies. I was standing beside a king.

All the winged people are fairies. I concluded.

I wondered if the pixies were their helpers. I hoped not. Those pixies, while they did lead me to the right place, were mischievous and troublesome. I would definitely be keeping my distance from the pixies.

Despite the pixies, everything about this place felt magical to me. I wished I could stay forever, but I didn't plan on staying long. I couldn't. My parents still needed to be rescued. I would learn as much as I could about my own powers and about Kilmar's dimension. Then I would leave when everyone was asleep. That was the plan.

Even though I was keeping everyone safe by going alone, it left my heart in shattered pieces. I didn't want to go alone. I was so scared to go through with this by myself, but I couldn't risk anyone else getting hurt. Me getting hurt, I could handle. But someone else getting hurt or even worse…I just couldn't live with that.

King Alaric fluttered over to me. I fought the urge to recoil as he landed gracefully in front of me. It wasn't that I was afraid of him. Everything about him was gentle. From the smile lines on his face to the way his eyes dipped at the corners. How could anyone be afraid of someone like King Alaric? Short answer: they couldn't.

There was something else bothering me. I was all too aware of the swords sheathed at the waists of all of the fairy men. Those long, sharp blades seemed cold and cruel, like ice. They felt so out of place here. The fairy men's hands twitched by their sides, as if they were just waiting for a chance to unsheathe their weapons. I feared if I even breathed the wrong way, they would hurt me.

He cupped my hands in his. His hands were rough and wrinkly like tree bark, yet his touch was softer than clouds. My hands shook in his. He studied me with intelligent green eyes that seemed to bore into my soul. I fought the urge to shrink under his gaze. Every instinct I had screamed for me to bolt away from that awful hut. Then King Alaric opened his mouth to speak.

The entire hut—that had been abuzz with murmurs and whispers—fell eerily silent.

"Do not be afraid. You are safe here," he assured me.

I released the breath I hadn't realized I was holding.

How had he known exactly what to say to make me feel better? I was astonished by this kind, old king.

"Thank you," I faltered, searching for the right way to address him, "Your majesty."

My voice caught at the foreign words. I hoped I had addressed him properly. I did not want to anger or offend the fairies. Fairies may sound all cute and sparkly in my world; however, in reality they were fierce and intimidating. At least the men were, except for King Alaric, who I was positive wouldn't hurt a fly. The women I had seen seemed kind, gentle, and graceful. They reminded me of my mother.

King Alaric turned to Will.

"Yes, I see now. She is powerful, but is she powerful enough to stop him?" King Alaric asked Will.

Stop him? Did he mean to stop Kilmar? That wasn't at all part of my plan. I didn't want to defeat Kilmar. I just wanted to save my parents.

"She is more powerful than she realizes," Grimes said before Will could respond.

For one small moment, I was shocked to see him here. Then the initial shock wore off, replaced by rage. He was one of the last people I wanted to see. He had helped save Oliver, but that didn't mean I trusted him, nor was I ready to forgive him. I fought the urge to glare at him.

King Alaric nodded to him solemnly.

"Let us hope you are right," he told Grimes.

I did a double take. Did they all really expect me, a fourteen-year-old girl from the middle of nowhere, to defeat a centuries old shadow king? He had all these demons and shadow creatures at his disposal. What did I have? I had light. They expected me to beat the ancient King of Darkness by being a freaking nightlight!

"I'm just a kid," I whispered.

Deep down I knew that wasn't true. I had never been just a kid, and I never would be. Knowing that didn't stop my fear.

I don't really think anything can stop fear. There are just things that outshine it, things that make you keep going despite it. After all, true courage is doing the right thing despite your own insurmountable fear.

Despite knowing this, I did not think of myself as courageous.

"My dear, you are so much more," King Alaric said in a kind voice. He offered me a soft, gentle smile that seemed genuine. Then he added, "Come, there is something I need to show you."

King Alaric flapped his wings gently and flew over to the door. I stole a glance at Will. To my surprise, he was already looking at me. Our eyes met, and I felt the rest of the world melt away at that moment. The look he gave me was filled with so many emotions, so many words that I didn't understand. There was so much I wanted to say to him at that moment, so many feelings that I didn't understand.

I was the first to look away, knowing that I needed to go with King Alaric. I heaved a long, heavy sigh before following King Alaric out the door.

A young fairy, probably around Will's age, started to

follow behind us. He had curly, ashy brown hair. He was definitely younger than most of the men. There were some guys that seemed a bit closer to his age, but not many. He was taller than me by at least five inches and everything about him was muscular and chiseled. His bronzed skin gave me the impression that he spent a lot of time out in the sun. His wings seemed to shift from reddish orange, to red, then reddish brown as he moved. Almost like fire. His caramel-colored eyes were intense and wild; greatly contrasting his stiff posture and tense movements.

"That won't be necessary, Hunter," King Alaric replied.

Hunter, as King Alaric had called him, straightened his shoulders indignantly. Hunter was taller than King Alaric and was much more muscular than him as well. Standing like that, he almost seemed intimidating.

"But Your Majesty, I am under orders to remain by your side at all times," Hunter argued.

King Alaric looked at him with sage eyes, giving him that same look he had given me, the kind where it feels like he's boring into your soul.

He wisely replied, "I am in no danger here. Besides, what I have to say is strictly between Celeste and myself."

Hunter caved under King Alaric's gaze. He sighed and bent in a stiff bow.

"As you wish, Your Majesty," he said in a forced formal voice.

King Alaric turned back towards the door. I watched as he fluttered through it. I looked around at the fairies; all of them looked at me with questioning eyes, except for Hunter, who was frowning and glaring at me as if I had personally offended him. I did not want to be stuck there with him any longer. I took that as my cue to follow King Alaric. Then I hurried to catch up with him.

When I caught up to him, he was crossing a rope bridge. I stepped onto it without thinking, just as I had done on my way to the hut. The rope bridge swayed under my feet, and I made the mistake of looking down. It was like looking over the edge of a skyscraper. We were so high that the massive golden river looked like a tiny creek. I gripped the rope railing so hard that my knuckles turned white. I fell to my feet as my head started spinning. I was never afraid of heights before; why was I being such a wuss about them now?

Maybe it wasn't just the heights scaring me. Maybe it was the massive weight that I had put on my shoulders; the weight that I was supposed to carry with my shoulders squared and my head held high. I was currently collapsing under that weight and the expectations all these people had for me.

I squeezed my eyes shut, trying to block the panic rising in my chest. I took short, sharp breaths, as I tried—and failed—to stay calm. I had never had a panic attack before, but I was pretty sure this is what it felt like.

"My dear, what is the matter?" King Alaric asked me.

His voice snapped me out of it.

I looked up to see him hovering in front of me. His feet were a couple of inches above the bridge. Despite the fact that neither of us were walking on the bridge, it still shook. I let go of the rope railing and wrapped my arms around myself. I soon realized that it wasn't the bridge shaking at all—it was me.

"N-nothing," I stuttered.

I was trying to be brave. King Alaric had so much faith in me. He thought I was this strong, powerful person that would be the world's saving grace. I still didn't even know half the things my powers could do, yet I was supposed to use them to defeat Kilmar? That kind of pressure has a way of bringing you down.

He looked at me skeptically. I didn't want to lie to him, so

I told him the truth.

"It's just, how am I supposed to defeat Kilmar? I don't even know how to use my powers," I worried.

I looked up at him, searching his eyes for answers as if I could find the answer to any problem in those wise green seas of knowledge.

"I cannot tell you how to go about defeating Kilmar," he said, placing a reassuring hand on my shoulder. "However, I can assure you that when the time comes, you will know what to do."

With that, he swiftly turned and continued fluttering across the bridge. I watched him for a moment, silently searching for the strength to stand. I took one steadying breath before I dragged myself to my feet.

Once across the rope bridge, we came to a stop on a familiar platform. This was the first platform I had come to. On my right I could see the spiral staircase I had climbed to get here. To my left, what I guessed was the giant healing branch stood straight and tall in the center of the tree. In front of me, in the center of the platform stood a tall, blonde boy.

NINETEEN

"Celeste?" he gasped.

"Oliver!" I cried.

I knew we hadn't known each other for very long, and we definitely weren't on a hugging basis yet, but I didn't care. I still ran to him; I couldn't help myself. Tears of joy and relief filled my eyes as I wrapped my arms around him. I felt some of the onerous weight that had piled up on top of me disappear.

I sighed with relief, and I squeezed him tighter. For a moment, he seemed too shocked to hug me back. At first, I even thought he wouldn't hug me back. Then his arms wrapped around me. I felt a feeling that had seemed so alien to me a few days ago but was becoming more familiar with every hug: safe.

Hugging Oliver didn't feel exactly like hugging Will. Where I got butterflies and my stomach turned to knots with Will, with Oliver I felt like I was hugging a friend, or maybe even a brother. There wasn't even a hint of romance with

Oliver.

Still, I didn't want to let go just yet, and I wouldn't have, but Oliver broke the silence. He coughed and gave a small laugh, because I was hugging him so tightly that was all he could manage.

"Can't breathe," he choked out.

I pulled away, offering a playful laugh in return.

"Sorry, I'm just so happy you're not—" I stopped myself before I could finish.

'Dead' felt like a forbidden word. I didn't want to say it in front of him. With my luck, if I said it, the universe would somehow find a way to really kill him.

"It's okay. You can say it," he gently assured me.

I shook my head, still unable to bring myself to say it. Instead, I looked him over, searching for any sign of scratches or bruises. There wasn't a single one. Still, I knew he had to be in pain. I knew from experience that pain wasn't always physical. Sometimes it could go deeper than a scratch or a bruise. It hurts more than a broken leg or a twisted ankle. Those kinds of things heal. This kind of pain doesn't heal. It leaves a lasting scar on your heart. It's the kind of pain that haunts you for the rest of your life.

"You're really okay?" I asked.

Somehow, I already knew he would tell me he was. I didn't have to ask. I needed to though. I needed to hear him tell me he was okay, because somehow that would make the guilt hurt less.

"Yeah," he replied with a grin, "I feel better than ever. These fairies really know their stuff!"

To anyone else, that smile would have seemed legit. I knew better. I could see the pain and the fear he was trying not to show. He couldn't hide it behind a happy facade, at least not from me. I knew that smile too well. I made it every time I came home from school in tears because I had been teased relentlessly at school or I had been called out in class by one of my teachers. I smiled like that whenever my mom got home from those long hard hours at a job she hated but kept anyway to support us. I smiled like that when I knew the last thing she wanted to see was me crying. That was the kind of smile someone makes when they are barely holding it together, but they don't want you to know.

Unshed tears glistened in the corners of Oliver's eyes. The whites of his eyes were bloodshot and red. His hands shook slightly.

I felt something snap inside of me at this sight.

"I'm so sorry," I struggled to say because of the lump that had formed in my throat. "This is all my fault."

He placed his shaky hand on my shoulder.

"Celeste, it's not your fault," he said.

I knew it was meant to be a reassuring gesture, but all his shaky hand did was bring me more guilt. I knew his words weren't true. It was definitely my fault; there was no denying that.

I shrugged his hand off, needing to be free of its shaking.

"Kilmar sent the scorpion after me. Not you. Not Will. Not Edward. Me," I snapped.

In retrospect, I wasn't being fair to him. I just couldn't help myself.

"I don't blame you," he reasoned.

His eyes pleaded with me to just let it go, but I couldn't. Every time I closed my eyes, I pictured that dreadful moment of him collapsing, that big ugly hole in his chest prominently displayed.

"I blame me!" I yelled at him.

Then my voice quivered as I whispered the truth that had been circling around inside my head since the moment we had been taken prisoner on that pirate ship—the words that had haunted me for so long.

"I blame me."

Then he did something that took me by surprise just as Will did. He pulled me into a hug.

I tensed at first, shocked. Then I hugged him back.

"I'm so sorry," I kept saying as tears trickled down my cheek.

"I don't blame you, and you shouldn't blame yourself. That scorpion was Kilmar's fault, not yours," he told me.

I didn't know what to say to that. I didn't believe him, so I simply shook my head.

He pulled away from me and placed his hands on his hips in mock sternness.

"Oh no! Don't shake your head at me! You know I'm right," he bantered.

I shook my head again. Why couldn't he see how wrong he was? Why did he have to insist on not blaming me?

He seemed to be able to tell how I felt.

"I believe it wasn't your fault. Please try to believe it too," he pleaded.

I wanted to argue, but I had just gotten him back. I didn't want to upset him, so I gave in and told him what he wanted to hear.

"I'll try," I told him.

Even I didn't believe me. My voice was dry and monotone as I forced out the words.

Oliver didn't appear satisfied. He opened his mouth to say something else. Before he could, someone cleared his throat very loudly behind us. I whipped my head around to find King Alaric looking at us expectantly.

Oh my gosh! I completely forgot he was here! I thought to myself.

My cheeks burned with shame and embarrassment. King Alaric had all these high expectations for me and yet he'd just witnessed all that.

"Sorry to interrupt, but we have more pressing matters to discuss," he said.

His formal tone sent chills down my spine. I had the sinking feeling in my gut that something bad was about to happen. I hoped not. I wasn't sure how much more any of us could take.

"Yes, of course. What's going on?" I asked. I tried to mask my fear, but my voice was an octave higher, and my words were squeaky.

Oliver moved closer to me. The gesture seemed odd to me, like he was being protective. We hadn't known each other long enough for him to be that protective of me, although if that hug meant anything it was that we were growing closer. Unless he knew something I didn't. Then there was a very high chance that this was going to be bad news.

"I assume the two of you are aware that you are the only halflings in the world?" He said it as more of a statement than a question. Still, Oliver and I nodded uneasily.

"Oliver, you have no idea where you came from, is that right?" King Alaric continued.

Oliver nodded again as he replied, "I don't even know my last name, or how old I am, or when the pirates found me."

The fairy king gave us an absent, "I see."

King Alaric flew nimbly over to the giant healing branch. He motioned for us to follow. Oliver and I hesitantly walked towards it. We exchanged nervous glances.

It became clear that Oliver knew as little as I did about what was going to happen. I felt like I was walking into a trap of some kind. I knew in my heart that King Alaric would never do anything to harm us; however, that didn't stop the paranoia from creeping into my mind and lighting my nerves on fire with fear.

"This is the tree of healing. It can heal physical injuries like the one inflicted on young Mr. Oliver, but it can also heal memories," King Alaric stated. He looked at Oliver and added. "All the answers to your past are buried deep in your memories, child. Both of you, put your hand on the tree and the tree will take it from there."

I reached out for the tree. Then I paused, my fingertips hovering inches from the rough bark of the tree.

"Wait a second! If it's Oliver's memories, why do I need to do it too?" I questioned.

It's not that I didn't want to help Oliver find his memories and retrieve his missing past. I just wasn't crazy about touching the magic memory healing tree.

"You'll see. Just trust the tree my dear," King Alaric said.

I sighed, resigning myself to my tree fate. The fairies had saved Oliver; I figured the least I could do was humor the old fairy king.

I put my hand on the tree beside Oliver's. I looked at our hands, only an inch apart, and I felt as if we were connected somehow. I can't explain it. I just did.

I closed my eyes and waited. Nothing happened. I opened my mouth to tell King Alaric when a barrage of hazy images flooded my mind.

No, not images. I realized. *Memories.*

Two people appeared: a man with strawberry blond hair and big amber eyes and a woman with blonde hair just like mine. The woman held a sleeping baby in her arms and the man held the hand of a young, blonde boy.

They stood in front of a house that seemed oddly familiar. I couldn't figure out why until I realized it was my house. Recognition surged through me at the sight of the woman. She was my mom. That meant that the man was my dad. I'd never seen a picture of him before. Only the statue in the Hall of Convocation. He was wearing human clothes—faded jeans and a white t-shirt under a worn flannel jacket—and his hair was messy. Definitely not someone I'd expect to be a leader of the Arbitrators. I assumed that I was the baby. If I was right, then who was the boy?

Mom and Dad were arguing, I could tell by the jerking hand movements and the way their mouths were set into scowls. I was too far away to hear what they were arguing about. It was like being in a movie theatre with headphones on. I wanted to get closer, but I didn't know how.

Somehow, as if it could hear my thoughts, the image zoomed in until I was close enough to hear them.

"You can't take him away!" Mom cried.

"Darling, it's the only way to keep him safe. The Convocation saw him. What if they took his power or worse?" Dad pointed out. His voice remained calm, but his expression was full of pain.

"Surely there's some other way! We could go into hiding or-or something! Please, Devon," she pleaded desperately.

Dad shook his head. "I'm sorry dear. Believe me if there were any other way—"

"But there isn't," Mom finished with a sigh. Her shoulders slumped as she seemed to realize that there was no escaping this. Then she looked down at me and added, "They're too young to remember this. At least they won't have to know the pain of losing each other. Not like we will."

Dad let go of the boy's hand and came over to hug Mom. She shifted me around so that he could hug her without squishing me.

"I could erase your memories of us if you'd like," Dad offered.

Mom didn't even consider it. She shook her head without a trace of conviction.

"Even though it hurts, I want to remember. I love both of you so much. I don't think I could forget you if I tried," Mom conceded.

He hugged her tighter. They stayed like that for a few short moments. Neither of them seemed to want to let go.

"It's time to say goodbye," Dad whispered gently.

Tears gleamed in Mom's eyes as she whispered, "Okay."

She pulled away from Dad and handed me to him. Then she took careful steps toward the boy. She bent down and caressed his face with her hands. Her voice was thick with emotion as she looked at him in his big blue eyes. "I love you so much Oliver," she told him, her voice soft and gentle like the petals of a flower. "You may not remember me, but I will never forget you. Goodbye."

The tears were streaming down her face as she turned to face Dad.

"Will I ever see either of you again?" she asked, her voice trembling.

"Yes, my love. I promise someday, somehow, we will see

each other again. Don't worry too much about Oliver. He will be in good hands," Dad assured Mom.

He handed me back to Mom and bent down to gently kiss my forehead.

"Goodbye, Celeste. I love you," he said.

I stared up at him with my tiny baby eyes. My eyes twinkled with questions, silently pleading with him not to go.

He kissed Mom on the cheek one last time before a swirling blue portal appeared. He grabbed Oliver's hand and together they walked through the portal. At the last second, Oliver turned around to Mom, his tiny face contorted in confusion.

"Mommy?" he said.

Then the portal engulfed him, and he disappeared.

After that there was silence. It was suffocating, the silence, and it seemed to suck the life out of Mom. Suddenly she burst into tears. She cradled me in her arms as she fell to her knees. Her gentle features turned red and puffy as tears streamed down her cheeks and sobs shook her shoulders.

I had never truly understood how hard it had been on Mom after Dad left. I knew she didn't like to talk about it; that was all. It must have been so hard on her having no one to turn to. She didn't just lose Dad; she lost her only son too. She lost Oliver. My brother.

All this time, she had been working long hours at a job she hated, her memories of Oliver and Dad haunting her each day. I marveled at the fact that she had found the strength to climb out of bed day after day, knowing she had a son out there, growing up without her. Thinking about it made me want to collapse to my knees beside her and cry too.

Suddenly, the memory shifted into a different scene. Dad stood holding Oliver's hand. They were on the beach of a tropical island. The waters were clear and beautiful, and the sun's magnificent rays sparkled off the dazzling surface of the water. The palm trees swayed in the ocean breeze like dancers moving to the beat of a song. Dad was talking to Captain Grimes, or at least it looked like the captain. He was younger and had no facial hair. His captain's hat gleamed fresh and new. He still had all of his teeth.

"I can keep him safe, but only if I don't tell him anything about where he came from. He won't know you or your family. He won't even begin to know who or even what he is until he comes of age, and his powers come," Grimes told Dad.

"As long as he's safe," Dad replied solemnly, "That's all that matters."

"You better hold up your end of the deal," Grimes demanded.

"I assure you. I will do everything in my power to make sure the Convocation doesn't meddle in your affairs," Dad promised.

Dad bent down to be eye to eye with Oliver.

"I have to go now son. You might not remember me when you grow up, but I will never forget you," Dad told him.

"I love you, Daddy," Oliver said.

He wrapped his tiny arms around Dad. They barely even went all the way around his front side, but he didn't seem to care. Dad hugged him back for a few short seconds before pulling away. Oliver looked at him like a scared little puppy. With big, questioning eyes that you don't want to look away from, but know you have to eventually.

"Goodbye, Oliver," Dad said. The sorrow in his eyes made my heart break. He turned away and a portal spiraled to life.

"Daddy!" cried Oliver.

He ran towards Dad, but it was too late. The portal had already closed, and Dad had gone with it. Tears streamed down little Oliver's cheeks as he sobbed. Captain Grimes came up behind him and scooped him up into his arms. Grimes gave a weak smile. Oliver did not return it. Instead, the tears turned into a raging storm, pouring down like never before.

"Come now, none of that. You'll be happy with us. You'll see," Grimes chided. He turned towards the shore.

Then the memory faded away and my eyes came back into focus. I stared at the complex bark of the tree. I reached up to wipe away tears I didn't even recall shedding. My hands shook and my legs became weak. I leaned against the tree for support.

Even though I didn't remember losing Oliver, I felt the pain of that loss now. My heart felt like it had been shattered into a million tiny pieces. I cried for Mom and Dad, for Oliver, and I cried for myself. I cried for all of us, for having to lose each other, for the life we could have had.

Wow! I cried a lot today. Honestly, I was fine with that. Even though I had the weight of the world on my shoulders, I was still just a fourteen-year-old girl. And sometimes, girls just need to cry. So, I did. I cried like I was a baby again.

I felt a hand on my shoulder and looked up to find Oliver. We stared at each other. Neither of us knew what to do or how to react. His cheeks were stained with tears. I didn't know boys could cry like that. I mean, everybody cries, but boys just don't do it as often, so it feels weird to see them cry.

I knew what we both wanted. We wanted to hold each other, embrace each other as siblings for the first time. So, I pulled him close to me. We cried together. Eventually, my tears turned from mourning to joy.

"I can't believe I have a brother," I said, my voice full of disbelief.

"I can't believe I have a family," he whispered.

After all this time, I had a brother. I couldn't help but recall all of those times I had to stick up for myself, all of the teasing and the bullying. All this time, I could have had a brother to defend me. It was all the Convocation's fault. They were the reason Oliver grew up without a family, on a stinky pirate ship, and with so many questions about his past. Just like that, my joy shifted to anger.

As new questions filled my mind, the anger shifted to confusion and curiosity.

"Wait a minute," I said as I turned to King Alaric. "How did you know about Oliver?"

He smiled slyly. This kind, gentle king didn't strike me as someone capable of being sly. I was finding out all kinds of new things today!

He replied, "Captain Grimes informed me of Oliver's unknown past, and I took it upon myself to make it known to the two of you."

"I can't believe he knew," Oliver muttered. "All these years. He. Knew."

I couldn't blame him. He had every right to feel confused. His entire world had just been flipped upside down. Or maybe, it had finally been flipped right side up.

TWENTY

"**I**f it's okay Your Majesty, could Oliver and I talk in private?" I asked, my voice dripping with so much fake enthusiasm that I barely recognized it. "It's just that we have so much to catch up on."

I knew it was probably not my place to ask King Alaric for anything, but this was really important. I needed to tell Oliver everything, especially my plan. I couldn't just ditch my brother after just getting him back, at least not without letting him know why or where I was going.

I just didn't want King Alaric to hear. This was going to stay between Oliver and me.

He gave me a skeptical look. In return, I gave him the most innocent smile I've ever made. Oliver just stood there, unsure of what to say or do.

King Alaric's expression softened.

"Of course. You two must have a lot to talk about. Would you like me to take you to the huts you'll be staying in?" he offered.

I had to do a double take. The king of the fairies had just offered to do me a favor. I figured these weren't very common things, so I should just take the offer.

"Thank you, Your Majesty! You're so kind," I said, my voice oozing as much flattery as I could muster.

King Alaric smiled at me approvingly. It was hard not to smirk. I knew I had just earned his trust and appreciation. I had a feeling that if I ever found myself in trouble, it would be handy to have the king of the fairies to call upon for help.

"Come along then," he said.

He walked back over the rope bridge. This time, I didn't falter as I stepped foot onto the shaky bridge. I'd found a new strength that kept me from wavering. I'd found Oliver, and I was going to find Mom and Dad. I had Will, and I had Edward. I have more friends and family now, in the midst of all this chaos, than I had a few weeks ago when I had lived a boring life back in Tennessee.

After we made it across the rope bridge and onto another platform, King Alaric turned left. A smaller rope bridge led up to a small hut. I walked across the bridge eagerly. My entire body was humming with nervous energy. I just wanted to be alone with my brother already.

Inside the cabin was a set of bunk beds, a small table with two wooden chairs, a couch and a kitchen. A green door on the left led to what I assumed was the bathroom and the blue one in the back led to a balcony. I would most likely be avoiding that particular part of the hut.

The hut itself was quite small, but there were only two of us living there, so it would be perfectly fine. There would only be two of us until I could figure out how to make a portal to Kilmar's realm. Then Oliver would be living on his own. Again.

I tried not to feel guilty about it. I hated that I had to leave him. He wouldn't be completely alone though. He would have Will and Edward. I was sure they would stay together. After all, neither of them could go back to Enceaf without getting in trouble for helping me.

Still, I hated leaving.

This is the only way to keep him safe, I reminded myself.

"I'll leave you two on your own now," King Alaric said. "I'm sure you've got lots of catching up to do."

I bowed to him respectfully and he gave me a nod of approval.

As soon as he was outside, I shut the door quietly and locked it discreetly. Then I walked over to the couch and sat down. Oliver stood like a statue. I could tell he felt uneasy, as if he somehow knew I was about to tell him something bad.

I patted the seat beside me to let Oliver know to sit down. Slowly, he moved towards me. Once he sat down, I turned toward him.

My voice was serious as I told him, "We need to talk."

"I can't let you do this by yourself. I just got you back I won't lose you again," Oliver said after I had filled him in on my plan.

"And I can't lose you either," I said, my voice thick with emotion.

I knew that my plan would likely get me badly injured or even killed, but it was the only plan I had. Anyone who helped me would be at the same risk. I couldn't handle anyone else's suffering being on my conscience. That meant this was my burden to bear alone.

"I won't try to stop you. Just let me help you. Please Celeste," he said.

I took a moment to consider it.

This was one argument I was clearly not going to win. Maybe if I let him think he was helping me, he would be satisfied. Then I could keep him safe and out of trouble—at least until I could figure out a way to make a portal to Kilmar. Then I could ditch him, and he wouldn't be able to follow me. It would be up to Will and Edward to keep him safe

The only problem in my plan was figuring out how to slip away without arousing suspicion. That was going to be hard. Oliver may have said he wouldn't try to stop me, but I have a feeling if he's there when I leave for Kilmar's dimension, he will try to stop me.

I needed to figure out the right time to slip away. I couldn't make it obvious, otherwise my friends would get suspicious.

One problem at a time, I chided myself.

I took a deep breath. Lately, I have gotten into a bad habit of letting my mind spiral out of control. It's kind of hard not to when I have so much to worry about.

"You really want to help me?" I asked. He nodded eagerly. "Keep Will from finding out. And Edward too."

"But—"

"They can't know," I cut him off.

I didn't want Will to get hurt; I also felt the need to keep Edward safe too. He'd been with us all this time. He'd been through the same things the rest of us had been through.

Speaking of Edward, I still wondered what his powers were, or if he had any at all. Those questions had been burning in the back of my mind for some time now; however, they felt irrelevant at the moment.

"Okay," Oliver said with a sigh.

He wrung his hands as a sense of awkwardness crept over the room. I rose from the couch with a heavy sigh. I looked over at the bed. I knew I should try to sleep, but first, I really wanted to shower. It had been days since I had showered. My hair was a tangled mess, I was covered in dirt, I had sand in places sand should never be, and being so gross made me feel terrible.

"I'm going to take a shower," I told Oliver as I made my way to the bathroom.

I couldn't help but marvel. Everything was beautiful in Sproot, even the bathrooms. The mirror's frame appeared to be made from gnarled branches or roots. The floor mat was woven from soft petals. The shower was an absurd combination of wooden pipes, gears, and spouts jutting out in a bunch of random places. It looked like something the Mad Hatter from Alice in Wonderland would make.

I stared at myself in the mirror. I was a mess. My clothes were in tatters. Twigs were tangled in my messy blonde hair, which was so dirty in some places, I looked like a brunette. I had dirt all over my face. My eyes were bloodshot from crying so much, and there were dark circles under my eyes. I was skinnier from not eating enough. An ugly scab ran across my neck from where Grimes had held his sword to it. I barely recognized myself.

I was in desperate need of a shower. I had absolutely no idea how to work it, so I started off spinning gears at random. I ended up getting blasted in the face with freezing cold, rainbow colored water. Then water that was much too hot shot out of a pipe near my feet, making me jump. I continued turning valves and shrieking when I was bombarded by ice cold or burning hot water that was every color imaginable.

Finally, after I had been shot at from every angle possible with all different temperatures, and literally every color of water in the world, I got the pipe above me to shower me with colorful water at a temperature that wouldn't freeze me to death or melt my skin off.

I stood there for some time, letting the colorful streams of water wash away the fear and stress of the past few weeks.

I could have stayed in that shower forever, but I knew I should get to sleep. After all, I had some hard days ahead of me. I needed to be well rested. I turned the gears to shut off the rainbow shower of death and stepped out of the shower onto the soft pink petal bathroom mat.

I searched the floor for my clothes, but they were nowhere to be seen. I did, however, find a silky pink nightgown, a white shawl that looked like it was meant for a grandma, and a pair of princess pink night slippers.

A small note card was propped up on top of the clothes. Inscribed on the note in intricate, beautiful cursive was this: We have taken your clothes for cleaning and mending. Do not fret. They shall be returned promptly in the morning.

I had no choice but to put on the frilly pink nightgown. I hated wearing pink; it washed me out. However, the soft fabric more than made up for the color. The silk felt like clouds on my skin. It fit me perfectly. I was amazed at how the fairies could make this ensemble fit perfectly without even knowing my size.

I decided not to wear the shawl, and I left it neatly folded with the slippers on top of it. As I exited the bathroom I heard the soft hum of snoring. Oliver appeared to have changed into a set of silky, blue pajamas. I giggled as he muttered some sleep nonsense about Mr. Squid eating his chocolate chip cookies. He turned over and muttered something else that I couldn't quite understand. I fought the laugh that was bubbling up in my throat.

I sighed as I settled into the bunk bed below him. I was still feeling restless, but I decided to try to sleep anyway.

It was by far one of the comfiest beds I had ever slept in. I felt like I was lying on a cloud. The linens smelled like pine. The pillows smelled of lavender. It reminded me of my home, back in Tennessee, because our detergent was lavender scented. All of this combined with the stress of the day made me want to go into hibernation for the winter.

I should have had no problem sleeping, but the longer I laid there, the more restless I became. I tossed and turned, unable to fall asleep. After a while I found myself staring absently at the boards above me. Oliver was snoring like a foghorn now. If the magical healing tree could heal someone on the verge of death, you would think it would fix his deviated septum while it was at it.

It didn't matter. It's not like I would have been able to sleep anyways. I still had a million thoughts and questions swimming through my head.

I thought about Oliver. He had lost so much. I'd known from the moment he told me he had the same powers as me that we were deeply connected. I hated that I missed so many years with him and despised the Convocation for being the cause of it. Why did they hate halflings so much anyway? What had we ever done to them?

Kilmar had said something about halflings betraying him, but that had all been a lie. He was just trying to manipulate me into doing what he wanted. Wasn't he?

My thoughts then turned to my parents. I imagined them in chains being subjected to all kinds of gruesome torture all for the sake of luring me to Kilmar. I had hated Dad for so long. All these years I thought he left because he didn't love us, but now I knew the opposite was true. I felt so guilty for pressing Mom to tell me more about Dad. I knew it had been hard on her when he left, having to raise me alone. She'd lost her only son too. I'd just made things even harder by constantly pushing her for more details.

I was determined to fix everything though. I would save them and then everything would be as it should be: the four of us together, one safe, happy family.

I knew what I needed to do: get to Kilmar's dimension and save my parents. To do that, I would have to first figure out how to make a portal that would take me there. Then, I would have to fight off whoever and whatever would be waiting for me when I got there. I would free my parents and try to escape before Kilmar discovered what I had done. That was if my plan worked the way it was supposed to and nothing unexpected happened. With my luck, it was bound to.

I knew pretty much nothing about Kilmar's dimension. I didn't even know what it was called. I knew it was the shadow dimension and Kilmar was the king of it. That was the extent of my knowledge. It would probably be helpful to learn more about his dimension before I snuck away to face a powerful shadow king on my own.

Wow, that sounds really reckless and stupid now that I'm thinking about it.

There was a small part of me that knew we would never be truly safe as long as Kilmar reigned. Still, nothing mattered more to me than getting my family back. Deep down in my gut, I had a feeling that even if I didn't face him this time, there would be a next time.

I sighed a deflated sigh.

Deciding whether or not to face Kilmar would have to wait until I got to his dimension. I really needed to figure out what it was called. Maybe I could ask Will or Edward in the morning.

The farther I let myself sink into this bottomless sea of spiraling thoughts, the bigger and scarier they started to seem.

They sucked the air out of my lungs as they bombarded me with a fresh wave of panic.

I couldn't breathe. I need some fresh air.

I threw the blankets off of me and scanned the room for my slippers. Since it was dark, I had a hard time finding them. I had looked over them maybe five or six times before my eyes settled on their dark outline on top of the sink. I decided to put the shawl on at the last moment since it had been a bit chilly earlier. I breathed heavily as I moved about the cabin, each breath sharp.

I rushed out the front door and took in huge breaths of fresh forest air. I gripped the railings of the platform the hut was connected to and looked down at the darkness below. The thought of falling off the edge was enough to send me stumbling backwards. The breeze blew gently through my hair, sending a chill down my spine. It wasn't quiet in Sproot. All the animals seemed to be around at night, and their cries echoed in the darkness below me. The wind howled as loudly as the wolves that I heard crying in the distance. Despite the chill, the breeze felt refreshing. I closed my eyes, taking deep breaths to calm my nerves and my mind. Then, a different sound caught my attention.

I heard two hushed voices. I looked around frantically, wondering if I had imagined it. Then I heard it again. It was coming from the other side of the platform. I took off tiptoeing towards the edge. I peeked my head over the side and had to suppress a gasp. I was shocked to see two familiar faces whispering on the platform below me: Will and Captain Grimes.

"Have you told her how you feel?" asked Captain Grimes.

"No, of course not! What if she doesn't feel the same way?" Will replied. His face was full of conviction and fear.

"But, what if she does?" Captain Grimes countered.

Who was she? Was there someone else Will had feelings for?

Jealousy flared inside of me like fire. Why would he like someone else?

"Look lad, I have a feeling you won't get another chance to do it. At least not for a long while. Tell Celeste how you really feel," he said as he placed a hand on Will's shoulder, "before it's too late."

I gasped at his profound words. They both looked up at me, the source of the noise. I scurried away from the edge as quickly as I could, not wanting them to know what I had heard. I fell backwards in my panicked effort to get out of their line of sight.

I landed with a thud on the wooden platform. I caught myself with my left hand. My right hand came shakily up to my mouth.

Will felt the same way I did, or at least I thought he did. How could he feel the same way when I wasn't really sure what I felt?

"Who's there?" I heard Will yell.

I knew his voice by heart by now. Despite the suspicion, it sent butterflies to my stomach.

My heart thumped madly in my chest as I prayed that he would decide it was nothing. I closed my eyes as if that could keep him from seeing me.

I stayed silent.

"Gees, lad. Paranoid much?" Grimes grumbled to Will.

"You would be too, if you had been kidnapped and enslaved by pirates," Will muttered back.

I heard Grimes laugh and tell Will he was returning to

Aquaria. I listened until I heard his heavy footsteps fade away.

"Umm. Celeste? What are you doing?" someone behind me said.

Still on the ground, I whipped my head around to see who had said it. I came to find a boy with hair as black as charcoal, and dark, mysterious brown eyes. His eyebrows were arched in question.

"Hey, Edward. N-nothing," I stammered.

"You're a terrible liar," he said dryly. He offered me his hand. I took it, and he pulled me to my feet.

"Yeah, I am," I replied.

I figured that he probably knew about Will's feelings already since they were best friends. I decided I did not want to tell him what I'd overheard.

"Care to enlighten me on why you were sitting on the ground looking like you've seen a ghost?" he prompted.

I shook my head. I definitely did not want to tell him. I wrung my hands as awkwardness settled over us like a thick fog. I needed something to break the silence. I also happened to have a question to ask him. I decided to kill two birds with one stone.

"I have a question for you," I said.

"What do you want to know?"

"What's your power?" I asked.

"I......don't have one," he mumbled morosely.

I fought back a gasp. Will said all Arbitrators have a power. I opened my mouth to speak, but Edward cut me off before I could utter a word.

"Look, I don't want to talk about it," he said.

I wanted to ask more questions but decided not to. It was his story to tell. Whether or not he told it was up to him. Changing the subject seemed like the best thing to do.

"So...........what color portal will I have to make to get us to Kilmar?" I asked him. My voice hitched on the word us. I practically forced it out.

I figured asking upfront would be more inconspicuous than trying to figure it out on my own. If I had to let him think that I needed to know so we could do it together, then I would. I would do whatever kept everyone safe.

"Black. Kilmar's dimension, Dread, is a shadow dimension. Being the king of shadows, he feeds off fear. So that's probably the emotion you'll have to feel to make a black portal," he explained.

"Okay, thanks," I said.

I had to try hard to keep my voice even. I was so excited. Not only had he answered my question, but he had figured out which emotion I would need to make the portal. I was even closer to getting my parents back.

And even closer to facing my fate. I thought.

I recalled the prophecy. Usually, I had trouble memorizing little things, but the unsettling words of the prophecy were burned into my mind. I already knew what the first part meant.

Shining bright,

Will be the savior of light.

Hidden away, out of reach.

They're safe within forbidden keep.

I was the savior of light. I was safely hidden away with my mom in Boringsville. That part was obvious. The next part:

Where shadows reap, a skirmish between darkness and day,

For both sides, there will be a price to pay.

If I was right, that part of the prophecy had been talking about me fighting Kilmar. He was the darkness because he is king of the shadows. I was day because of my light powers. The end also tied into that:

Powers great and strong,

Will battle for right and wrong.

The greater force will win, with great sacrifice to end.

I had a feeling it was describing some kind of battle that would take place in Dread. I was praying with every piece of my heart that I wouldn't have to fight Kilmar. I didn't think I would win if it came down to it. Honestly, the rest of the lines scared me more than anything.

Betrayal of the light,

They'll be stuck in a plight.

If I was the light, that meant someone was going to betray me. I would rather be hurt than betrayed. Getting injured is painful, but betrayal hurts way more. Who would it be that betrayed me? Grimes? That one fairy, Hunter, the way he looked at me...could it be him? No. Neither of these seemed like great answers. How could they betray me when they hadn't even earned my trust? It would make more sense if it was someone I trusted.

Edward must have seen the way my sleep-deprived mind was spiraling, and the way I was losing my concentration on our conversation.

"You should probably get some rest," he said. It sounded so abrupt, as if he wanted to be done with the conversation too.

"Yeah, you're right," I said as I turned and started walking back toward my hut.

After thirty or so steps, I risked looking back at him. He was staring at me coldly. I wondered if my question about his powers had offended him. Or maybe he was onto me, and he knew what I was planning to leave. Could he be the one that would betray me? What if he was?

His eyes softened and he offered me a dry, "Goodnight Celeste."

There was something in his voice, something I couldn't quite place. I was tired and it had been a long day, so I chalked it up to sleep deprived delusion.

"Goodnight Edward."

I walked back to my hut.

The last thing I felt like doing was sleeping. I still had so many questions. At least now I know how to make the portal. I could most likely use some practice, but I also knew I could make one without practice if I had to. Although I still felt antsy, I laid down on the bed. As soon as my head hit the pillow, I was out like a light.

TWENTY-ONE

My dreams were a horrible collage of nightmares about my parents. Their screams echoed through every scene. In some, their lifeless bodies were strung up from the ceiling with ropes. In others, they stared at me with lifeless eyes that were black with shadows. In the worst ones, their hands reached out for me, begging me to save them. Then they stopped asking for saving and instead turned to blaming.

Celeste, why didn't you save us?

You should have tried harder!

Don't you love us?

These horrible accusations echoed in my mind along with the screams.

I wanted to scream, but I couldn't. I had no voice. I was useless. There was nothing I could do but watch in disgust and horror.

As guilt consumed me, I sank into a dark hole. It carried

me down, down, down until I saw light—Wait, light? Maybe it was carrying me up—I heard my parents calling out to me as I was torn farther and farther from them.

It's your fault, they said, *It's your fault. It's your fault.*

"No!" I screamed. I sat up abruptly.

I breathed heavily as the fear of what I had seen latched onto me with cold claws, refusing to let go. Cold sweat ran down my back like ice. For a moment, I was unsure where I was. Then, I remembered, the forest realm, Oliver, fairies, healing tree, Will. I was safe. It had only been a dream. Or at least, I thought it was just a dream. I put my hand over my heart, which was still racing like it was trying to win the Indy 500.

"You good?" Oliver asked from the bunk above me. The bed rattled as he climbed down.

"Yeah, just nightmares," I said as a chill ran down my spine. I shivered from the feeling.

Every time I go to sleep now I have nightmares. And every time I thought I would be used to them. I never was.

"Do you want to talk about it?" Oliver asked. He sat down at the foot of my bed. It tilted towards him slightly. I curled my feet up to my chest and rocked back and forth.

I didn't really want to talk about it, but the dreams were getting worse. I supposed it wouldn't hurt to talk about it, just a little. He was my brother, and he wanted to help. I wasn't going to shut him out, not when I was planning on leaving.

"Ever since I woke up on the beach in Aquaria after my encounter with the Convocation," I started, voice shaking, "I've been having these terrible nightmares of Mom and Dad. Before it was always just them being tortured."

"That's awful, Celeste. Why didn't you tell anyone?" he asked.

"I hoped that if I didn't say anything they'd go away, but they didn't. They just got so much worse," I said. A single tear slipped down my cheek, but I fought back the rest. I really didn't want to cry. I didn't think it was possible for me to shed any more tears.

"What do you mean?" Oliver asked. I felt a lump form in my throat as I tried to figure out how to explain my gruesome, abstract dreams.

"It was horrible. They were dead and Kilmar had them strung up by rope like mangled dolls. Their eyes…." I trailed off. I squeezed my own eyes shut.

I gulped and tried to continue. "Their screams….the screams scare me the most. The screaming never stops. It's relentless in every dream."

Then I couldn't hold back the tears that slipped down my face, burning with fear and shame as they trailed down my cheeks.

He reached out and wiped away a few tears from my cheek. Warmth spread through my face from the places he'd touched. His hand settled on the side of my face, caressing it. I leaned my head into his hand.

"It's okay," he whispered gently. "We'll get them back."

"What if we can't? What if…." I paused, trying to find the courage to say the rest of it, "What if he kills them?"

"We won't let it happen," he said soothingly. Determination rang through his words.

"It's all my fault. Kilmar took them to get to me," I mumbled.

"Celeste, look at me," he commanded.

I didn't want to look at him. I didn't want to face him when I knew that it was my fault. It didn't matter what he said, nothing would change the fact that it was true.

Sweet, naive Oliver tried anyway to make me feel better.

"None of it is your fault," he said. "It's Kilmar's fault. Guilt is like a weight that weighs you down to the point that you can't get back up. I already told you that. Please take my advice. Don't carry that burden."

His words were so touching. I couldn't believe I'd been missing him all my life. My heart overflowed with emotion. I couldn't get any words past the lump in my throat, so I did something else. I tackled him with the biggest, most crushing, sisterly hug I could give him. I wrapped my arms around him, and he did the same for me.

"I love you, sis," he said. I could tell he was testing the waters, waiting to see if I would call him my brother too. Of course I did.

"I love you too bro," I replied.

Sitting there holding onto Oliver, I felt like I was grasping the one part of my life that was stable. It's funny how we hadn't known each other for more than a week or two and yet it still felt as if we had been siblings all our lives. I loved him as if I had grown up with him, and I knew he loved me the same.

I figure we could have stayed there for eternity, neither one of us wanting to let go. However, I am only human—huh, actually I guess that particular phrase doesn't apply to me anymore. Whatever, I still required food. My stomach growled, reminding me that it was time for breakfast.

My cheeks turned red as Oliver pulled away, laughing.

"You should get dressed, then we can go see what's for breakfast," Oliver said. I could tell he was trying—and mostly failing—to stifle a laugh.

"But they took my clothes," I said, blushing.

Then I noticed that Oliver was wearing different clothes too. Simple blue pajama pants and a long-sleeved shirt. They looked like they were made from the same material; the only difference was that his had tiny comical pixies embroidered onto them.

"Oh, yeah. Maybe they left our clothes somewhere for us," he said, as our clothing predicament finally dawned on him.

"We should go look around then," I said.

He stood up, giving me a better view of the pixies on his PJs. I couldn't take it anymore. I doubled over with laughter. I laughed until my stomach hurt, and I couldn't breathe.

"What's so funny?" Oliver asked, clearly miffed that I hadn't bothered including him in my joke.

"You have pixies on your PJ's!" I chuckled before bursting into another hysterical fit of laughter.

"Real mature," he grumbled, although a smile twitched at the edge of his mouth.

Then he walked off in search of our clothes. I really liked the pixie-themed clothes and would not have minded watching Oliver wear them the rest of the day. Even if it did mean I was stuck in the frilly nightgown. It would have been worth it.

Grinning from the thought, I walked off toward the bathroom to help search for our clothes.

I walked into the bathroom since that was the last place I had seen my clothes. Unfortunately, they were not there. Shoulders slumped in disappointment; I turned to walk back out the door.

"Aha!" Oliver screamed as he thrust our clothes up into the air. He pumped his fists triumphantly.

"Great job!" I said. Then in a serious voice I told him,

"Now give me my clothes, so I can get out of this frilly nightgown."

He grinned, seeming to understand that I hated the frilly pinkness of my nightgown as much as he hated the silly pixies of his PJs. He offered me my clothes, and I snatched them out of his hands.

"Thank you, Oliver," I said as I went into the bathroom. I looked down at my nightgown. "And goodbye nightgown."

I shut the door and practically ripped the frilly gown off me. My clothes were clean and mended. All the scorch marks, dirt, sand, smells, and holes were gone.

As I exited the bathroom, I was shocked to see Oliver was not in his old clothes. He wore a dashing green jerkin. The edges were lined with silver, making it look as if it had been dusted in starlight. The sleeves hugged his biceps tightly, making them stand out. His pants were simple, the same color green as the jerkin, but without the silver. He looked so grown up. I'd never really thought about the fact that he was older than me. Standing there looking at him, he seemed to have aged a few years. He was tall and actually quite handsome. Not in a "I like him" way, because that would be weird, but in a "I'm so proud to call him my brother" way.

"What's wrong?" he asked. Concern was etched into every handsome feature.

"Nothing, you just look so much older," I said. Then I blushed at how stupid it must have sounded.

"I guess these are a step up from my usually dirty clothes," he said, blushing.

I smiled warmly and said, "They definitely are! Come on, let's go get some breakfast."

I walked toward the door, Oliver at my heels. As I reached for the door handle, someone simultaneously knocked from the other side. I opened the door to find Will and Edward. Will's jerkin was the same style as Oliver's, although it was slightly baggier on his arms. His was blue, the same color blue as the clothes he'd worn the day we met. Edward's outfit was black. It made his dark brown eyes pop. Dressed like that, Edward actually seemed handsome. I guess I had simply never noticed. I had been too busy looking at Will, just like I was doing now. I was trying so hard not to stare at Will, but I couldn't help it. I couldn't help but remember what I'd heard that night. I tried to shake the thought, but it continued to hover in my mind.

"Hey guys! What are you doing here?" I asked. I tried to sound casual, but it came out a bit squeaky.

"We came to see if you wanted to get breakfast with us," Will said.

Our eyes met, I could see him trying to figure out why I was acting so strange. That color blue looked absolutely dazzling on him. His blue eyes sparkled in a mesmerizing way.

"We would love to," I said, looking away.

"Great. Can we go now? I'm starving!" Oliver whined. I elbowed him in the ribs.

"Hey," he said. I could tell he was trying to sound hurt, but the smile he failed to suppress gave him away.

"Follow us," Edward said.

I stayed by Oliver's side as we walked. Honestly, I felt like it was the best thing to do. I felt awkward standing next to Will with what I had overheard. I was worried Edward suspected me of something. There was a lot of stuff I was holding from everyone: My plan to save my parents, my encounter with Kilmar, my feelings for Will, and the fact that I knew Will had feelings for me. So, he had a lot to suspect me of.

Oliver made me feel safe. I guess that's what it's supposed

to be like with older siblings. When you need someone to talk to, but you feel like no one else will understand, they listen. Sometimes you feel like you just need a hug or a shoulder to cry on, and an older sibling will be there to hold you while you cry. When you get into fights, they'll be right there to fight alongside you. You may argue with each other, but you'll always make up, because you can't stay mad at each other.

I found myself feeling sorry that I'd missed growing up with a brother. Then I looked at him, and I saw that I could still get to experience that. At least until I had to leave. I'd already established a connection with him.

As we walked, our hands gently brushed each other's. After a few steps he intertwined his fingers with mine. I smiled and gave his hand a soft squeeze. We walked like that for a while, hand in hand, neither one of us wanting to end the quiet sibling moment. Then Will slowed his pace until we were right beside each other. Oliver immediately let go and moved a few feet ahead so that he was beside Edward.

I wondered if he knew about Will's feelings for me. Was it that obvious? I had an even scarier thought. What if he knew about my feelings for Will? Whatever the case was, I was not eager to be left alone with Will.

I looked at Oliver pleadingly. Our eyes met and we seemed to have a silent conversation. It went something like this:

Please don't go.

Sorry, you're on your own.

Don't leave me alone with him!

You'll be fine.

Please....

Then he walked up beside Edward to give us some space.

Great, I thought. *Just great.*

"I just thought you should know, the fairies are vegetarians. They firmly believe that all life is important. So just be careful what you say about the food," Will warned me.

He didn't look at me as he spoke, which I was grateful for. I was worried if he looked at me, he would see right through all the walls I had put up around my heart and catch a glimpse of those feelings I had buried deep within the darkest crevices of my heart.

"So don't talk about meat. Got it. Thanks for the tip," I said. I tried to offer a smile and make my voice sound light. However, my smile faded, and my voice was a little too serious.

"What's wrong?" he asked. This time he looked straight at me. I could see his eyes searching my face for signs of what was wrong.

"Nothing," I lied. "I just didn't sleep well is all."

I held my breath as I waited for Will to say something.

"That makes sense. You've had a rough three weeks," he finally said. The last two words caught my attention. Three weeks. Has it really been three weeks? Had my parents been stuck with Kilmar for three whole weeks? Panic settled into me, making my chest tighten. They had been stuck for three weeks and here I was about to go have a casual breakfast with my new brother and friends. I felt stupid and selfish.

I knew I couldn't wait any longer. There was no way I could sit at that table and eat while knowing how long my parents had been stuck with Kilmar. I needed to get to them as soon as possible.

"I–um forgot something back at the hut," I said. "You guys go ahead. I'll meet up with you when I get back."

I didn't even wait to see if they believed my excuse or not. I didn't care anyway. All I cared about was getting to my parents. I turned and ran at full speed back towards the hut. As I ran, I thought about everything I was leaving behind. Oliver, Will, and even Edward had all become like family to me. Well, Oliver really was my family. Still, I was determined not to lose any of them, or my parents. If protecting them meant giving my life, I would do it in a heartbeat. I hoped it wouldn't come to that, but if it did, I would.

As I ran, all my fear and panic was replaced by a sort of numb determination. The only thing I felt was my desire to get to where I needed to go. I had to run across so many bridges and platforms that when I finally made it to the hut, I was out of breath. My throat was dry from running. My heart thumped madly in my chest. I rubbed my side where it was sore from running.

After standing outside the door to catch my breath, I hurried inside the hut. I absently shut the door behind me without bothering to lock it. Then I set to work, trying to open a portal to Dread.

TWENTY-TWO

Edward said I needed to focus on my fear. He'd said that Kilmar fed off fear. The only problem was that I felt numb inside. I tried to think of things that scared me. I imagined spiders, heights, drowning, scorpions. None of them could spur me. Maybe those things weren't strong enough. I knew one thing that scared me most: losing the people I loved.

I remembered how it felt to watch Oliver be stabbed by the scorpion. I imagined the blank look in Oliver's eyes. I thought I'd lost him forever.

Then, I imagined the portal opening in front of me. I felt a small tug in my gut. A very small portal opened. It began to close almost instantly. I needed stronger emotions. I thought of my parents, and the fact that they could be dead because of me. The portal opened again, bigger this time. It still started to close, although it closed slower.

I scrambled to think of something that scared me more than anything else. Unfortunately, that was when Will walked through the door. His jaw dropped and his eyes grew wide.

"Celeste? What are you doing?" he asked.

Standing there, looking at him, I realized what scared me the most, and that was losing him. With that startling realization, I was thrown out of my numbness. All the pain, loss, and guilt came crashing back on me.

I found it hard to get words past the lump that had formed in my throat. I saw the portal grow larger and stabilize, but I couldn't make myself move. I couldn't make myself leave him just yet.

"I have to do this alone," I choked out. Tears burned like fire in my eyes.

"No, you don't. Oliver, Edward, and me, we can all help you if you let us," he said.

Why did they have to keep saying that? Couldn't they see that I was doing this to protect them? I couldn't do that if they wouldn't let me do this alone. Oliver had asked me not to carry the burden of guilt by myself. Fine, he could help me with that burden, but this one, this one I had to carry alone.

Will hadn't moved since he'd arrived, but suddenly, he reached out for my hands. I recoiled and he stopped.

"You don't understand," I sobbed through the tears that were now streaming down my cheeks.

"Then help me understand," he said gently.

"I can't let Kilmar hurt anyone else I love," I cried. I struggled to hold open the portal as I looked at Will. I let the L word slip. He caught on to it.

"Do you love me?" Will asked sincerely.

I turned away. How could I answer that? I did, didn't I? I wanted to tell him. I wanted to tell him how much he meant to me, that I couldn't imagine my life without him, that when I looked to my uncertain future, he was always there.

"I care about you, Will, and I don't want you to get hurt."

I knew it wasn't the answer he was looking for. It wasn't the answer I wanted to give either. But I did love him, right? If I told him that, there was no way he would ever let me leave.

"Celeste, please," Will begged, "don't go."

His voice cracked. If I had the heart to look him in the eyes, I imagine I would have seen fresh tears slipping down his cheeks. My own tears made my vision blurry as I turned back toward the portal. I didn't struggle to keep it open. I had all the fear I needed surging through my heart.

"Goodbye, Will," I whispered as I dove through the portal. The words were so quiet that I wasn't sure he could hear them. They held a sense of finality to them, the kind that breaks you inside.

On the other side, I landed on a cold stone surface. I tumbled across it until I came to a stop. I looked up to find that I was in a dark wasteland. Black mountains towered over me; their shadows were as dark as the dark side of the moon. There was hardly any light, only a faint glow coming from one of the valleys. I could still see, but only barely. I figured that the source of the light was probably where I needed to go, but I wasn't sure I had the strength to move on.

The reality of my situation hit me like a freight train. I was alone, in a desolate shadowy dimension, where an evil king awaited with my parents. I'd just left the only boy I had ever had a crush on, my brother, my friends, and the fairies behind. I wrapped my arms around myself and cried. I fell to my knees as sobs shook my body. I felt selfish for crying. I needed to keep going and get to my parents, but I couldn't stop the tears.

I couldn't have been there for even a minute, before someone spoke behind me.

"Celeste?" said the voice. I instantly recognized that voice.

"Will?" I cried as I stood and turned to face him. He stood about two yards away from me, his perfect face set with determination.

Seeing him should have made me feel better, but it didn't. It just gave me one more thing that I could lose.

"I told you not to come!" I shouted at him.

His eyes grew wide at my sudden outburst. Then he did something that surprised me. He smiled and came closer. Tears still slid down my cheeks as I watched him take slow strides towards me.

"You also told me you cared about me," he said.

He stopped about two feet away from me. I couldn't find the strength to speak, so I didn't respond. Will stepped even closer and took my hand. I didn't recoil at his touch. Instead, I looked him in the eyes, those big, beautiful sapphire blue eyes.

"I couldn't let you go without letting you know that I care about you too," he said.

This shouldn't have surprised me, since I already knew he had feelings for me. However, his words still lit a fire in my heart that had long since begun to sputter out. That fire seemed to dry my tears. It gave me the courage to speak.

"I won't make you leave, but I need you to promise me something," I said, still gripping his hand like a lifeline.

"Anything," he said. There was something in his voice that made me blush, and it filled my stomach with butterflies.

"Promise me that no matter what happens to me, you'll get my parents out of there," I said. My voice was cold and solemn, so much so that I barely recognized it as my own.

"Why? What's going to happen to you?" Will said, clearly puzzled. He didn't know what I knew about Kilmar's plan. He didn't know we were walking into a trap. I didn't want to tell him.

"Just promise me!" I yelled at him.

"Okay, okay! I promise!" he said.

I could tell he knew that I was keeping something from him, but he didn't ask about it. I was grateful for that.

"Come on," I told him, "We need to hurry."

I'd made it to Dread, but I still needed to get to Kilmar. That was about as far as my plan went. I had no idea what would happen when I finally made it to Kilmar. I had no idea what could possibly be waiting for me. I decided to put it out of my mind until we got to Kilmar. For the moment, I needed to focus on climbing down this dark mountain.

I had been naive enough to think that climbing down the mountain would be easy, since going downhill was always easier. I couldn't have been more wrong. It was more of a cliff than a mountain. We had to make our way along a path that couldn't have been more than a foot wide. The edge of it dropped off into a dark, pitch-black abyss.

The rock that made up the mountain was so rough and sharp that it dug into my hand when I gripped it, cutting into my palms. In other places it was so smooth that I could barely hold on. It was also very dark. I could barely see a few feet in front of me.

At one point, the path narrowed out even more. I put my foot out thinking that there would be solid ground there, but there was only air. I fell forward, and I would have slipped into the darkness if Will hadn't caught me. As much as I hadn't wanted him to come, at that moment, I was relieved that he had.

"Th-thanks," I mumbled as I stared down into the darkness. A shiver ran down my spine. I had a feeling if I fell, I would never hit the bottom, I would just continue falling forever.

"Don't mention it," he said brightly. His cheerful tone seemed so out of place in the darkness of Dread.

He flashed a confident smile that made my cheeks burn. Butterflies took flight, fluttering around in my stomach. I had missed feeling that way. That terrible fear of losing the people I loved had clouded my mind like a black fog, shrouding the love I had been feeling for Will. Now, that fear was still there, but not because I was going to lose them. No matter what it took, I would save them. Even if it meant I might get myself killed. I had known going into this that there was a chance I could die. I had made my peace with it.

I stood up, slightly embarrassed, but thanks to Will uninjured. I dusted myself off, although I couldn't even see if there was dirt on me or not because of how dark it was. At least that meant Will couldn't see my cheeks flushing.

As we got farther down the mountain, the path started to slope. At first it was barely noticeable. Just a slight incline and smoother rock. Gradually though, the incline grew sharper. I grasped the rocky wall behind me, searching for a handhold. I could hear Will doing the same.

"How long do you think it will be before it gets too steep?" Will asked, mirroring my own fears.

I was about to answer back that I had no idea, when my feet slipped out from under me.

"Will!" I screamed as I slid down the slope.

Will cried out behind me as he slipped too.

"Try to stop!" he yelled back.

I tried using my legs to stop, but the stone was too smooth. I reached out to touch the wall, but I could only find air. It grew so dark that I couldn't see anything.

"I can't!" I cried.

Intense fear surged through me as I slid downward uncontrollably. There weren't even any turns or hills, it was just this intense falling and sliding sensation. I hated that feeling. Between falling from the portal in the sky, to the slide in the forest, and now this, I was really tired of falling.

I was afraid our little horror ride might go on forever. It didn't though. It started to even out, only slightly at first. Then gradually, the ride became less steep. My heart hammered in my chest as I waited for it to level out completely.

I started to see light up ahead. It started off as a faint, little dot in the distance. However, as I came closer, it grew bigger and brighter. It reminded me of the dream I'd had the night before. The one where I was being pulled toward the light.

"Am I the only one seeing the light?" Will yelled. He was very close to me now, based on how loud his voice was. There was no need to yell, but I didn't tell him that. I wasn't in a joking mood. I knew what that light meant. I was getting closer to Kilmar and closer to saving my parents.

"Oh, I see it alright," I said. There wasn't a bit of sarcasm or amusement in my voice as I spoke. I didn't try to mask my fear behind a joke or fake happiness. I didn't want to be fake with Will.

Suddenly, there was a burst of light on either side of me. Torches mounted to the walls of a hallway-sized cavern blazed to life, seemingly on their own. It gave me chills.

As our stone slide ended, we slid across the stone floor until coming to a complete stop on the cavern floor. I grunted as Will ran into me.

"Sorry," he said, his cheeks turning bright red, "I couldn't stop."

"It's fine," I said as I stood, my cheeks burning as well.

At that moment, I wished it was still dark, so that he couldn't see how red my cheeks were.

Once we had both regained our bearings, I decided we needed to continue on.

"We need to follow the torches. They'll lead us to Kilmar," I told Will. I didn't know how I knew, I just had a feeling.

As we walked, Will's fingers brushed against mine, sending tingles through my hand. I intertwined my hands with his. For so long, I had wanted to do that. Now, I finally felt as if I could. This was so much different than holding Oliver's hand. Will's hands were strong and comfortable. My hand fit perfectly in his, as if it was meant to be there.

I knew then that I needed to tell him I loved him, before it was too late, but I was afraid he wouldn't feel the same, which was stupid since I had heard him confess that he cared about me. Still, what if he changed his mind? I was so scared of being rejected. I was also kind of hoping he would say he loved me first. That would give me a fantastic opportunity to share my feelings.

As we walked, my focus shifted from our entwined hands to the torches that blazed on the walls. Something about the torches seemed odd to me. As we passed by, the flames would erupt from the top and then they died down once we were farther away.

"That is so freaky," Will muttered beside me.

"It is," I agreed.

I wondered if Kilmar was controlling this dimension. It was strange how the path hadn't changed until just after Will had spoken of it. Then, there were the torches. Kilmar was the King of Shadows, so he probably hated light. He wanted me to come, and I needed light to see where I was going. Maybe he was providing me with as little light as possible to give me just enough to see where to go.

"What are you thinking about?" Will asked as we walked. I jumped, startled from my thoughts.

"A lot of things. Why do you ask?" I replied.

I wished I had a book on how to explain how to play chess—preferably the kind that had "For Dummies" in the title, because that is what I felt like. I was a huge dummy playing Kilmar's little game. His game was like chess in a way. You had to make sacrifices to win. I felt like I was the pawn, and the pawns usually died.

"You always get this far away look in your eyes. You look like you're bearing the weight of the world on your shoulders," he said. I didn't look at him. I looked at my feet instead.

"I kind of am," I said. "It's on me to defeat Kilmar."

"You don't have to do it alone," he said.

He stopped and turned to face me. I looked up from my feet to see his handsome face full of an emotion that I couldn't quite read. Was that pride, or maybe determination? Or something more?

"You're right," I said, trying to believe the words, "I have you."

I looked back down at my feet, letting go of his hand. My hands felt so out of place by my side instead of in his hand. I just couldn't bring myself to hold his hand again. I hated keeping so much from him now that I understood how I felt about him. He deserved to know that we were walking into a trap, but I was worried he might try to talk me out of it. I couldn't let that happen.

"What are you not telling me?" Will asked.

I sighed and frowned at my feet, since that was all I could bring myself to look at.

This was it. I wasn't going to lie to him anymore.

"It's a trap," I said, my voice barely a whisper.

"What do you mean?" he whispered back.

"He wanted me to come," I said, my voice still quiet. "My parents are the bait."

"That's why you made me promise to save them," Will guessed. I nodded.

"It's okay," Will said.

He pulled me into a hug. I let my head settle on his shoulder and willed his words to be true. I had grown to love his hugs, even if the cause of them was usually not happy. I loved the feeling of his strong, reassuring arms holding me. I loved his hugs, and I loved him.

"Thank you for coming with me. I know I tried to push you away, and I didn't tell you everything. I'm sorry. I thought I had to do this alone, but you're right, I don't," I muttered in his ear. I knew there were still some things I would have to do alone, but I wasn't completely on my own.

"What does Kilmar want from you?" Will asked.

"My powers. Halflings took his so he wants to take mine," I replied, my voice shaky. "It's the only way he can get his power back."

I heard a sharp intake of breath from Will. I lifted my head off his shoulder and pulled back to look at him.

"I was told that the halflings helped Kilmar. The ancient Arbitrators made the halflings out to be bad guys. Why wouldn't the Convocation have told us the truth?" Will said, his eyes wide.

"The Convocation doesn't tell you a lot of things," I muttered bitterly. They hadn't told him why they needed me.

They hadn't told him they planned on taking my powers. They hadn't told Will that they would be completely uprooting my life by bringing me to Enceaf. I couldn't help but remember how they treated me. They lied a lot.

"We're going to defeat Kilmar. Then we'll let all of the Arbitrators know what really happened," Will said. His initial shock seemed to be replaced by sheer determination.

"Thanks. We really should keep going," I told him.

He nodded in agreement. I turned to face the darkness. After taking a deep breath, I stepped forward, expecting the next torches to blaze to life ahead of me, but they didn't. Instead, the torches went out completely, engulfing me in darkness.

Fear made a cold chill run down my spine. I started to think that the darkness would last forever.

Then, the next torches blazed to life in front of me. I gasped when their light illuminated a large black gate. It was only half the size of Enceaf's, but still quite large. The gate seemed to be made of a shiny black rock. It was the same rock the rest of this awful place was made of. Two large braziers blazed with fire at the top of the gate. This wasn't the same fire that was currently providing the room with light. This fire was inky black. The flames danced like shadows. I wondered if that was what they really were. It was the shadow dimension, so it made sense. What didn't make sense was the fact that it still enabled me to see. I could see perfectly fine. In fact, I could make out every detail of the large gate.

The pattern on the gate filled me with terror. It was made of a series of irregular shapes all following a circular pattern.

A spider web, I realized.

That wasn't the scariest part though. Carved into the middle of the spiderweb was something that made my blood run cold. A looming figure was carved into it. Claws reached out from it, and sharp teeth hung from its mouth. Its eyes were the only thing with color. They were dark red. I guessed they were made of rubies.

I knew that figure all too well. It was Kilmar.

"That thing is so creepy," Will said.

I looked over at him. He wrinkled his nose at the gate. Will, sweet, innocent Will. I smiled at him. Despite the fact that I had tried my hardest to push my love for him away, he still managed to make me love him. Somehow, he had nudged his way past the walls I had built around my heart, so that he could have a piece of it that was completely his.

This warm, lovey-doviness was suddenly replaced by a cold chill that ran down my spine. The temperature of the air around us dropped drastically. It was so cold that I could see the cloud of mist from my breath.

"Something is wrong," I said, not even trying to mask my panic.

"You think?" Will said sarcastically.

"Now is not the time for sarcasm!" I told him sternly.

"It's always the time for sarcasm!" he retorted.

I tried to glare at him, but my frown melted at the sight of his face. A slight smile tugged at the corners of my mouth despite my efforts to contain it.

How weird was that? I was sure there was something wrong or that we were possibly about to die, yet I still couldn't help but smile at him.

I rubbed my hands against my arms, my fingertips sliding across the goosebumps that had appeared. Although I couldn't tell if it was from fear or the cold, I shivered. Will wrapped an arm around me. It didn't really help, but it felt nice to have him so close. It also felt kind of weird.

Our relationship or whatever this was had moved very fast. I mean, we hadn't even admitted to each other that we loved each other. We had skirted around the edges of it, but we hadn't actually taken that leap yet. I wasn't even sure if we were more than friends yet.

He definitely treated me like more than a friend, but he wasn't even my boyfriend yet. We had never made it official. He was just someone I cared about and really liked being around, someone I loved. Wasn't that the definition of a boyfriend? I groaned internally. Why did this have to be so complicated?

My internal strife was interrupted when the torches flickered. I stiffened as I watched them. The flickering was not bad at first, but then it got worse. The flickering turned to sputtering. The fire on the torches continued to fade until the torches' light diminished completely.

Suddenly, something pushed me away from Will. I felt his arm drop away from my shoulders. I stumbled alone in the darkness, crying out for Will. It didn't matter how many times I cried his name, or how many times I screamed. There wasn't an answer.

I screamed until my throat was raw and my voice was barely audible anymore. I felt hopeless and helpless.

Then I remembered something: I could make light.

Wow, I am so stupid. I thought.

Here I was wasting my time wandering aimlessly through the pitch black, utter darkness, when this entire time, I could create my own light.

I didn't care what color light I made; I just wanted to do whatever was easiest. I focused on an emotion that had become very easy to feel: Anger.

I focused on how angry I was at Kilmar for taking my

parents. I was also still angry at Johnny for how terrible he'd treated me in school. Honestly, I was a little angry with Will for following me after I specifically told him not to. That didn't really make sense since I loved being with him.

Whatever, it gave me more to fuel the flame that was burning inside my heart, growing larger and larger with every passing second. Suddenly, I glowed bright red, illuminating the cavern. Except, it wasn't the cavern anymore. I was in a vast coliseum. Unlike the traditional ones in Rome, this one was made of black stone. Shadow monsters like the scorpion and demons like the one I had encountered on my way to Enceaf, occupied the seats. They reminded me of passionate fans, waiting anxiously for a game to start. They cheered and pumped their fists in the air, shouting the name that had occupied my nightmares: Kilmar.

I looked for Will, but I could not find him. I started to panic.

Then I saw them. On the opposite side of the arena, in a cage made of what appeared to be shadows, there were three people: Will, Mom, and Dad.

TWENTY-THREE

T ears welled in my eyes as we stared at each other in shock. My parents each had a few scratches and bruises on their faces, but otherwise they seemed to be okay. I wanted to see them so badly.

I started running towards them, my vision blurred by tears and my heart overwhelmed by emotions. My glow faded as my anger was washed away completely. I was halfway there when they started waving and shouting at me. I slowed my pace, but only slightly. Their cries seemed muffled, which should have seemed weird to me. However, I was so happy to see them that I didn't let it deter me.

That was a mistake. As I picked up my speed again, I ran into something hard. My chest burned and I felt like there was fire, burning through my bones. I was thrown backwards with such force that I tumbled across the ground. My arms and legs twitched uncontrollably, and my body seized. I recognized this pain. The same thing happened when I touched the forcefield in Enceaf. I realized it must've been an invisible forcefield.

I could hear Will and my parents calling my name. Everything hurt, and their voices were so far away. The pain had stopped with the forcefield in Enceaf. This pain sunk deeper though. It sank deep into my bones. My mind grew hazy from pain and consciousness began to float away from me. I remembered how the darkness could numb me, numb all the pain. I wanted to sink back into it as I had done before.

Then there was a voice I didn't quite recognize. It spoke so softly I could barely hear it. Then it grew louder.

Celeste, the voice said. It was deep, but not gruff. *You can do this. Don't give in to the shadows.*

Shadows? Was that why the pain felt different? I decided it didn't matter. I just wanted the pain to go away.

I tried. I really did. I just can't do it. I thought.

I slammed my eyes shut as if I could block out the voice, but I couldn't.

The voice pushed on. *Your mother and I believe in you.*

My brain was foggy, so it took me a moment to realize who the voice belonged to. Tears welled up in my eyes when I finally did.

Dad?

It's me.

Those two words alone gave me the strength to fight the shadows. A new emotion filled me. One I had never experienced that strongly before. This new emotion swelled inside my heart, driving out the shadows that had buried themselves within me. I felt like there was a heavy weight on my chest that had been lifted off me by the strength of this emotion.

I opened my eyes, and my entire body was glowing. I could feel the power surging through me, returning my strength. Light started swirling around me. There wasn't any color to describe it. It was simply pure, powerful light. It was every color and no color at all at the same time. I felt it lift me up, then my feet left the ground. I floated higher and higher, the lights forming a swirling cyclone around me.

"Kilmar!" I cried. My voice didn't sound like mine. It boomed, echoing throughout the colosseum. It was deep and menacing.

A dark tornado of shadows appeared before me. Its swirl slowly faded away to reveal Kilmar. He was hovering maybe two feet off the ground. He was much bigger than me. Kilmar was at least half the height of the coliseum, and the coliseum was massive. I couldn't see his feet. A cloak of shadows covered his body, and a hood covered his face. I could only see his eyes. Those terrible glowing red eyes.

"So, you've come to try and defeat me?"

"I came for my family, but killing you would be a plus," I said. I meant it as a joke, but my booming voice echoed throughout the coliseum cancelled out some of the funniness.

Despite my booming voice, I was terrified. Was I really doing this? Was I actually challenging Kilmar to fight? Even though I had been through so much since my fight with Johnny, I was still that same girl. I still didn't know how to back down from a fight.

The lines of the prophecy echoed in my mind:

Powers great and strong,

Will battle for right and wrong.

The greater force will win, with great sacrifice to end.

I prayed with all my heart that I would be the greater force and that I would be the one to win. Even if that meant making a great sacrifice.

"They are free to go," Kilmar said.

With a wave of his hand the shadow prison disappeared. My parents and Will stood there gazing at me. I suppose my swirling light cyclone could have been what was leaving them speechless. Or maybe it was the fact that I had just called them my family, all of them, including Will. That's what he was to me.

I looked at Will, tears welling up in my eyes. As much as it hurt, it was time for them to leave.

"Get my parents out of here, Will. Promise me you'll keep them safe," I said.

I fought back the tears that threatened to spill onto my cheeks. I didn't want them to see me crying.

"We're not leaving," Dad said. I felt a surge of appreciation for Dad. He was willing to stay here and risk his own life to protect me. I loved him for that, but why did he have to be so difficult? Couldn't he see that I was trying to save them?

"Take them to Sproot," I told Will. Then, to all of them, I added, "I love you guys. Tell Oliver I love him."

I heard my parents gasp. My mom muttered Oliver's name and covered her mouth. Dad wrapped his arms around her. They both seemed happy and shocked to hear the name of their long-lost son.

I hoped this wouldn't be the last time I saw Will. Just in case it was, there was something I couldn't let him leave without doing.

I let my cyclone diminish enough so that I could get close to Will. He reached up and caressed my cheek. I just couldn't help myself. I pulled him in and kissed him. It wasn't a big slobbery kiss like you see in human movies. It was just a simple kiss. It was the kind that that leaves a bit of warmth on your lips and a special something in your heart.

As I pulled away, he whispered three words into my ears.

"I love you."

"I love you too," I whispered back. "Go, now."

A portal appeared behind them.

I turned away, not wanting to see their faces as they left. Kilmar laughed maniacally. Then he turned to my family.

"Leaving so soon?" someone said. It had come from somewhere behind Kilmar.

The voice sounded familiar somehow, but I couldn't quite place it. I gasped as someone stepped out from behind Kilmar. My parents cried out in shock. Will, sweet Will stood there dumb founded. Even the monsters in the stand quit their grumbling and started shushing each other, as if they had come to watch a show and it had just begun.

"Edward?" I cried.

"Finally! Do you have any idea how long I've been waiting for this? For weeks I've kept up this charade of being your friend, Celeste," he said. He wrinkled his nose as if he were smelling something awful. I gaped at him, horrified.

"Why-how-what?" I stammered. I searched my memories looking for any signs I had missed. I remembered my last night in Sproot. When I asked him how to get to Dread, he knew exactly how to get here. That didn't seem suspicious at the time. How could I not have noticed?

"So, this is what the prophecy meant," I muttered to myself.

I remembered the words of the prophecy:

Betrayal of the light,

They'll be stuck in a plight.

Edward was the betrayer. I should have seen the signs. I should have paid closer attention.

"Yes, Edward has been watching you, Celeste. All this time he had been helping me, telling me where you were and what you were doing," Kilmar beamed. "He betrayed you."

Kilmar smiled. This wasn't just his fault. It was Edward's too. I recalled the shadow scorpion. It had come out of nowhere, and it had almost killed Oliver. If it wasn't for Grimes and the fairies, he would have died. Anger flared inside me, weakening my cyclone.

I opened my mouth to yell a whole lot of words that my mom would have washed my mouth out with soap for saying, but Will spoke before I could say anything.

"Were you ever really my friend?" Will asked.

I turned around to look at Will, who was supposed to have left already. He didn't look at me, only Edward. Edward's expression softened at Will's sorrowful words. His mouth moved as if he wanted to say something. He must have never found the right words. Instead Kilmar spoke for him.

"Of course not!" He boomed. "He has no friends."

Edward looked away. I thought he was going to cry.

"I've always been your friend, I never wanted to hurt you," he said solemnly.

For a moment I believed him. He was a victim too because his mind was being poisoned by Kilmar's words.

Then his face twisted into a sneer. Suddenly, he burst out laughing. He laughed hysterically, doubling over from it. When he finally composed himself, he wiped away a fake tear.

"Sorry, I just couldn't pretend that I actually cared about

any of you anymore. No Will. I was never your friend. I only pretended to befriend you once I knew you had contacted the halfling," he said.

His face was full of pride. He was proud of all the horrible things he'd done. I couldn't believe it.

I looked over at Will, who was looking down at his feet, clearly hurt. The anger clouded my mind. Edward had been the reason Oliver got hurt. He was the reason my parents were taken prisoner, and he had hurt Will. I was tired of him hurting the people I loved. The more I thought about it, the angrier I got. My cyclone faded away, the love I had felt before was now consumed by anger. My feet touched back to the ground, and I was left standing there with my fists clenched, teeth gritted, and glowing bright red.

Celeste, calm down. You can't beat him with your anger. I heard my father's voice in my head again.

I jumped. It was really weirding me out that he was talking to me in my head.

Sorry. I didn't mean to scare you.

It's alright, I thought. Then I thought to him, *How do you even do this? How can you talk to me in my mind?*

I'm a telepath…..but that's not important. You need to do whatever you did earlier. It's the only way to defeat Kilmar. He replied in my mind.

I let my glow fade, bottling up my anger and saving it for later. Then, I turned to look at him, trying to read his expression.

Don't look at me! He shouted in my mind.

I flinched from the volume of his voice. I snapped my head back to Kilmar and Edward.

He can't know I'm talking to you, otherwise you'd lose the element of surprise. He said a bit more softly.

I thought it was so creepy the way he just talked to me in my mind. His voice was so loud too. I felt like he was screaming at my brain. Even when he spoke more softly, my skull felt like it was vibrating.

I don't really know how I did that. I felt a really strong surge of love and it just sort of happened. I told him.

If he was expecting me to do that again, I wasn't sure I could. I was so angry with Edward for betraying us. I felt like an idiot. He didn't just hurt me; he hurt Will too. Messing with me was one thing, but messing with someone I love was another. I wasn't really feeling the love. That was a problem since I needed love to fuel the cyclone thing I did earlier. Also, there was another problem. Since my cyclone and glow had been extinguished, I was starting to realize how much it had drained me. I was so tired. My limbs felt like lead. Even if I could figure out how to do it, I wasn't sure I would have the energy to do it again. I was stuck between a rock and a hard place.

I need you to try, Dad urged me.

I bit my lips, unsure of what to do. I didn't want to tell him I could do it, because I was pretty sure I couldn't. That wasn't what he was asking. He only asked me to try. I could do that. I could try—on one condition.

I promise I'll try, but you, Mom, and Will, need to leave. I told him.

I looked over at him. He shook his head. He barely moved it, but I could tell what he was trying to say. *No.*

"You've been awfully quiet over there Celeste," Kilmar pointed out.

My attention snapped back to him. Edward looked over at me. He glared at me, his skeptical gaze seeming to peer into my soul.

"I think it's time for my parents and Will to go," I said to him, not wanting to directly answer his question.

Edward frowned. Then I looked at Kilmar. Kilmar's eyes settled on me. They had a malicious gleam to them, as if he couldn't wait to take my powers.

"As I said, they are free to go," Kilmar said with a roll of his red eyes.

I glanced at Will.

"I'm not leaving you," he told me.

"You made me a promise," I reminded him. Something on his face changed. He seemed to realize that I would never let him stay.

He nodded and turned to Mom and Dad.

"We have to go," he told them. His voice was strong and sure, except for the part where it cracked. That sounded slightly less brave.

"No. I already left her once, I won't do it again," Dad said.

My mom's eyes were wet with tears as she looked at me. I walked over to them.

"What do you think you're doing?" cried Edward.

"Saying goodbye," I snapped without looking at him.

I kept my eyes on my parents. My voice was as steady as my heartbeat. Everything was silent as I made my way over. All I could hear was the steady thumping of my heart in my ears.

I had always wondered what to do or say if I ever met my dad again. Luckily, I knew exactly what to do. I wrapped my arms around him and gave him a huge bear hug. He squeezed me back. Then he reached out for my mom, pulling her in too.

He ran his hands through my hair, softly humming his song, the same one I had sung over and over again when no one was looking.

Songbird sing.

Songbird fly.

Songbird soaring through the night.

Songbird sing,

Songbird soar.

See the dawn rise once more.

Songbird sing.

Fly away.

Songbird bring a brand-new day.

I hummed along, letting the words sink into my heart like an anthem.

"You remember our song?" Dad asked.

I bit my lip, trying to find the right words to say. There was so much to say and so little time.

"I always thought you left because you didn't love us. I know now that's not true. For a while though, I wanted nothing to do with you, but mom and I still sang our song. I still had to keep part of you with me. I think deep down, I always knew you loved me. I guess it just took all of this for me to see it," I told him.

I put my head against his chest. I loved the safety and the comfort of his arms. I wondered if he would feel upset that I had said that. If he was, he sure did a good job of hiding it. He hugged even tighter.

I never realized how much I missed having a dad. I always thought I couldn't miss it because I never had one, and you can't miss something you never had. However, he was always with me. Every day of my life. He never left my heart.

As a kid, mom would take me out to eat sometimes. I remembered seeing all the other kids with their dads. I stared at them longingly, wishing I had a dad to fill the void in my heart that my own dad had created by leaving. I envied them for knowing the love of a father. Meanwhile, I had been oblivious to the love Dad showed for me every single day, by staying in Enceaf and keeping the Convocation away.

Mom pulled away from our little group hug first, wiping fresh tears off her cheek.

"Did you really find Oliver?" Mom asked.

Her voice was filled with fragile hope. She had been through so much already. She seemed so broken. I had never seen her this way before: shaky, uncertain, her shoulders slightly slumped. She had always been the strong one. This time it was my turn to be the strong one.

"I did. It's a long story, one that I don't have time to tell you right now," I said.

"I love you both," I said. I gave them one last hug.

Come back to us. Dad's voice whispered softly in my head.

I didn't even jump this time. It was as if he had said it extra softly this time. The words felt like slightly less than a whisper in my mind.

"I will," I said aloud.

Then I turned to Will. He took my hand, rubbing his thumb soothingly across its surface.

"I can't believe I finally kissed a boy, and it happened in this place," I told him. I laughed, half bitter, half disbelief.

"So, I'm your first kiss?" He asked sheepishly.

"Am I yours?" I asked, not quite willing to admit it just yet.

"Of course," he said. "You are by far the most special girl I have ever met. I know we haven't known each other for very long and we're really young, but we've been through so much together. I'd love the chance to call you my girlfriend."

My heart fluttered the same way it did when I first met him, except it didn't feel stupid this time. I felt like I had invisible wings wrapping around my heart, lifting me higher and higher. They lifted me up and away from the fear and the pain. Then those wings disappeared and dropped me with a painful thud back to the ground as I realized that I couldn't tell him yes.

"I know we have. I think you're an incredible guy. It's just...." I trailed off.

"Just what?" He pushed.

I could see the desperation in his eyes and hear the hurt in his voice. It was better for him to hurt now than to be broken later.

"I'm scared. What if I don't make it out of here? I know what it's like to lose the people you love. I can't put you through that kind of pain," I told him.

I turned away from him as tears started to well up in my eyes. I didn't want him to see me cry. Not again.

There's been too much crying already. I thought.

"Celeste, please—" he begged.

He grabbed my hand, sending tingles of warmth through it. As much as I needed that warmth in the cold darkness of Dread, I couldn't let him stay. I yanked my hand from his grip, and faced away from him.

"Please just leave," I pleaded.

"But you said you love me. You don't just leave the people you love. I'm staying," he insisted.

The hurt in his voice made my heart break. I just needed him to leave already.

"I was wrong. I-I didn't mean it," I lied. "I don't love you."

It pained me so much to say those words. By the look on Will's face, I could tell it hurt him more. I hated hurting him. However, hurt was better than dead. I couldn't keep from hurting him, but I could keep him alive.

"You don't really feel that way. You can't," he pleaded.

He was making this so difficult.

"Just go!" I spat back at him.

Out of the corner of my eye, I saw him bow his head, shaking it in defeat. Then there was the sound of shuffling feet as they went through the portal. After that I heard nothing but the resumed muttering of the monsters. I instantly regretted my words. I hated leaving things like that with Will. I felt so stupid. Shame made my face burn red. At least he and my parents would be okay. That was what mattered most.

TWENTY-FOUR

"**F**inally!" whined Edward. "I almost barfed watching your stupid little goodbye."

I clenched my fists as the shame on my face turned to fiery rage.

"No, don't go! Please, I love you!" he said mockingly. He spoke in a high squeaky voice that I knew was meant to be an imitation of me.

His words made the fiery rage turn into an inferno. Here I was trying to say a heartfelt goodbye and Edward was making fun of me for it. I hated him. I hated Kilmar. I hated this whole freaking dimension.

"At least I actually have people that care about me!" I screamed back at him.

He recoiled and looked at me like I was a monster. I knew that look well because I looked at him the same way. My words disgusted him. So that was his weak spot, having no one that cared about him.

After glancing back at Kilmar, he straightened up, holding his head a little higher as he spoke. He was trying not to let me get to him. However, I had already gotten in his head. He was just as angry with me as I was with him.

"You think you know everything about me, don't you?" he growled in a cold and bitter voice.

"After my powers came, there wasn't anyone left who cared about me," he said.

He looked off into the distance, and his face turned sour with a frown.

"You said you didn't have any," I pointed out.

I was so confused. He had told me in Sproot that he didn't have any powers. He seemed so genuinely upset by my asking about it that I didn't think he was lying. However, all this time I had thought he was my friend too. He had been lying about that, and I had still believed him. I guess it was possible he had lied about having powers too.

"That's what I told my parents. My powers were so frightening that I was afraid of what they would say if they found out. So, I made sure they didn't find out," he said.

I stared at him, appalled by his words. How could he pretend to lose something that was so important in the eyes of the Arbitrators?

"Why would you hide your powers? I know they're scary at first, but it gets easier," I told him.

I was beginning to understand why he was so bitter. He had probably been looked down on his whole life. I knew that power was something the Arbitrators valued. It was also something they feared. If you had power, you were accepted. If you had no power, you were scorned. If you had too much power, you had to be eliminated. I had learned the last one the hard way.

"You just don't get it do you?" he growled.

"No, I don't," I snapped.

I was so frustrated with him. I was fighting so hard to control the anger boiling inside me. I tried to hush the fearful whispers that were hidden below the surface of my heart. Something in my gut warned me that something bad was going to happen. I didn't listen. I couldn't listen. If I did, I would probably end up screaming like a sissy and running out as fast as my legs could carry me.

"Do you have any idea what it's like to know you have to either be feared or looked down on for the rest of your life?"

"When I came to Enceaf the Convocation was terrified of me. They looked down on me because they feared me. They literally tried to kill me because they knew that I was more powerful than all of them. So yes, Edward, I do know how it feels," I said.

Throughout the crowd of shadow monsters and demons, I heard a chorus of mutters.

"Ooooooo!"

"Burn!"

"Dang!"

There were a few other words in the mix that I didn't understand. However, they sounded very similar to some human words that I would have gotten in a lot of trouble for uttering.

I wondered if it was possible for them to learn human cuss words. I guess they had somehow managed to learn some human slang, even if it was a bit out of date.

Edward's face turned bright red. It was clear that he was embarrassed. I watched as his shame turned to anger. He clenched his fists. Wisps of shadows curled around his hands.

The temperature in the room dropped. My ears popped from the sudden change in air pressure.

I shrank away, as intense fear had overtaken me. Fear that I couldn't explain. I knew I shouldn't be afraid. I had faced far scarier things than this. He was just a teenage boy. I knew I could handle him. Yet, I couldn't shake the breathtaking, blood chilling fear.

"I think it's time for me to show you my powers," he said. He gritted his teeth like he was in pain or under strain.

I wondered if his powers drained him the same way mine drained me. I didn't have too much time to dwell on the thought.

He thrust his hands towards me and two beams of shadows shot like missiles at me. I dodged the first one, but the second nailed me in the chest. I cried out as sharp pain shot through my chest. I collapsed to the ground. I felt like someone had just driven a knife into my chest.

Edward twisted his hands and just like that the pain got a whole lot worse. I felt like he was twisting the imaginary knife he had just driven into me. I screamed a bloodcurdling scream of pure agony. My cries echoed throughout the colosseum, and everything went silent.

"You want to say something else or have you had enough?" he roared.

I tried to get up.

"Clearly you haven't learned your lesson," he sneered.

He shot another shadow missile at me. It nailed me in the shoulder this time. I crumpled back to the ground, screaming in pain.

I looked up at him. Pain made the world hazy. I struggled to keep my head up as my eyelids grew heavy.

"Enough!" Boomed Kilmar.

He took his mangled, claw-like hands and grabbed Edward by the neck. Edward grabbed at Kilmar's hands, but they wouldn't budge. He gagged and made a series of muffled grunts that were probably meant to be words.

"I need her alive!" Kilmar barked. "If you kill her, I will kill you. Then I will make an example out of you for anyone else who dares to defy me. Do you understand?"

With his airway cut off he couldn't reply. He struggled through a nod. Kilmar released his grip, and Edward collapsed to the floor. Edward coughed and gagged, rubbing his neck where it was red. With wide, crazy, bloodshot eyes he looked over at where I sat on my knees, struggling to stay upright.

"Get out of my sight," Kilmar grumbled.

"Yes, my King," Edward said shakily.

Then he scrambled out of the way. I watched as he ran toward a staircase at the bottom of the stands that led out of the coliseum.

What a coward. I thought.

Kilmar turned his attention back to me.

"Get up," he commanded.

"I can't," I whispered.

I knew he couldn't hear me in that loud coliseum with the crowd of demons and shadow monsters cheering and shouting at us.

I didn't really want to do anything Kilmar said. That wasn't why I didn't get up though. I simply didn't have the strength. I was physically in so much pain that I could barely lift my head. My chest ached. It felt like someone was poking me with a thousand tiny needles each time I moved.

Mentally, I was so tired of fighting for my life. Honestly, I was fine with not getting up ever again if that meant I didn't have to fight anymore. I was so tired of fighting, of being in pain, of always being afraid, of constantly being in danger, and watching the people I love get hurt. I was tired of being feared by the Convocation and of never getting a break. I was sick and tired of having all this pressure put on me to save the world.

Why should I fight to save a world that was filled with people who had done me wrong, people who had tried to kill me, people who had hurt me, and people who feared me? I thought bitterly.

Then I remembered something. I remembered why I had kept fighting, even when it was hard; even when it felt impossible to win. I was fighting for my family. I was fighting for the fairies, the pirates, even the humans. As much as I hated to admit it, I was fighting for the Arbitrators too. It wasn't all the Arbitrators' fault that the Convocation had treated me so harshly.

All of them would die if I gave up and let Kilmar take my powers. Their dimensions would be overrun by shadows and demons. There would be no light left in the world. There would be no joy, no love, no peace, and no life. It would be a barren waste land filled with shadows and dark, deadly terrains like Dread's.

If I gave in now, I would surely die. I thought of my family. What would they think if they knew I had let Kilmar win? Would they ever forgive me? It would leave them heartbroken if I died in vain. I'd fight Kilmar even if it killed me. When had I ever been the type to go down without a fight?

I clenched my fists and gritted my teeth. I struggled back to my feet, grunting in pain. Every muscle in my body ached.

The crowd cheered as I turned to face Kilmar.

"Ready to hand over your powers?" Kilmar asked.

"Nope. Not yet, but I'll make you a deal. If you beat me, you can have my powers," I told him through gritted teeth.

"Oh, come now. That's too easy," he snickered.

I chose to ignore his snarky, overconfident comment.

"However, if I win, then I get to kill you. Do you accept?" I replied. I tried to sound confident, while my voice trembled slightly.

"I accept your offer, Celeste Rowan. It will be a swift and easy victory," Kilmar boasted.

"I wouldn't be so sure," I muttered under my breath.

I was terrified of what I had just committed to. I had just sealed my own fate. The last line of the prophecy was about to be fulfilled.

The greater force will win, with great sacrifice to end.

This was going to end in a sacrifice. I hoped it wouldn't be my life I was sacrificing. Honestly, I wasn't very hopeful on that front. I didn't think I could beat Kilmar. That wasn't going to stop me from trying though. Sure, he was more powerful, bigger, and stronger. But I had something he didn't. I had my family. Although they weren't with me physically, they would never leave my heart. The thought of Will and the way I had left things with him, left me aching to get back to him. I wanted to set things right, and I could only do that if I beat Kilmar.

The more I thought about them, the more love swelled in my heart. I felt like a hot air balloon. The love filled me until I started to float off the ground, literally. I felt my feet lift off the ground. My body began to glow. I felt the pain in my chest and shoulder lessen until it didn't hurt at all. It was as if the pain and fear were ropes anchoring me to the ground, and they had just been cut by the unbreakable force of love. I was free.

I floated higher as I thought about all the love I had felt since I had started this crazy journey. My mind flashed back to when Will took me to the Convocation and revealed that Dad had been secretly protecting me and keeping me safe all these years. That was the first time that I realized Dad loved me. That was also the first time that I allowed myself to truly love him.

I recalled the healing tree in Sproot, when it showed me that Oliver was my brother. I never thought I could love someone so much, but I do. I love Oliver as much as you can possibly love a brother.

I thought of my mom, who had raised me for fourteen years alone, with the burden of her past weighing on her. All those nights she came home late and exhausted from work, but still made an effort to spend time with me. I loved her so much that I didn't think I could possibly love her more.

Then of course, there's Will. I had tried for so long to deny my feelings for him. I had so much going on with saving my parents and then Oliver almost died and then all the other crazy things that were happening. It just didn't seem like the right time to fall in love. Also, I thought it was impossible to fall in love with someone you hadn't known for very long. I thought that only happened in the princess movies I watched when I was little. Then I realized that I could love him, and that it didn't matter if I knew him for a day or for my entire life. I would love him anyway. He'd told me he loved me. I told him I loved him too. Then, I kissed him. And that kiss was the best kiss you could possibly have in a place like Dread.

Once I was sure I was ready, I called out to Kilmar.

"Let's finish this Kilmar!" I yelled.

"You think a little light will hurt me? You were a fool to challenge me!" he replied.

He turned to address the crowd of monsters and demons.

"Are you ready for a fight?" he cried.

He held his hand up to his hood where I imagined his ear

would be. The crowd erupted with cheers and applause. I felt like he was the ringleader of a circus, getting the crowd excited to watch him tame a wild beast.

His eyes were wild and crazy, like a madman's. Of course, he was one, so that checks out.

I willed the light to surge in front of me, forming a sphere of white light.

"You think a night light can hurt me?" he said with a booming laugh.

"Yes. I do," I said shortly.

I hurled the ball of light at him. It spun wickedly, and it grew bigger as it flew toward him. He stood there staring at it in horror. Then it slammed into his right leg. He fell to the ground with a thud, crying out in pain. His fiery red eyes turned angry as he grumbled and stood up.

I gasped. His hood had been thrown back to reveal his terrifying excuse for a face. For the first time, I got to see who he really was under the hood. His face was a void of shadowy darkness. He had no mouth, no nose, no ears, only glowing red eyes.

"I told you that nightlight wouldn't hurt me!" he cried.

The crowd cheered as their king stood pumping his clawlike fists in the air. They couldn't see the way he refused to put any weight on his right leg, but I saw it. A triumphant smile crawled across my face. I had injured him, not fatally, but a few more hits like that in the right places and it could become fatal.

"Now that you have shown me a taste of your power, perhaps it's time I give you a taste of mine," he called over the roaring crowd.

Before I could react, there was a mass of shadows flying toward me from all sides. I couldn't move; there was nowhere for me to go. I could only stand there until it slammed into me. I tumbled backwards, sliding across the floor from the force of the impact. My glow flickered for a moment as a terrifying fear tore through me. I had already felt this way once, when Edward's shadows hit me.

It isn't your fear that's scaring you. It's the shadows. You can't let them win, I told myself.

I thought about my family and everything I loved again. That was what would fuel me. That was what kept me going all this time and it was what would keep me fighting now. My glow steadied as I fought the surge of fear. I felt like the two feelings were fighting a raging battle inside my heart. Eventually, the love won out and the fear disappeared.

My body ached, but the pain wasn't unbearable. I got back to my feet. My powers surged and I lifted back into the air. Kilmar glared at me.

"That should have killed you," he said.

He sounded shocked and very angry. I heard a collective gasp from the crowd. It was apparent they had been thinking the same thing Kilmar had; I should have been dead. I was still very much alive and even more determined than before.

"Guess this won't be as easy as you thought it would," I said with a smirk.

Kilmar fumed. If he had a face, I'm sure his cheeks would have been red with rage. Shadows gathered around his hands. I willed a larger sphere of white light to form in front of me. I let it grow bigger and bigger until it surrounded me completely, like a force field. Kilmar's shadows surged towards me. They collided with my light. For a moment everything seemed to stop. The monsters were silent, nobody moved. Then there was a massive boom, and a blast wave composed of a mixture of my light and Kilmar's shadows rolled across the coliseum. I was thrown backward into one of the massive stone support pillars. The back of my head slammed into the pillar. I crumpled to the ground, and everything went black.

TWENTY-FIVE

I wasn't sure how long I had passed out, but it couldn't have been long. I groaned as I came to. There was a faint light all around me. Although it was small, it seemed to sear my eyes with blinding pain. I wanted to shut out the light by closing my eyes. It didn't work. It burned brightly even behind my eyelids. I couldn't stop it. I didn't know where it was coming from, and I didn't know where I was. For one terrifying moment, I didn't even know who I was. All I knew was that my head was pounding, throbbing, and aching.

Then, in a rush that made my head spin, it all came back to me. I sat up abruptly, instantly regretting it as the world tilted sideways and my vision turned yellow. Or maybe it was me that tilted sideways. I couldn't register which one was true. Either way, I felt like I was on a rollercoaster. Dark spots danced across my vision. I leaned against the pillar, closed my eyes, and took a deep breath.

At least it is quiet. I thought to myself. Then I realized something was wrong. *Something's not right. Those monsters and demons in the stands should not be this quiet.*

I opened my eyes and gazed across the coliseum. The stands were completely empty. All the monsters and demons that had occupied the stands were gone. I couldn't believe it.

"No way," I whispered in disbelief.

I used the pillar for support and pulled myself to my feet. The world started to spin again, and I fought the urge to puke. My head felt like it was being used for a drum solo. There was a constant ringing in my ears that wouldn't go away.

I shifted my focus from the pain to Kilmar. He was on his knees struggling to get up. I knew this was my chance to finish him off and I knew what I had to do. I also knew what it would cost to make a surge of power strong enough to defeat him: my spark. That was the only way to destroy him.

How ironic; I would be giving him exactly what he wanted, all my power, and yet, he would die without ever being able to use it.

Just because I knew that it was what had to be done, that didn't mean it was easy. There was a very high chance it would kill me. That's the sacrifice I was willing to make for the sake of the world.

Deep down in my heart I believed that there was a chance that maybe, just maybe I could survive. I could live with my family and Will. We could go back to Sproot and live in the fairy village. For the first time in a really long time, I could truly be happy. First, I had to save the world from Kilmar.

I took a shaky step forward, then another. Each step brought me closer to Kilmar until I stood only a few feet from him.

"Have you come to give up?" Kilmar said in a gruff, hoarse voice. His red, glowing eyes had dimmed slightly, as if he was beginning to realize he was going to lose, as if he were giving up hope.

I didn't answer him. I looked down at my hands. They were still glowing like the rest of my body. That wasn't going to be enough to beat him. I needed more. I needed everything I had. Love may have been the most powerful emotion I had felt by far, but love wasn't all of me. After all, I'm not perfect. Nobody is. I'm also full of anger, sadness, grief, and fear. I was full of happiness and hope, jealousy and frustration, embarrassment and pride. Who could forget shame, confusion, bitterness, and even excitement? All of these emotions hold their own kind of power, and all of them made me who I was.

I took a deep breath and closed my eyes. I searched through every single memory I had, just as I had done so many times before. Except this time, I wasn't just searching for one singular emotion, I was looking for every emotion.

I felt like I was watching a movie of my entire life in my mind. It all felt so surreal. Every little memory was like another scene being played. Every person, every place, everything I had been through, it all made me who I was. Those memories, good or bad, old or new, they all gave me strength.

I vaguely felt myself lift off the ground. Then there was a swoosh of air around me. I opened my eyes, and a thousand different colors were swirling around me in a dazzling sphere of light.

I felt a faint tugging sensation in my gut, although this time, it was less of a tug and more like a painful stretching of a muscle I wasn't meant to use. I knew it was my spark. I was using it up. I felt like that muscle in my gut stretched more and more until I felt something inside me snap.

The sphere of light that swirled around me surged inward. Then a beam of colorful light shot out of it and straight into the spot where Kilmar's heart would be if he actually had one. He let out a blood chilling scream. I watched as his eyes changed from red to the same color as the light.

"Nooooooo!" he wailed.

Then, he started crumbling to black dust. His claws went first. He screamed louder and louder as the rest of his body started to turn to dust too. I knew that if I lived to survive this, I would never forget his screams. Finally, his head was the last thing to disappear. As it went, he let out one more sudden, piercing scream. Even after he was gone, his scream echoed around the coliseum.

Suddenly, the sphere of light around me imploded on itself. There was a pain in my gut, like someone had driven a knife into it, and the knife was twisting as it drove deeper inside of me.

Then gravity took over, and I started falling. I felt the rush of air in my face as I fell and the ground grew closer.

All around me, the coliseum started collapsing. I watched as the massive pillars fell one by one. I realized that the dimension was collapsing, and it would collapse on top of me. I didn't have the strength to make a portal or even move. A silent tear slipped down my cheek as I realized this was the end. I said a silent goodbye to my parents, Oliver, and Will.

This is it, I thought. *I did it. I won.*

Somehow, I had managed to find the light inside of me even in a world full of darkness. I was stuck in a dark, destitute place meant only for shadows. I had wiped out all the darkness of this dimension. No one would ever have to fear the name Kilmar again. Dread would become a place of memory.

Perhaps someday, the Convocation would know what I had done. They would know that I had saved the world. They wouldn't fear me then. I probably wouldn't be alive for them to fear me anyway. They could at least be kinder to Oliver and my parents.

I didn't want to die. Dying sucks, and it's absolutely terrifying. It isn't just the idea of dying, but the thought of everything you'll leave behind. I would never get to tell my family goodbye. They would still be a family together, but I was heartbroken that I wouldn't be a part of it. They would have a happy life, whether that was in Sproot or back in the human dimension, Fortest.

What scared me most was the idea of never getting to fix things with Will. He probably thought I didn't love him, but that couldn't have been less true. I loved him like a poet loves to write. I needed him like the earth needs the sun. I needed him like I needed air to breathe. I felt the same passion for him that a dancer feels for music. The thought of him never knowing this was enough to keep me holding on. It left a small part of me holding onto living.

As I fell, and the ground came dangerously close, I clung to the thought of him. I braced myself for the inevitable impact.

Suddenly, there was a burst of green light. A green portal opened below me, and I fell through it.

TWENTY-SIX

I tumbled across a wooden surface. I looked up to see familiar huts. Small beams of sunlight seeped in through the canopy of leaves above me. The bright vivid colors of the leaves were like a beacon of hope in my heart.

I made it. I thought. I....

My thoughts trailed off as I suddenly found it hard to think. The longer I lay there, staring up at the leaves above me and the sky that peeked through the green canopy, the more the colors seemed to dim. My eyelids grew heavy. My consciousness was like the colors. It was so evident and full of life before, but it was fading away with every passing second.

I heard a series of vague thuds that shook the platform. I guessed it was footsteps because a few seconds later there was a pair of blue eyes staring into mine. The boy leaning over me had a worried expression on his face that scrunched up his handsome features. I felt a tug in my heart, like there was something I was forgetting. I knew there was a name that went with that face and those piercing blue eyes. I just couldn't seem to remember what it was.

Then there were voices, quiet voices that I knew I recognized because they filled my heart with a warm fuzzy feeling. The people behind those voices were people I knew I held close to my heart. They were getting so far away, too far for me to get back to them. Their worried tones filled me with fear, fear that I didn't have the energy to deal with. I let myself float away from those voices, tuning out the fear and despair they brought with them.

Eventually, I floated so far that I couldn't feel the pain anymore. I couldn't feel my body at all. I kept floating farther and farther.

A thought pricked my mind. There was something I needed to do, someone I needed to get back too. I just couldn't remember what or who.

Suddenly there was a voice filling my head. It was strong and steady. I wanted to tune it out like the rest, but I couldn't. This one wasn't talking out loud. It was ringing inside my head.

It's going to be okay.

That's all the voice said. I had heard that voice before. I knew I had. However, I couldn't place it. Nevertheless, I clung to those words and held them close to my heart as I faded farther and farther away from everything. Soon, I lost touch with the world.

If this is dying, I thought. *It isn't so bad.*

I drifted aimlessly. It was so quiet and peaceful. Yet the entire time, I felt that there was something missing. I couldn't decide if it was within me or if it was something else. Every time I thought about it, a faint image of blue eyes, a warm smile, and brown hair flickered across my mind. Then, before I could focus on it, it would float away. I couldn't focus on anything, because there was nothing but me there in that place.

There was nothing else there. Just nothingness. It reminded me of something. I couldn't remember what though. I couldn't remember anything. I had no idea where or who I was. I didn't care, I was safe. I had no worries, fears, or doubts. I didn't have any other feelings either. I didn't feel happy, amused, or hopeful. I felt one thing. I felt hollow. I felt like something vital inside of me was missing. It left an empty hole inside of me that made me itch to get it back. If getting it back meant pain, I didn't want it back. I was fine with being incomplete if that meant being safe.

After some time, voices started to float through the nothingness. All of them spoke in a desperate tone. I wanted to understand what they were saying, but I couldn't. I only ever managed to grasp a word or two before the voices were whisked away, along with my urge to understand. Then I would be left floating again, like a leaf carried by a breeze.

Then it all changed. I started hanging on to the voices. Little fragments of sentences started to piece together until I understood their desperate pleas. I finally understood what they were saying.

Please wake up.

Come back to us.

We miss you.

We love you.

They kept begging me constantly. I tried to ignore them. They were a little bit annoying. I just wanted to be left alone in the peace and quiet of this nothingness place.

I don't know how to get back. I thought helplessly.

What if I didn't want to? I couldn't remember what I had left behind. What if it was something awful? What if they are lying? I couldn't even remember who the voices were. What if they only wanted me to come back because they wanted to hurt me? There were so many things that I didn't know and couldn't remember. For the first time in so long, I felt afraid.

However, a feeling stronger than the fear still lingered inside of me. That hollow, emptiness. What if that thing that was missing was the thing that was waiting for me to come back?

I knew then that I had to go back. Even if I didn't know where I was going back to. There was no way I could live with that feeling any longer.

I'm ready. I thought. That thought echoed around me. The echoes turned into a rush of words. They grew louder and louder, pounding and thumping in my ears. The loud sound became too overwhelming for me to handle. I spiraled down, down, down, needing to be free of it.

Suddenly, I stopped spiraling, and the noise faded to a steady *thu-thump*. I listened to it for a moment.

Thu-thump, thu-thump, thu-thump.

I took a deep breath, thankful that the rush had stopped. Then I realized something: I could feel my body again. I could feel my arms and legs and feet and toes. Unfortunately, that also meant I could feel a truckload of pain that had been dumped on top of me. I took another deep breath, and another, and another. It helped ease the pain a bit, but I had a feeling it would be a long time before I would stop hurting.

I opened my eyes, wincing at the bright light that stung my corneas. I blinked a few times before my eyes finally adjusted to the light. I looked around. I was in a hut, slightly smaller than the one I had stayed in during my time in Sproot. I was on a soft cot similar to the ones I'd seen in human hospitals. A few rays of light came in from the windows, illuminating the hut.

I felt hot from being under the blankets, so I pulled my arms out from under them. That's when I realized I was back in my pink nightgown I had worn my first time in Sproot. Although I felt like a silly little girl in the posh, pink nightgown, the silliness of it made me smile.

On the other side of the hut someone was sitting in a chair, staring back at me with beautiful, piercing blue eyes. The sight of him took the breath out of my lungs. Everything came rushing back to me in a terrifying flash.

"You're awake," he gasped. His mouth hung open and his dazzling blue eyes widened.

"Yeah," I said as I sat up. Then I winced as a million tiny needles shot through me.

His features shifted and tiny lines formed on his forehead.

"Being awake hurts," I said. I gave him a halfhearted laugh. A heavy feeling had settled over us.

I bit my lip trying to figure out what to say.

"Will?" I said.

He looked down at his feet. I didn't want him to do that. I wanted him to look at me with his blue eyes that always made me smile. I wanted him to hug me and to tell me that everything was okay and that I was safe.

Before any of that could happen, I needed to set things right.

"I know I said some things in Dread," I started. "They probably made you feel like I don't love you."

The tears started to fall from my eyes, and I didn't fight them. I didn't have the strength to.

"I was just so afraid of what could happen to me, and what that would do to you, that I pushed you away," I continued.

Will started walking over to me then. As his eyes met mine, I knew what I needed to say.

"Now I'm really regretting it because I do love you, Will. I love you so much that it hurts."

He sat on the edge of my bed beside me. My heart hammered in my chest and butterflies took off, doing thousands of loopty-loops in my stomach.

He smiled at me. The kind of smile that someone makes when they finally get something they've been pining for. The one where you're so happy that your lips drift up on one side to form a lopsided grin. The kind of smile that made me melt.

"You don't just mean the world to me, Celeste. You are my world."

Then he leaned in and his lips met mine. His lips were soft like petals as they brushed against my own. Our breathing fell into sync with each other. His hands found my waist and mine came to rest on his cheeks. I'd kissed him before, but this time it was even better. The longer we sat there, holding each other, the more love surged through my heart.

My main thought: *Man, he is such a good kisser.*

As we kissed, I pulled him closer to me, running my hands through his movie star dark brown hair. Every touch sent fire through my veins. Every second, electricity crackled in my bones. Fireworks went off in my heart. I don't know what kissing is supposed to feel like, but I was pretty sure it was this. And this kiss? This kiss was everything.

Then he pulled away, looking at me with those sapphire blue eyes. We didn't have to say it again. Our kiss had said it better than any words could. I loved him, he loved me, and that's how it was going to stay.

"Does the offer to be your girlfriend still stand?" I said, half fear, half exhilaration at the thought.

"Would I have kissed you if it didn't?" he pointed out.

I laughed. He pulled me into a hug, and I leaned my head

on his chest.

So, this is what being in love is. I thought.

I could have stayed that way forever. I didn't want to interrupt our moment, but there was something I still needed to know. I bit my lip, almost too scared to ask.

"Are my parents here?" I asked.

I had fought so hard to have a family again. I wanted to see them so badly that it hurt. Or maybe that was the almost dying. The almost dying had hurt a lot more than I had expected it too. I guess I should have expected that though. That's why it's called almost dying.

"They've been here a lot. Your mom practically never leaves your side. I had to convince her to take a break for a while. Your parents and Oliver have been so worried about you," he said.

I was so excited to see them that I couldn't help but ask.

"Can I see them?" I asked.

"Of course! I'll go get them," he stood up and started moving toward the door.

As he walked away, I realized there was one more thing I needed to know.

"Will?" I asked.

He stopped mid stride, turning to look back at me.

"Yeah, Celeste?"

"How long has it been?" I whispered.

He looked down at his feet. He fiddled with the bottom of his shirt, something I'd never seen him do. He was clearly nervous, and he didn't answer me.

"Will," I spoke up a bit more, "How long has it been?"

He closed his eyes and took a deep breath. Fear made my chest tighten. Was it really that bad? Was it days or weeks? Surely it couldn't be more than that. Finally, Will answered me.

"It's been two months, Celeste," he said without looking up. "You used up almost all of your spark. Y-you almost died. What happened after I left?"

I thought about telling him what happened. I wanted to. The fear and sadness in his eyes made me want to spill every single detail. I just...couldn't. I couldn't relive what had happened, not when the pain was still so fresh. Thinking about it and even talking about it felt like rubbing salt in an open wound.

I shook my head as all the words I knew he wanted to say formed a lump in my throat.

He sighed as he seemed to realize I wasn't ready to tell him yet. He opened the door and left without saying another word.

While there were a million different thoughts in my head, one stayed stuck to the surface:

How could it have been two months?

That was the only thing I could think about as I laid in my bed. I wondered how much I had missed. Will seemed different somehow. He appeared older and more mature. He seemed taller and more muscular as well. How could he have changed in two months? If he'd changed, how much did my family change? Were they happy without me? I wondered if my parents were angry with me for making them leave. They had to have been so scared when I tumbled back into Sproot. Would they forgive me for putting them through all that?

I stared out the window. A purple bird flew by. Then there was a small breeze that made the large leaves rustle. The room was so peaceful compared to the turmoil inside my heart.

Although my body ached and my limbs were stiff, I suddenly felt confined to my bed. I decided I needed some fresh air. I sat up slowly and instantly regretted it. I was so dizzy that I almost hurled.

It's been two months; I need to get out of this bed. I thought to myself.

I threw back my covers and swung my legs over the side of the bed. A wave of nausea hit me, but I gritted my teeth.

I saved the world, so I should be able to get out of this bed.

My feet touched the ground. The wooden floor was cool beneath my feet. I hesitated for a moment before putting weight on my feet and standing. I almost face planted as I stood. My head started to spin, and I almost fell. I walked over to the window and leaned against the windowsill for support. I stood there for a while, losing myself in thought.

A knock at my door startled me from my thoughts.

"Come in," I called as I turned around to face the door.

My mom gently opened the door. As soon as she saw me, she burst into tears. She ran across the room and strangled me with a hug. She cried into my hair, which was kind of gross because she got my hair wet and snotty, but sweet at the same time.

"I can't believe you're awake," she said when she finally composed herself.

"Me either," I said.

I wanted to say more, but I started to feel lightheaded. My mom must have noticed, because she demanded that I sit back down before I wore myself out. I happily obliged. I plopped down on the bed, letting my legs dangle over the side.

She sat with me and wrapped her arms around me. She

hummed a tune that I had never heard before, but it was one of the most beautiful songs I'd ever heard. The old me would have been embarrassed and pulled away. However, after everything I'd been through, after everything I'd fought for, I never wanted it to end.

"I don't recognize that song. Where did you learn it?" I asked her.

"The fairies taught it to me. It's supposed to be a healing song," she said.

She got this far away look in her eye that made me wonder if she'd sang it to me while I was unconscious. I wondered how many times she'd sat by my bedside hoping and praying for me to wake up. I wondered if Dad and Oliver had done the same.

"Where are Dad and Oliver?" I asked.

Then I realized it sounded like I didn't want her there. I opened my mouth to clarify, but before I could, she smiled brightly at me.

"They should be here any minute now. They have been out helping in the forest," she said happily. Her voice had this light airiness to it that I hadn't heard in a long time. "Things have changed a lot since you killed Kilmar."

His name sent a chill through my body. I remembered his screams as I killed him. Those awful, terrible screams. They were worse than the ones from my nightmares about my parents.

"What are they doing in the forest?" I asked, wanting to change the subject.

"The parts of the forest that were overrun by shadows are coming back to life. They're helping the fairies clear out the dead trees to make more room for the new ones," she said, "Of course, it is taking forever because the fairies insist on having a little funeral for every single tree since they believe that all life is important. I agree, but come on, they're just trees."

"Huh," I whispered in awe. That was all I could manage at that moment. So much had changed in the two months I had been unconscious.

Suddenly, as if my mom had somehow spoken them into existence, Dad and Oliver burst into the room.

"Celeste!" Oliver shouted as he wrapped me in a hug.

"Little tight," I wheezed.

He stepped back with a smile on his face. Oliver had the kind of smile that made me want to smile too, and I did. I smiled so big my face hurt.

"Sorry," he said, "It's just so good to see you awake."

"It's good to be awake. I can't believe it's really been two months," I said.

His smile dropped and his shoulders fell. It was like watching a flower wilt. I felt horrible for making them go through so much. I felt like a heavy weight had settled over all of us. The room suddenly felt too small, and it was harder to breathe.

Dad put a hand on each of our shoulders.

"What matters now is that we are all together and we are all safe," he said.

It was something a dad would say. I was starting to see why people like having them so much. They are pretty cool.

Dad pulled us both into a hug. My mom wrapped her arms around us too. We weren't a perfect family, but what family is perfect? We loved each other more than anything else in the world. Which is saying a lot, because with all these new dimensions, my world was a whole lot bigger.

EPILOGUE

I sat with my legs hung over the edge of a platform, looking out at the forest. The sunset made the vibrant colors of the forest pop, and the light made the surface of the golden river glisten and glimmer with a mesmerizing shine. There was a warm breeze blowing through the air. The breeze made my hair bounce and twirl. I took a deep breath, taking in the breathtaking scenery. I sat there for a while, my mind swirling with thoughts. I had a lot to think about.

It's funny to think about how this whole crazy journey started with me wanting answers about my dad. In the end, I had gotten so much more than just answers. I got him back. I also got Oliver, Will, and a new home in Sproot.

My thoughts were interrupted by Will coming over and sitting down beside me.

"I've been looking for you. What are you doing out here?

Shouldn't you be inside resting?" he asked.

I wanted to groan. He sounded like my mom.

"I needed some fresh air, so I came out here," I said casually.

I decided not to mention the fact that I had gotten very dizzy while walking out here, so I had to sit down. As much as I hated to admit it, I still had a while to go before I would be fully recovered. I had lost almost my entire spark. That wasn't the kind of thing that healed in a day. I hoped it would heal eventually, but there was also a chance it could never heal at all. It could be in a few years, or it could be never.

"Do you want to talk about what happened to you in Dread?" He asked.

I stared off into the sunset. I didn't really want to, but I figured he wouldn't stop asking me until I caved and told him. I could tell him a little bit.

"I'll tell you about it one day, I promise. For now, how about one question?" I asked him.

"How did you escape?" he asked.

"Escape? What do you mean? I came through a portal," I said. "You saw me."

I looked at him like he was crazy. They'd seen me come through the portal. He had been the first one there.

"You used up your spark to defeat Kilmar though, so how could you have made the portal?" he asked.

I stared blankly at him. I searched my memories of that moment. My blood went cold as I had a startling realization.

"Kilmar was dead, the demons and monsters were dead, and I was too weak to make it," I said in dismay, "there was only one other person there…"

My voice trailed off. I couldn't bring myself to finish. It just didn't make any sense.

"Edward," Will finished for me.

Why would he of all people help me escape? He tried to kill me while I was there.

I shook my head and asked, "But why would he save me?"

Will stared off into the sunset. He bit his lip.

"I don't know. We can deal with it later. For now, I just want to be here with you," he replied.

"I'd like that," I said.

I laid my head on his shoulder. I felt his arms wrap around me. As we sat there together, watching the sunset, I felt safe and loved.

I knew that there was still much to come with the Convocation and with Edward, but Will was right. Those things could wait. In the meantime, I wanted to enjoy my new life, because even though it wasn't perfect, it was a life worth living.

A NOTE FROM THE AUTHOR

To all of my readers, I want to thank you for giving my writing a chance. I am not as experienced as other authors and I may not be as good as them either, but you still chose to read my book anyway. That makes me incredibly lucky and blessed to have all of you.

A common question I get asked when writing is where I get my inspiration for my book. All my characters are modeled off of people that I have met, heard about, and admire. I don't have very many people that I dislike, and I can assure you that my characters are not based on those people. Why do I model them off real people? Although these characters are only fictional, the feelings they inspire are real.

Throughout my writing process, there were times when I wanted to give up. I was very much considering it. Still, I'm so glad that I didn't because I get to share all the stories and characters that have only ever existed in my imagination with you. This book will always be a part of me and my life. Now, so will all of you, my wonderful readers.

When I was writing this book, I felt like I was setting my imagination free. I discovered a part of myself that I had never seen before. I learned that when we don't set any limits to our imagination, we can create entire worlds (even if those worlds are fictional).

No matter where this writing journey takes me, I am thankful for the readers who picked up my book and decided to read it.

ACKNOWLEDGEMENT

I was so very blessed to have many amazing people helping me throughout the process of writing this book. I could never truly thank you enough for everything you have done for me. Although I know I could never repay you, I want to thank you from the bottom of my heart for being there for me, guiding me, and pushing me to be the best author I can be.

There are a few special people who have helped me more than anyone else, and I want to thank them.

Mom and Dad, I want to thank you first because you heard it first. You were encouraging me even when my book was nothing but an idea in my head. Before I had even put a pencil to paper, you were already there, guiding me. There were so many times when I was ready to give up, and you encouraged me to keep going. Your support has meant so much to me. More than you will ever know.

Mrs. Jade, thank you for all of your feedback and support. Your feedback and ideas were fundamental in the beginning editing stage of my book. Without you, this book would have so many plot holes. I could never have done this without your help. You have no idea how thankful I am for you.

Aunt Jennifer, I can't even begin to express how thankful I am for you. You have supported me throughout the entire process of writing this book. Whenever I doubted myself, you always came through with a round of encouraging words that lifted me up and gave me the confidence to keep writing. I don't think I would have ever finished this book without you.

Mrs. Key, you are an amazing person and are so supportive. It meant so much to me that you took the time to read and edit this novel. Thank you so much!

Aunt Nancy, it meant so much to me that you were willing to edit my novel. It meant a lot to me to have an actual technical writer editing this novel. Thank you for taking so much time to edit my novel.

Lastly, I want to thank Leland. I don't think you realize how much you have helped me. All of your editing suggestions and plot hole fixes were such a big help during the beginning editing stage. It made me feel so much more confident about my writing to have someone my age beta-reading it. I know that I couldn't have done this without you. You, Leland, are such a kind person and you have always been an amazing friend.

You may not realize it, but this book would not have happened without all of you. Whether you have read it, encouraged me, given me feedback, or all of the above, I am grateful and blessed to have you all in my life. Thank you, everyone, for all you have done.

ABOUT THE AUTHOR

Christy Stalnaker Photography

Berkley June Hutson is the author of the *Celeste Rowan* series. At fourteen, she published her first novel, *Celeste Rowan: Find The Light*. She realized her passion for writing in sixth grade when she began writing *Celeste Rowan: Find The Light*, and she has fallen in love with writing ever since. She lives with her family in Alabama. She enjoys volleyball, music, reading, and an embarrassing amount of hot tea in her free time.

Find her online at berkleyjunehutson.com. She invites you to stay tuned by following her on:

    Instagram @authorberkley.hutson

    Facebook @Author Berkley June Hutson

www.ingramcontent.com/pod-product-compliance
Lightning Source LLC
Chambersburg PA
CBHW020122120726
47903CB00007B/2066